Book One of the Dragon of the Month Club Series

Iain Reading

Artwork Sketches "The Book World" and
"Professor Möbius" by Isabella Chen

ISBN-10: 1505633664
ISBN-13: 978-1505633665

this book is dedicated to lost friendships

Other books by this author:

Kitty Hawk and the Curse of the Yukon Gold
Kitty Hawk and the Hunt for Hemingway's Ghost
Kitty Hawk and the Icelandic Intrigue
Kitty Hawk and the Tragedy of the RMS Titanic
Kitty Hawk and the Mystery of the Masterpieces
The Guild of the Wizards of Waterfire
The Hemingway Complex (non-fiction)

www.kittyhawkworld.com
www.wizardsofwaterfire.com
www.dragonofthemonthclub.com
www.iainreading.com
www.secretworldonline.com

table of contents

the dragon of the month club

chapter one
a very unlikely friendship

The very unlikely friendship of Ayana Fall and Tyler Travers began on a Tuesday afternoon in the maze of bookshelves at the back of the old library. It was so far back, in fact, that hardly any natural light penetrated there, and the only illumination came from the ancient incandescent light bulbs in the tacky iron fixtures hanging from the ceiling.

So it was quite dark. And to make matters worse, it was also very dusty. The weekly shelf cleanings that the staff conducted seemed to have little effect so far back in the library. If you dared to sneeze, you would be rewarded with a shower of dust mites and even the occasional feather (who knows how THAT got back there?), which would make you sneeze again... and again and again, until you had to hurry back to the more civilised parts of the library just to catch your breath.

In this lovely place full of books (and I say that with absolute sincerity and not a hint of sarcasm) the unlikely friendship of Ayana and Tyler began, somewhere between a three volume history of the anatomy of earthworms and a handy five hundred and forty-six page (plus appendices!) illustrated guide to the indigenous mosses of Iceland,.

Ayana was new in town, just having moved to the rather small city of Medicine Hat, Alberta. Her family was from Vancouver. She was born there, and it was the only home she'd ever known. But her father had walked out on her and her mother, leaving them to fend for themselves. And her mother had lost her job, and the only work she could find was back in her hometown in the middle of nowhere set amidst the endless pale brown flat expanse of the Canadian prairies.

She almost cried when she first saw it—everything as flat as a pancake instead of the towering beautiful rocky mountains she was used to. Dusty and dry instead of lush green rainforests and open blue sea. Small and boring instead of endless possibilities.

New school. No friends.

But all of that was nothing compared to Ayana's *real* problem: Heather van der Sloot.

Heather was the 'it' girl of Ayana's new school. The beautiful one. The supposedly cool one. The one that everyone wanted to be friends with. And for some reason that Ayana could not possibly imagine, Heather had it in for her.

It was painfully obvious from the very first day of the new school year. Ayana had arrived early to pick up some forms from the school office before heading to her first class. No one was there when she arrived, so she picked a seat near the back at the far end of the class near the corner.

"You're in my spot," she heard a voice say from the hallway door.

Ayana looked up and saw three girls standing there. One tall and pretty girl with long, straight brown hair and a perfectly matched outfit was standing in the middle of the group with two others on either side obviously desperately trying to look like her.

"I'm sorry," Ayana said. "I didn't know there were assigned seats."

"There's not," the girl replied, smirking at Ayana as she quickly gathered her books. "I just don't want you sitting there."

Ayana didn't know what to say.

Is this for real? she thought, and moved to another desk.

"That's my desk," one of Heather's clones said nastily as Ayana set her books on one of the places four seats closer to the front.

"Oh," Ayana replied, lifting her stack of books again and trying another one.

"Nope," the first girl said as Ayana was about to sit down at another desk three rows over.

"Then where?" Ayana replied, getting angry.

The class was filling up with other students, all of them keeping a respectful distance from the group of girls as they filed inside, flowing around them like a river.

"Nice clothes," Heather said maliciously, her voice dripping with sarcasm as she and her entourage headed to the corner desks to take their seats.

Ayana stared down at her threadbare, second-hand clothing and blushed in shame. It was all her mother could afford.

"Be nice to the new girl, Heather," Ayana heard an adult voice say from somewhere behind her. A tall thin man in a corduroy jacket strutted into the room carrying an iPad in one hand and a paper cup of coffee in the other. It was Mr Wens, the first period math teacher, and Ayana was relieved that finally someone was there to stand up for her. Unfortunately, it was the first *and* the last time that would ever happen.

Over the course of the next few weeks, Ayana would learn that no one ever stood up to Heather van der Sloot. Her parents were local supporters of the arts or something like that, and wealthy, at least by the standards of the small town world of Medicine Hat; well respected and even feared. Her father owned a successful contracting company that had employed a lot of people and put food on the tables of a lot of local families. Not the kind of people you necessarily wanted on your bad side, in other words.

But as I said, for some reason that's exactly where Ayana had ended up: on Heather van der Sloot's bad side.

"Where ya goin', Ivana?" Heather asked one day after school, appearing out of nowhere from some side steps as Ayana was about to start across the Finley Bridge toward downtown and the Dairy Queen where she was supposed to meet up with her mother. Heather always called Ayana by the wrong name on purpose, just to be mean.

"Nowhere," Ayana said, twisting her body to slip past them and continue down the sidewalk.

"I hope you're going shopping," Heather replied, side-stepping in front of her before she could sneak past. "Your clothes are looking a bit ratty."

Heather reached out and tugged on Ayana's shirt collar. Ayana twisted again and tried to pull away.

"Leave me alone," she said, again trying to slip past the three of them. This time she was successful and started across the bridge, walking quickly with her books clutched close to her body as she went.

Ayana hoped that Heather would just give up after her one biting insult and then go find something better to do. She usually did, but for some reason Heather was in an especially nasty mood that day and followed after her across the bridge, her and her clones keeping pace with Ayana as she constantly sped up in an attempt to outrun them.

"You'd better hurry," Heather taunted her from behind. "The Salvation Army's about to close."

"Just leave me alone, Heather!" Ayana yelled over her shoulder. Heather was close now, too close, and Ayana was too late to react.

Heather pushed her from behind, planting her hands squarely on Ayana's shoulders and shoving her to the concrete. Ayana's books scattered all over the place as she put up her hands to protect herself, scraping her knee and both palms in the process.

Ayana crawled off to one side, away from the three other girls. Her hands and knees were stinging painfully as she tried to gather up her books.

Is Heather crazy or something? she thought, keeping one eye on them as she slowly stacked her books.

"What's this?" she heard Heather say as she reached down to pick up one of Ayana's handwritten notebooks. "Is this a diary or something? Is there anything about me in here?"

"Give that back!" Ayana cried as Heather yanked the notebook open and flipped through the pages. It wasn't a diary. It was Ayana's book of notes for some stories she was thinking of writing.

Heather pulled away as Ayana tried to reach for the notebook. One of the clones—a girl named Tristan—roughly pushed Ayana away again.

"What is all of this?" Heather asked, sneering as she flipped through page after page of Ayana's innermost thoughts and ideas. "Sea monsters? Tentacles?"

"Just give it back, Heather!" Ayana cried again, trying to push past Tricia to recover her notebook.

Heather smiled a horrible crooked smile—one that would have been quite ugly had she not been so pretty—and without a word of warning she tossed the notebook over the bridge's railing, sending it spinning through the air like a Frisbee on its way down to the waters of the river below.

"Noooo!!!!!!" Ayana shrieked, leaping to her feet and springing across to the railing to catch it, but it was too late. The notebook was gone, flapping and tumbling like some awkward paper bird.

For a moment, Ayana considered climbing the railing and jumping after it but it was a long way down, and it didn't take a genius to realise that the fall would probably kill her. All she could do was watch helplessly as the notebook fluttered downward and hit the surface of the water with a muffled splash, and then it simply floated there, face open to one of its pages filled with Ayana's handwriting and a sketch of some tangled tentacles squirming their way across the page.

Ayana clenched her fists as she watched the current carry her precious notebook away. It was too light to sink, and so it rested on the surface, pages turning in the wind as if some unseen being was flipping through it. In a matter of seconds, it floated under the bridge, and she knew that if she hurried to the other side she would see it emerge again downstream like a token in some twisted and horrid game of Poohsticks.

Tears were welling in Ayana's eyes, overflowing and coursing down her cheeks. She wanted to do something. She wanted to hurt Heather for doing this—anything to make her pay. But as she glanced up into Heather's eyes, she saw something that made her reconsider.

Heather is crazy, Ayana thought. *She has to be. Who would do something like this?*

"Don't cry, you big baby," Heather mocked, her voice spiteful and cold. "Sea monsters belong in the water, don't they?"

Ayana wanted to jump at her and hurt her. But she turned and ran the other way instead, as fast as she could across the rest of the bridge toward the other side, crying uncontrollably as she went.

Glancing over her shoulder as she ran she saw that Heather and the clones had finally given up on her. With a casual flip of their hair in unison, they turned and headed the other direction.

Ayana's pace slowed as she reached the end of the bridge and watched them disappear down the stairs to where they'd appeared from in the first place. She was safe—for the moment anyway.

"What's the matter, young lady?" a kindly old woman with a stroller asked as she passed by Ayana on her way to the bridge.

Ayana turned her head away, embarrassed.

"Nothing," she said and quickly ducked down the long sloping stretch of lawn next to City Hall to get away. She didn't want anyone to see her right now, not even her mother who was probably already waiting for her at Dairy Queen.

I have to get out of here, Ayana thought in a panic, the tears flowing down her cheeks again. She hurried down the lawn and out along the road that ran parallel to the river. She looked at the water and imagined her notebook still floating somewhere miles downstream. By now, the dirty greenish brown water was probably soaking into its pages, staining them with some kind of filthy tie-dye patterns on the pages, seeping into the cardboard covers and weighing them down until the whole book would simply sink to the bottom.

Ayana couldn't bear the thought of it, and new tears formed on the heels of the old ones. She was completely losing it. A jogger on the other side of the street was looking at her strangely. She had to find somewhere to hide until she could pull herself together.

The library was the closest building Ayana could find, and she rushed up the hillside and pushed open the heavy glass doors leading to the inside. It wasn't the first time she'd been there. Her mother and she had come there on their first weekend in the city to apply for library cards. Ayana knew that the library was divided into two parts—one modern and new and busy, all glass and steel and sunlight; and the other much older, cold stone and empty, with dimly lit corridors.

Empty and dimly lit was exactly what Ayana needed at that moment. She turned her head to avoid the eyes of an older couple who were on their way out the door, and she ducked down the closest stairs into the older part of the library.

Still keeping her head down she hurried past the checkout desk where a grumpy-looking middle-aged woman with narrow glasses and her hair tied back into a painful ponytail was sitting. The librarian looked like she wanted to say something to Ayana— perhaps tell her to slow down or something—but she remained silent instead, much to Ayana's relief.

Just a bit further, Ayana told herself as she wove her way past the map section with its wide flat drawers full of maps. She moved on past the backstage doors of the theatre and between the double row of old-fashioned thick reference books sitting on top of heavy wooden pedestals, their dense covers and pages open to the last spot that someone had turned to, if anyone ever actually used them, probably some time before Ayana was even born. The last book on Ayana's left, a massive dictionary.

Interstitial

...was the last word at the bottom of the page. She caught the text out of the corner of her eye as she glanced back to make sure she was completely alone.

(adj.) relating to or situated in the small spaces or gaps that lie between things.

Reassured that there was not a single other human being anywhere in sight, Ayana plunged into the final rows of shelves at the very back end of the library and waded into the dusty darkness.

A single narrow shaft of sunlight from some unseen window was streaming across the very end of the last row brilliantly illuminating the dance of the dust mites pirouetting through the air, but this row was so far back that not even that brave sliver of light could bring more than just a pale luminance to the ancient and heavy banks of books.

Ayana crumpled to the floor just underneath the blade of sunlight, floundering around until her knees were pulled up to her chest and her face was buried in her hands. She began to cry full on now. The floodgates in her head opened, and every ounce of hurt and pain and disappointment and frustration came suddenly rocketing to the surface.

Her father running off and leaving her and her mother all alone. She hated him. But loved him. But hated him.

Moving from her beautiful home in British Columbia where there were trees everywhere to this awful and dirty brown place on the prairies with its stupid name. She'd seen the Wizard of Oz. She knew what happened out here where the land was flat: tornados.

And of course, Heather van der Sloot. How could anyone possibly be so mean? So vicious. Ayana hated her too.

All of these thoughts flashed through Ayana's head, one after the other like the end credits of a movie rushing by. But mostly she just cried. She cried like never before in her entire life. She cried until she simply had no more tears left, and her eyes were swollen and red, and rivers of sniffling snot were threatening to run out of her nose.

Wiping her sleeve across her face, Ayana finally looked up and stared at the row of books in front of her. Directly across was an enormous book with a thick linen cover and tiny writing along the spine. Something about the mosses of Iceland, but Ayana's attention was distracted elsewhere because peering over the top of the weighty book from the next row of bookshelves was a pair of pale blue blinking eyes.

Ayana was startled and immediately pulled herself upright, wiping her nose with her sleeve again trying to compose herself.

"Who are you?" she asked, frightened. "What do you want?"

The eyes just blinked and stared back at her, looking every bit as scared as she was, if not a little more.

"Sorry," she heard the muffled and tiny voice of a boy say from the other side of the shelf. The eyes blinked one last time and disappeared from sight.

Ayana just sat there too surprised to move.

A few seconds later the eyes appeared again, this time attached to an entire head and face that was now peeking around the corner of the bookshelf above her. The boy was about Ayana's age with slightly ruffled and messy brown hair and a concerned and frightened look on his face.

"What do you want?" Ayana demanded, pulling herself up even straighter and trying to make herself look presentable.

"I heard you crying," the boy said, poking his head and body even farther out until Ayana could see what he was wearing. It looked like the kind of cheap suit you would see on mannequins in the Sears store.

"What are you wearing?" Ayana asked.

The boy looked down at himself and blushed.

"Picture day at school," he replied.

Ayana nodded. That made sense. No one would ever leave the house looking like that otherwise.

"What school?" she asked.

The boy hesitated for a moment.

"Vincent Massey," he said.

Ayana nodded again.

"Riverside," she said.

"Pardon me?"

"Riverside School," Ayana repeated. "I go to Riverside."

"Oh."

"No picture day for us today," Ayana observed distantly.

"Oh," the boy repeated.

The boy stepped a little farther out from the shelves until he was completely visible. As he did, Ayana could see tucked into the lapel of the jacket a small fuzzy grey blob that looked like a small animal was trying to burrow its way inside.

Ayana stared at the furry little ball and frowned.

"What's that?" she asked.

The boy looked down and blushed again.

"Rabbit's foot," he said, pulling it out of his jacket and stuffing it into his pocket. "You know?"

"Right," Ayana replied.

"For good luck," the boy explained.

"Right," Ayama said, giggling slightly.

The boy blushed some more and shifted his feet nervously.

"I'm Tyler," he said, nervously sticking out his hand toward Ayana.

Ayana giggled again and scooted forward, reaching up to formally shake his hand.

"Ayana," she said as she slid her cold hand into his warm one and shook it.

And with that strangely formal and awkward introduction began a very unlikely friendship.

chapter two
the book

Following their most unlikely of beginnings, the friendship of Ayana and Tyler grew quickly, and before they knew it, they were the best of friends, meeting up with each other almost every day. Sometimes they met up with Ayana's mother after school at the downtown Dairy Queen for ice cream. Other times they climbed the edges of the coulee behind Ayana's school and went to Tyler's house where they did their homework together in his room. But most of the time, they just agreed to meet up at the place where they'd both accidentally bumped into each other on that very first day—amongst the dusty old bookshelves of the old library at the row between the history of the anatomy of earthworms and the illustrated guide to the indigenous mosses of Iceland.

It was on just such a day that Ayana and Tyler first discovered *THE BOOK*—a name that would be forever capitalised in their minds whenever either of them dared to utter the phrase aloud.

It was a magical book. That much was clear almost from the outset, so perhaps the manner in which these two unlikely friends happened to come across it was magical as well.

It all started on a typical Friday afternoon. Ayana and Tyler had agreed to meet at the library right after school. Tyler had a dentist appointment and would either be a few minutes late or a few minutes early, depending on how long that took. Not surprisingly Tyler was a few minutes late. This could have been expected since Tyler took dentist appointments *very* seriously. For weeks ahead of time he would be sure to brush his teeth five times every single day—once when waking up, once after breakfast, once after lunch, once after dinner, and once again before bed—which was two more times a day than he usually did. (He normally deemed the wake-up and after dinner steps unnecessary.) All of this was in addition to flossing, rinsing, and otherwise generally trying to keep his teeth in the best possible shape for the check-up.

To Tyler, going to the dentist was like studying for a test in school. Failure was not an option. So it shouldn't be much of a surprise that once he was actually in the dental chair, he expected the dentist to be every bit as thorough as he was, a process that required a bit more time than it normally would with less fastidious patients.

So Tyler was late.

And so, when he finally arrived, he hurried down the stairs and quickly navigated through the maze of shelves at the back of the library and found Ayana sitting there, crouched on the floor, sobbing her eyes out.

Tyler sighed heavily. He could already guess what must have happened: Heather van der Sloot... again.

He took off his backpack and set it on the floor. Folding his legs under him, he lowered himself down until he was sitting next to Ayana, not too close, of course, but as close as he dared to.

"What happened this time?" Tyler asked.

Ayana sobbed and buried her face even deeper in her hands. After a moment her left arm shot out, pointing an accusing finger toward a stack of soiled and dishevelled papers lying in a heap on an empty space on the shelf opposite them.

"That," Ayana cried, her voice thin and cracking.

Tyler stared at the papers, and it took him a moment to realise what they were.

"Your poems," he gasped.

Tyler had to take a breath and swallow. Ayana's poems were a work of art, neatly written in careful flowing script, one to a page. Ayana carried them with her sometimes in a stiff green cardboard folder with trees on it that had little strings that you used to tie it shut.

Ayana nodded, still sobbing.

"She threw them all over the playground," she said, her voice raspy. "She grabbed my tree folder away from me and threw them everywhere. I... I ...."

Ayana stuttered and couldn't speak for a second.

"I don't know if I got them all back," she finally said, finishing her thought. "I think I lost some."

Tyler nodded and crawled over on one knee to pick up the chaotic stack of papers. He sorted through them, one by one, trying to put them back into some kind of order. They were smeared and scratched and crumpled. One even had a dirty footprint stamped squarely on it.

Normally Ayana wouldn't even let Tyler glance at one of her poems, so he was surprised that she wasn't bothered by his looking through all of them now. She clearly wasn't thinking straight, so he tried to make as neat a stack out of them as possible and set it down on the carpet in the middle of the row of shelves.

"There are a lot there," he said, sitting close to her again. "Maybe you *did* get them all."

Ayana shrugged her shoulders hopelessly.

"It doesn't matter," she said, staring blankly at the pile of papers. "I don't care."

Tyler felt a sudden squeeze around his heart. He had no idea what he was supposed to do to make Ayana feel better.

But as his mind was racing, trying to think of something, the universe intervened.

"I hate her, Tyler," Ayana said. "I HATE her!"

On this second last syllable, Ayana kicked at the opposite shelves with the heel of her shoe, making the wooden frame shudder and some of the books rattle around. One particular book—a small, thin one high up on the very top shelf—tipped forward as if in slow motion until it was hanging precariously at an impossible angle, almost as if it was levitating, before tumbling end over end to the floor.

Tyler tried to catch it but he was too slow, and instead it crashed into the stack of papers, scattering them slightly, before it fell flat on its back, right side up right in front of them.

how to conjure your very own dragon in six easy steps

...read the front cover of *THE BOOK* in bright yellow letters against a wavy blue background.

Tyler frowned and Ayana stopped crying for a moment. They both stared at *THE BOOK* with wide-open eyes, neither of them quite able to believe what they were seeing.

"How to conjure a dragon?" Ayana asked, kneeling forward to grab *THE BOOK*.

Tyler crawled next to her as she opened the front cover.

THE BOOK was very thin—more like a pamphlet, really— with no table of contents, no copyright page, no dedication page. There wasn't even an indication of who the author might be. It just went straight into the first chapter, which was entitled:

the water dragon

"A water dragon?" Tyler read over Ayana's warm shoulder.

Underneath the chapter title was a brief list of the various characteristics of the water dragon.

category: lesser dragon
difficulty: medium
classification: common

Below that was a basic introduction and explanation of the dragon followed by some advice to those who might want to conjure one:

this spell is a relatively simple one, but be forewarned that the water dragon is a damp and clumsy creature, prone to making messes and causing trouble. It is recommended to have plenty of towels at hand when undertaking this conjuring.

Underneath this brief introduction was a list of materials needed to actually conjure the dragon.

required material(s): water, towels (optional)

And last but not least came the instructions, six simple steps to conjuring your very own dragon. Tyler could hardly believe what he was reading. The steps were so simple. Just a series of strangely specific hand gestures performed by two people simultaneously. The instructions even had little helpful sketches to help you understand what to do.

It reminded Tyler of IKEA assembly instructions when his parents bought new furniture and let him put it together for them. But that was furniture made of wood and fabric and those little IKEA screws that needed a special tool to screw them in. This was supposed to be a dragon, whatever that meant. How could such simplistic instructions possibly result in assembling *anything*, much less an actual dragon?

"We *have* to try this!" Ayana said excitedly.

Tyler was sceptical. *How can this possibly be real?* He took *THE BOOK* from Ayana and scanned the pages of introduction and instruction for a second time.

"I don't know," he said hesitantly. But that's when Tyler looked at Ayana and saw her staring back at him. Gone were the tears of pain that had been streaming down her face just a minute earlier. Gone was the anger and frustration that had led to their discovery of *THE BOOK* in the first place. All that was left written on her beautiful face was the wide-eyed thrill of discovery and excitement and unwavering belief that something as crazy as this dragon book might actually work.

What have we got to lose? Tyler thought, smiling at Ayana's newfound enthusiasm. *Besides, at least Ayana is happy again and not thinking about Heather van der Sloot.*

"Okay," Tyler said. "Let's do it!"

Ayana smiled broadly and grabbed *THE BOOK* from Tyler, pulling herself to her feet as she did so.

"Come on," she said, gesturing for him to follow her to the checkout desk so they could sign the book out.

"What about your poems?" Tyler asked, glancing at the rumpled pages stacked loosely in the middle of the aisle.

Ayana winced. "Just leave them," she said angrily and walked off, leaving Tyler standing there all by himself.

Frowning, Tyler reached down, carefully gathering the poems together and sliding them into his backpack.

"Wait up!" he called after Ayana, hurrying to catch up. But Ayana was already at the checkout desk where grumpy Ms. Bergstrom was busy at the end of the day sorting through a mound of recently returned library books.

"Excuse me," he heard Ayana say, her voice thin and distant. "I'd like to sign this book out please."

"Come back tomorrow," Ms. Bergstrom replied coldly, without looking up from her book sorting. "The library is closing. No sign-outs after five thirty."

"But I'd really like to sign this book out today," Ayana replied, smiling sweetly as she pulled herself onto her tiptoes to peer over the edge of the counter. "Do you think you could maybe make an exception just this one time?"

Ms. Bergstrom continued sorting, obliviously unsympathetic.

"No sign-outs after five thirty," she repeated, pausing only long enough to point one stubby finger at the sign on the wall behind her head.

No sign-outs after five thirty, the sign read.

"Okay, sorry," Ayana said, lowering herself again before taking a step backward. "I'll come back again for it tomorrow."

As Tyler approached, Ayana took another step back and appeared to nonchalantly turn as if she were heading back toward the shelves to replace the book. But as she did so, she was making a series of frantic hand gestures to Tyler behind the cover of the counter where Ms. Bergstrom couldn't see.

Tyler frowned. What in the world was she doing? He watched her free hand flailing at him crazily while she waved with her other hand, the one with *THE BOOK* in it. *Does she want me to do something with the book?*

Tyler stopped cold when he realised what she wanted. She wanted him to grab *THE BOOK* without Ms. Bergstrom seeing.

And then what? Tyler already knew the answer. She wanted him to take the book and sneak it out of the library. She wanted him to steal it.

It's not stealing, he could almost hear Ayana's voice saying to him inside his head. *We're just borrowing it, like we would have done properly if stupid Ms. Bergstrom would have let us.*

Tyler started to sweat nervously. Ayana was silently waving him over more frantically than ever.

Just do it! a voice in Tyler's head told him. *Ms. Bergstrom is going to get suspicious if you keep standing in the middle of the library looking like an idiot.*

But Tyler was frightened. He'd never stolen anything before. Okay, if you consider stealing change from his mother's purse to go to the store and buy candy, then I guess that might count, technically. But he never took more than a dollar in total, so it wasn't *really* stealing, was it? Plus, that was his mother. This was the public library.

What if I get caught? Tyler worried, but it was too late. His feet were already walking forward, and Ayana was already sidestepping toward him.

"Meet me at your house," she whispered as she brushed past him, close enough that he could smell the apple shampoo her mother always bought for her. In one quick fluid motion, she slipped the thin book into his jacket as she passed by then on toward the back of the library once again. Tyler kept going, tense and nervous as he continued toward the exit with *THE BOOK* crammed underneath his hot, sweating armpit.

Ms. Bergstrom glanced at him as he walked past the checkout desk.

"Have a good night, Tyler," she said, friendly but still unsmiling. Tyler had been a regular at the library for years.

"Thank you, Ms. B... Bookstrom," Tyler stuttered in reply. "I mean, Ms. Bergstrom."

Tyler blushed conspicuously, but Ms. Bergstrom didn't seem to notice, and Tyler continued out the doors and up the stairs without her saying another word.

As he stepped out into the cool outside air, Tyler felt a sudden rush of relief wash over him. But he knew he wasn't home free just yet. He continued glancing over his shoulder as he headed across the parking lot, half-expecting to see Ms. Bergstrom rushing up behind him with her thick arms outstretched, ready to grab him. By the time he reached the crosswalk at the intersection and the light turned green, he was already running. He didn't stop until he ran all the way home, in through the front door, past his mother in the kitchen, and all the way up the stairs to his bedroom where he closed the door behind him and looked around desperately for a place to hide *THE BOOK*.

Tyler lifted his mattress and quickly slipped THE BOOK underneath, carefully replacing the bedspread afterward. He took a step back, worrying that it looked too suspicious. Shaking his head, he ironed the quilt flat with the palm of his hand until it looked perfect.

Now it looks TOO perfect, he thought, panicking. His room was kind of a mess, with books lying around all over the place, including several strewn across his bed. The perfectly flattened corner of the quilt stuck out like a sore thumb, so Tyler repeated the entire process for a second time, rumpling the blankets and flattening them out again more naturally.

He took another step back to examine his handiwork. He still wasn't satisfied. What if his mother came in and saw that one corner of his bed was perfectly made up? She would be suspicious.

But by then it was too late. Downstairs he heard the ring of the doorbell and the sound of someone answering it.

Tyler panicked.

It's Ms. Bergstrom and the police! he thought, looking around his room for a place to hide.

But of course it wasn't.

"Tyler! Ayana's here!" his mother called out. A second later, he heard the sound of Ayana's footsteps pounding up the stairs and down the hall toward him.

"Hey," Ayana said, breathless from running as she burst in through the bedroom door. "Do you have the book?"

Tyler shushed her.

"Not so loud!" he whispered. "My mother might hear you!"

Ayana rolled her eyes as she slipped off her jacket and threw it over the chair at Tyler's desk.

"Do you have it or not?" she asked.

"Of course I do," he replied. "I hid it."

Ayana looked at him, her eyes flashing.

"Well, get it out," she said, grinning. "We're going to conjure a water dragon."

chapter three
the water dragon

Tyler glanced out toward the hallway to make sure the coast was clear before he lifted the corner of the quilt that he'd just finished patting down to carefully to hide *THE BOOK*. It was a very colourful quilt, with a repeating pattern of stars and planets and galaxies. All of Tyler's quilts were colourful. His mother bought them for him specially that way.

Tyler slipped *THE BOOK* out from its hiding place and handed it to Ayana. She took it and pushed some random books that were lying on Tyler's bed out of the way and flopped down. Tyler sat next to her, reading over her shoulder.

"We need some water," Ayana said, reading the instructions. "Do you have a bucket or something?"

"A bucket?!?" Tyler asked, surprised. "Why so much water? Didn't you read what the book said?"

Tyler pointed to a final note at the end of the instructions:

note: the more water you use, the bigger the dragon will be. and don't forget that smaller dragons are easier to conjure than larger ones.

"Of course I read that," Ayana replied, frowning impatiently.

"And?" Tyler asked. "Don't you think maybe we should start a bit smaller? Like just a glass of water?"

Ayana rolled her eyes.

"Fine," she said. "You go grab that and I'll get some towels from the bathroom."

Tyler nodded and the two of them headed for the hallway, parting ways at the door. Tyler went left and downstairs to the kitchen for a glass of water while Ayana made for the bathroom down the hall to get some towels.

"Are you kids doing some homework?" Tyler's mother asked cheerily as he breezed into the kitchen.

"Uh huh," Tyler replied, trying not to look suspicious. "Homework."

Grabbing a glass from the cupboard and a litre-sized bottle of water from the fridge, he headed back upstairs where Ayana was already waiting with a stack of towels piled on the bed.

"Let's do this," Ayana said, grinning from ear to ear as she sat cross-legged across from Tyler on the bed.

Tyler carefully poured half a glass of water and set the bottle on the floor next to the bed. Ayana lay *THE BOOK* flat next to them, propping it open by pinning it down with one of the books on Tyler's bed.

"Put the water between us," Ayana directed, making space for Tyler to balance the glass where she could grab it with her toes and hold it in place. Her socks were green with a single red heart on each big toe.

"Okay, what now?" Tyler asked, leaning over to check the instructions.

"First we name it," Ayana said.

before undertaking the conjuring steps you must first name your dragon. doing this allows you to conjure and un-conjure the dragon as needed. (don't worry—un-conjuring a dragon does not harm it in any way, and the dragon can be re-conjured at any time. to temporarily un-conjure a dragon, simply say its name backward.)

Tyler thought about this for a second.

"How about the name Watery?" he said.

Ayana frowned and wrinkled her nose. She shook her head.

"How about Splashy?" she suggested.

"Okay," Tyler agreed. Ayana always was better at naming things.

"We name our dragon Splashy," Ayana said aloud to no one in particular. Neither of them was quite sure how this worked or even if it *would* work. Tyler already had his doubts.

Ayana leaned over to read further.

"Step one, starting positions," she said, extending her hands and arranging them the way the diagram on the page showed. "Now you."

Tyler reached out with his hands, also leaning over to check the diagram, carefully placing them in the proper configuration relative to Ayana's. It was tricky. The pictures were helpful, but they were still just mere two-dimensional representations of a complicated three-dimensional arrangement of fingers and hands and arms.

"I think that's right," Tyler said, checking and re-checking the diagrams against what their actual hands were doing.

"Okay. Then step two," Ayana said. "I go first."

Carefully, deliberately, Ayana followed the instructions on the page, twisting her right hand slowly palm up and waving it underneath the sort of box of hands in the air formed by the spell's starting position.

"Now me," Tyler whispered, bringing his left hand down and curling his fingers into a tight fist.

"And now me," Ayana said, awkwardly lowering her other hand, slowly bringing it down like she was trying to compress the air between them.

"And me," Tyler said, curling his right hand around, flipping it face down on top of the new strange configuration.

Ayana checked the result then continued.

"Step three," she said, moving her hands again and following the instructions as carefully as she could.

The two of them worked slowly through each of the steps in turn, doing their best to recreate the complex motions and figures in the air between them. It was incredibly difficult to do— much harder then it looked on paper.

"Now all hands face up," Ayana said as they reached the sixth and final step, which called for both of them to simultaneously lift and turn their hands palms upward like they were making some kind of offering.

Ayana closed one eye expectantly as their hands reached the final positions of the complicated spell. But nothing happened. She waited a few more seconds, hoping, but it was soon clear that it hadn't worked.

"Crap," Ayana said, frowning. "We must have done something wrong."

"Maybe the whole thing's just a joke," Tyler suggested.

Ayana shook her head.

"No," she replied emphatically. "We just didn't do it right. We were too jerky and awkward. The hand motions have to be smooth and graceful."

Tyler looked at her quizzically.

"How do you know?" he asked.

Ayana shrugged.

"I just know," she said. "Now, go again."

Carefully the two of them put their hands back into the starting positions as indicated by the diagrams under step one. Again they worked their way through the steps, one at a time, each of them moving their hands according to the detailed instructions until they reached the final step, curving their hands upward and lifting.

But still nothing happened.

"Again," Ayana said, moving her hands back to the starting position. "We're getting better at it."

"Okay," Tyler agreed, putting his hands obediently back into position but secretly thinking that his earlier impression had been right—the whole thing was just a big joke.

Ayana was right about one thing, however. As the two of them worked through the steps again and again and again, they were getting better. The elaborate hand motions gradually became more familiar, and they were able to execute them more gracefully and precisely with each repetition.

Not that it helped much, though. With each new attempt, their form was getting better and better, but still nothing happened.

I wonder what time it is, Tyler's stomach growled as his hands moved through step five and he waited for Ayana to finish her part. *It has to be dinnertime pretty soon.*

"Step six," Ayana whispered, her attention acutely focussed on the hand motions of the spell.

"Step six," Tyler echoed as the two of them carefully rotated their palms upward like they'd done dozens of times before.

But this time was different.

This time something happened.

Something utterly incredible.

As the two of them slowly turned their palms upward into their final positions the most unbelievable thing happened. The water in the glass perched between Ayana's toes suddenly came to life, bubbling and boiling and bursting into the air as a large rippling sphere.

The sphere of water moved incredibly quickly, passing between their hands in a flash, startling both of them and causing them to pull their hands back before finishing their final motions.

Unfortunately, the instant their hands pulled away, the spell was broken and the water sphere suddenly lost cohesion, tumbling onto the bed between them.

"Ahh!" Tyler cried, pulling even further back as the blob of water broke and splashed all over the place, soaking Ayana's socks and feet.

"Did you *see* that?!??" Ayana squealed gleefully.

Tyler nodded. He *had* seen it. He couldn't believe it, but he'd definitely seen it. He immediately grabbed a towel to dry off the bedspread and Ayana's feet.

Ayana pushed the towel away and pulled off her socks, tossing them onto the floor as she grinned maniacally.

"Again!" she cried, pointing to the water bottle on the floor. "More water! We have to try again!"

Tyler couldn't have agreed more and quickly grabbed the water bottle. With shaking hands, he refilled the glass, and Ayana ripped off her socks so that she'd have a better grip on the water glass. She grabbed it with her bare toes and held it between them. Her toenails were painted with bright purple nail polish.

"Careful...." Ayana's voice was quivery with excitement as she tried to steady her own hands into starting position. "We have to do this right."

Tyler nodded silently, lifting his hands and trying to force them to stop trembling. They both took a couple of deep breaths then looked at each other.

"Go," Tyler whispered reverently, and they began the spell once again, smoothly running through the steps and motions until they came to the final lift at the very end. This time they were prepared, however, and as the gurgling sphere of water rose into the air between them, they both gasped in amazement, but their hands stayed firm and followed through the spell's final step.

With their hands stretched out toward each other, palms up, they watched in complete astonishment as the ball of water hovered in mid-air and slowly rippled and morphed into the shape of a tiny watery dragon.

It was unbelievable that the spell had actually worked, but the proof of it was right there in front of their eyes: a tiny little dragon made completely out of water. Ayana moved her head from left to right to examine it, careful to keep her hands in position as she did so.

The dragon looked just as you'd expect a tiny dragon made out of water to look. It had an elongated reptilian body with shiny watery scales running the length of its flanks and ridged tail, and a long curling neck ending in a proud horned head and narrow mouth with tiny sparkling teeth. When its formation was complete, they saw four legs with powerful-looking claws on its feet and elegant, curving wings spanning above.

Ayana gasped again at the beauty of it. The wings unfolded to twice the size of the rest of the creature and it gradually began to flap them, grappling against the air in an attempt to stay aloft.

"It's trying to fly!" Ayana cried, ducking her head as droplets of water flew in her face from the claws at the dragon's wingtips.

The rhythm of its wings quickly increased as the tiny dragon struggled to get control of its unfamiliar new body, bouncing from one side of Tyler's room to the other. Water was flying everywhere now, sending Ayana and Tyler ducking for cover as the dragon clumsily flapped and bumped past Tyler's desk chair and knocked his lamp onto the floor. The dragon sailed across the room toward the bookshelf, water streaming behind it as Tyler tried to chase after it with a towel to protect his books.

The dragon's tiny snout ricocheted off the corner of the shelf and water soaked the spines of the books as it frantically whipped his wings about to regain control, diving back across the room toward Ayana.

"My homework!" Tyler cried, tossing Ayana a towel so she could protect the pile of hand-written pages neatly stacked at the corner of his desk. Ayana unfolded the towel and laid it over top of the papers before they got too soaking wet.

The dragon changed direction again, this time flapping its way toward the ceiling, its wings cutting furiously through the air as it gained altitude, spraying water across the entire room as it ascended.

The volume of water now descending in trickles and droplets throughout the room was making everything absolutely wet. It was like standing under a tiny flying lawn sprinkler.

Clearly, the amount of water the dragon was capable of flapping off into the air far exceeded the original small glass of water they'd used to conjure it in the first place. If they didn't stop it soon, Tyler's room was going to be a complete soaking wet mess, if it wasn't already, that is.

"Are you kids okay up there?" Tyler's mother called up from the bottom of the stairs. "You're making an awful racket."

"Do something!" Tyler whispered to Ayana desperately. The dragon now bumped its head against the light fixture on Tyler's ceiling, sending little tendrils of steam hissing off the hot light bulb.

Ayana nodded and closed her eyes for a second, thinking.

"Yishapsla," she finally said, wrinkling her forehead in concentration. "Yishlapsa. No, wait."

It took Tyler a second to figure out what she was trying to do. She was trying to say the dragon's name backward and undo the spell.

What is Splashy backward?!? Tyler thought in desperation, closing his eyes as he tried to sound out the letters.

"Yhsalps!" Ayana cried triumphantly, opening her eyes in time to see their tiny water dragon vanish into thin air. The watery sound of flapping wet wings suddenly disappeared, and all that was left was the quiet patter of water dripping from nearly every surface in the entire room.

Ayana and Tyler looked at each other in disbelief then burst into laughter. Tyler's room was soaked. There was water *everywhere*, but the two of them couldn't stop laughing.

"Did you *see* that?!?" Ayana grinned as she brushed her wet hair out of her face and stared up at the dripping ceiling.

Tyler was about to answer when the door to his room swung open and his mother peered inside.

"What in the world is going on in here?" she asked, looking concerned and confused as she glanced around the soaking wet room and the two soaking wet laughing children inside of it. "Why is everything so wet?"

"We were trying to do a magic trick with water," Ayana explained truthfully, quickly regaining her composure. "And it went a bit wonky."

Tyler's mother raised her eyebrows and looked around the room in disbelief.

"I'll say it went a bit wonky," she finally said. "You'd better get some more towels and clean up this mess."

"Yes, Mrs. Travers," Ayana replied respectfully. "We will."

"And next time try your magic tricks in the bathroom where nothing can get ruined if it gets wet."

"We will, Mom," Tyler said as they followed his mother out into the hall where she grabbed a big stack of towels from the linen closet.

"And be good," she added with a smile as she handed them the towels and headed back down the stairs toward the kitchen. "Dinner's in half an hour."

"We will," Tyler replied, and they watched her disappear down the steps before hurrying back to the soaking wet disaster zone that was Tyler's room.

"We have to try that again!" Ayana whispered excitedly to Tyler as the two of them soaked up all the excess water in his bedroom.

Tyler nodded eagerly.

"No kidding we will," he said, patting down the spines of his books and wiping the little pools of water on the bookshelves. "But in the bathroom, just like my mom said."

Ayana's eyes got wide.

"In the bathtub!" she cried. "Imagine how big a dragon we could make if we filled the bathtub! Or the swimming pool!"

Tyler looked at her and was about to tell her how absolutely crazy she was. But she looked so adorable standing there on her tiptoes patting the water off the glass face of Tyler's moon clock that he decided not to say anything at all. He just smiled and watched her working.

If she really wanted to conjure a swimming pool-sized water dragon, then who was he to stop her?

chapter four
the dragon of the month club

Ayana and Tyler didn't know it yet, but conjuring a swimming pool-sized dragon is not a very easy thing to accomplish. In fact, as far as they were concerned, it was basically impossible since it requires a level of skill and concentration that neither of them would achieve for many, many years. But that didn't stop them from trying many other experiments that same night in conjuring different types and sizes of water dragons.

After cleaning Tyler's bedroom as best they could, Ayana called her mother to tell her she was staying over for dinner, as she often did. But as they ate, the two of them could hardly sit still, so they gobbled up Tyler's mother's schnitzel and potatoes as quickly as they could and excused themselves from the table.

"Good luck with your magic tricks!" Tyler's mother smiled at them as they jumped from the table and left their dishes by the sink on their way upstairs. Tyler's father looked confused.

"Thank you!" Ayana called over her shoulder as she and Tyler pounded up the stairs and headed for the hallway bathroom. It was the one that only Tyler used and was therefore the easiest to waterproof by clearing the counters of anything that might get wet or knocked over.

When they were ready, they both climbed into the large, empty bathtub and sat across from each other with a glass of water positioned between them. *THE BOOK* was open on the floor nearby, and they each took a moment to refresh their memory of the various steps and motions required to execute the spell.

Once they were satisfied that they remembered it correctly, they placed their hands in starting position and began to weave the air to conjure the dragon. It took them three tries to get it right, but when they did, the same incredible thing happened: the tiny watery form of a little dragon formed and unfolded its wet, liquid wings right in front of them.

His name was *Bathtub*, in honour of where they were conjuring

25

him, and Tyler was already giggling at saying his name backward to un-conjure him: *But-htab.*

Bathtub flapped and fluttered awkwardly into the air while Ayana and Tyler stared up at him wide-eyed, their faces wet from the flying water. He bounced around the small room, ricocheting off the shower curtain and mirrors, rebounding here and there as they watched until he finally seemed to get a hang of things and found a place to land.

Ayana stared at him in amazement as he perched himself on the edge of the bathroom counter, licking his watery claws with a tiny transparent tongue.

"Here, *Bathtub*, here boy," she called out to him, extending her finger gingerly toward him.

The tiny dragon stared at her for a moment then slowly craned its neck forward to sniff her hand, blowing minuscule droplets of water out of its nostrils as it did so.

"He likes you," Tyler whispered in amazement.

The dragon took two steps forward and extended its little tongue to lick the tip of Ayana's finger. It felt like being licked by the cold, wet tongue of a hamster or hedgehog.

"You try," Ayana said, pushing Tyler forward.

Tyler reached out his hand, holding it as still as possible to avoid startling the little creature. Slowly the little dragon crept forward, sniffing cautiously until it nudged its tiny horned nose against the side of Tyler's hand.

"See?" Ayana said, grinning. "He likes you too."

Ayana held out her hand and watched as the dragon climbed onto her palm, its wet feet leaving tiny clawed footprints on the bathroom counter behind it. She tilted her head forward and let the dragon nuzzle its nose against hers. Droplets of water ran down the side of her nose, magnifying the freckles as they went.

"It's so cute!" she breathed in awe. "You're so cute, aren't you?"

Tyler watched her and imagined what it would be like to nuzzle his own nose against Ayana's.

"We have to try another one," Ayana said, eyes closed.

"What about *Bathtub*?" Tyler asked. "What happens to him when we un-conjure him?"

Ayana opened her eyes and thought about this for a second.

"You read what the book said," she replied. "Un-conjuring water dragons doesn't hurt them. We can always bring him back again."

Tyler thought about this then nodded slowly.

"Okay," he said finally.

Ayana smiled and spoke the dragon's name backward.

"*But-htab*," she said, and *Bathtub* dutifully winked temporarily out of existence.

"Where do you think they go when you un-conjure them?" Tyler asked uneasily.

Ayana shrugged her shoulders. Her mind was already on the next dragon they would conjure.

"Do you have any food colouring?" she asked, barely able to contain her excitement.

"Food colouring?" Tyler asked, confused.

Instead of a dragon made out of plain old water, Ayana wanted to conjure a coloured dragon—maybe green or red or purple— made from water mixed with food colouring.

As they would soon discover, this actually didn't work. As much as they tried, they simply couldn't get coloured water to work. They tried food colouring, Kool-Aid, even strawberry tea, but nothing worked. Tyler thought maybe there was something about the impurity of it that interfered with the spell.

Ayana was disappointed, but that didn't stop them from experimenting further.

Strangely enough, salt water worked extremely well for conjuring. The resulting dragon (named *Salty*—Tyler's idea) looked quite similar to *Bathtub*, but with a slightly scalier and courser skin texture. The more salt they added (*Salty 2* and *Salty 3*), the rougher the dragon skin appeared to be.

Soda water also worked quite well and resulted (unsurprisingly) in a rather bubble-filled dragon (*Bubbly*—Tyler's idea again) that fizzed and popped even when standing perfectly still on the bathroom counter, nose-to-nose with Ayana.

Ayana and Tyler also discovered that using water from different countries around the world also made a difference in the appearance of the resulting dragon. *Evian* water from France, for example, resulted in a dragon with a longer and much narrower worm-like body than the normal filtered tap water from Tyler's fridge had made. Unfortunately, that particular dragon had been especially difficult for Ayana and Tyler to un-conjure since Ayana had named it *François*—a suitable name but one that was somewhat difficult to say backward.

Fortunately, to aid in their experiments, Tyler's parents had several different brands of mineral water in the house. To their disappointment, however, most of these were just normal water purified using a mysterious process known as reverse osmosis, which didn't seem to make any kind of difference at all.

But by a stroke of luck they also had a couple of other exotic mineral waters from around the world including *Jana* water from Croatia, which resulted in a short, stocky little dragon they called *Boris*, and *Waiākea* water from Hawaii, which resulted in a rather Asian-looking dragon they called *Mahalo*.

"We have to get more water," Ayana observed solemnly as Tyler un-conjured *Mahalo*. They were silent a moment as they watched him evaporate into thin air.

"Definitely," Tyler agreed, his voice sounding far away as he pondered this, but then he nodded enthusiastically and made some careful notes in a blank notebook he'd dedicated to writing down their observations about the various dragons had conjured.

Ayana stifled a yawn. It was getting late.

"I should probably go," she said, disappointed. "But we totally have to get more water."

"The health food store my parents shop at has all sorts of weird water from around the world," Tyler said, snapping his notebook shut and picking the dragon conjuring book off the floor.

"Tomorrow we try a bigger dragon," Ayana said, her eyes boring into Tyler's to make him promise. "Bucket sized."

But Tyler wasn't listening. He was staring down at the cover of the *THE BOOK*—the dragon conjuring book that had fallen off the shelves of the library and straight into their hands just a few hours earlier.

"Look," Tyler said, barely breathing. "The cover...."

Ayana looked over Tyler's shoulder and frowned. At first she didn't notice what he was staring at, but then she saw it.

The name of *THE BOOK* had changed, and so had the cover.

Previously the cover had been blue—a pale watery blue—with big friendly yellow letters that read: *how to conjure your very own dragon in six easy steps.*

But now the cover was the colour of the sky just before sunrise, an endless deep blue against an infinite field of stars, and written across this background in letters the colour of a faraway distant rainbow were the following words:

the dragon of the month club
(or how to conjure your very own dragon in six easy steps)

"The dragon of the month club?" Ayana exclaimed. "I don't get it. What happened to the book we found?"

Tyler hesitated.

"I think this is it," he replied. "It's the same book. It just changed."

Ayana stared.

"But what's the dragon of the month club?" she asked.

"I don't know," Tyler replied, flipping absently through the pages to check whether anything else had changed.

Tyler frowned.

"Was this page here before?" he asked, jabbing the last page with his finger.

Ayana looked down. Printed on the final page of *THE BOOK* were two blank forms complete with dotted lines around them

"There's no way that was there before," Ayana said, shaking her head slowly. "I *definitely* would have noticed it."

"I didn't think so either," Tyler replied.

now that you've successfully conjured your first dragon, you are eligible to join the exclusive dragon of the month club. signing up is easy. just fill out the forms below and drop them into any mailbox.

Following the text at the top of the page there were two blank registration forms.

dragon of the month club registration form

name:
favourite colour:
favourite food:
favourite animal:
favourite jelly bean:
favourite flavour of ice cream:
favourite school subject:
swim or fly:
cake or pie:

signed: _____

"There's no blank space for your address," Tyler observed. "How will they know where you live?"

Ayana shrugged. "Maybe they don't need to?" she suggested, grabbing Tyler by the arm. "Come on! We're filling these out and dropping them in the mailbox at the end of your street before I go home."

Ayana pulled Tyler to his feet and dragged him down the hall. Pushing open the door to his bedroom with her foot, she immediately headed for his desk, pulling open the top drawer and extracting a pair of scissors.

With a few quick snips, Ayana clipped the two registration forms and handed one to Tyler along with a pen.

"Fill yours out," she said. "And I'll do mine."

"Okay," Tyler readily agreed and the two of them sat down to fill out their forms. The questions were easy, and it only took a few seconds to complete the entire form.

dragon of the month club registration form

name: **Tyler Travers**
favourite colour: **Blue**
favourite food: **Pizza**
favourite animal: **Dogs**
favourite jelly bean: **Sour Apple**
favourite flavour of ice cream: **Chocolate**
favourite school subject: **Science**
swim or fly: **Swim**
cake or pie: **Cake**

signed: _Tyler Travers_

"And now an envelope," Ayana said, handing her form to Tyler while she rummaged around his desk.

Tyler couldn't resist sneaking a look at Ayana's form while she was searching.

dragon of the month club registration form

name: _Ayana Fall_
favourite colour: _Purple_
favourite food: _Ravioli_
favourite animal: _Dragons_
favourite jelly bean: _Buttered Popcorn_
favourite flavour of ice cream: _Pistachio_
favourite school subject: _Recess_
swim or fly: _Fly_
cake or pie: _Pie_

signed: _Ayana Fall_

Pistachio ice cream? Tyler never would have thought her the pistachio type. He'd have to remember that.

"Okay, got it," Ayana cried, holding up a brand new crisp white envelope. "I knew you'd have one."

Ayana took both registration forms and dropped them inside, licking the glue on the flap at the edge of the envelope and sealing it shut.

"Wait a minute," Tyler said, frowning. "Where do we send it? They don't say anything about what address we're supposed to put on it?"

Ayana shrugged again. Details like this didn't seem to bother her in the least.

"Maybe we don't *need* an address," she said, grabbing her coat and quickly pulling it over her shoulders. "Come on, grab your jacket. I have to get home, and I want us to mail this tonight."

"But how will it get to where it's supposed to go without an address?" Tyler asked, grabbing *THE BOOK* and shrugging into his own jacket as Ayana impatiently pulled him out of the door and down the stairs.

"Bye, Mr. and Mrs. Travers!" Ayana called out toward the living room as she pulled open the front door and dragged Tyler outside.

"What about stamps?" Tyler asked stubbornly.

Ayana stopped in her tracks.

"It's a magic book," she said impatiently. "The forms don't need addresses or stamps to get where they're going."

Tyler frowned.

"But how do you know all that?" he asked. "How can you be so sure?"

Ayana thought about this for a second.

"I just am," she finally answered and pulled Tyler toward the end of the block to where a bright red Canada Post mailbox was waiting.

Tyler's block was empty except for a few late evening walkers out with their dogs. By the time the two of them reached the mailbox, even those had disappeared, and they had the street to themselves. A strange silence seemed to fill the air around them, as if the entire world was holding its breath in anticipation of some momentous event about to happen.

"Are you ready?" Ayana asked, yanking open the mailbox and holding the envelope above the dark, yawning chasm inside.

Tyler gulped and nodded. He was as ready as he'd ever been.

"Here goes," Ayana said, and she dropped the envelope into the slot.

Tyler heard it slide down the throat of the mailbox and hit the bottom with a muffled clunk.

They both waited, breathlessly.

"Is that it?" Tyler finally asked after several long moments of silence.

Ayana was frowning. She had been expecting something dramatic to happen.

"I guess so," Ayana sighed in disappointment.

But that wasn't it.

"Ayana, look!" Tyler cried, staring down at *THE BOOK*. While Ayana had been sighing, he'd flipped it open to the last page again, and was surprised to see that *THE BOOK* had changed yet again. The clipped remnants of the registration forms were now gone and had been replaced by a brand new final page.

Ayana and Tyler were speechless. There was nothing for them to do but stare at each other with their mouths open in disbelief.

dear Ayana and Tyler,

congratulations! you are now officially members of the dragon of the month club! membership in this exclusive club has many exciting benefits, including the monthly release of a brand new dragon. check back in this book at twelve o'clock noon on the thirteenth of every month to see each new dragon of the month as it is revealed.

conjure and collect them all! limit of one type of dragon at a time!

most of all, have fun!

yours truly

Vanity Logansky

Vanity Logansky

Dragon of the Month Club
Department of Membership Inquiries
Room 32b
137 Faraday Park Circle
London W1
United Kingdom

chapter five
the steam dragon

Over the course of the months that followed, Ayana and Tyler made a special point of getting together on the thirteenth of every month to sit impatiently and wait for the clock to strike noon so that they could see the new dragon that was revealed.

The reveal was done in typical Dragon of the Month Club fashion with additional pages appearing out of nowhere at the end of *THE BOOK*. And as time wore on, *THE BOOK* grew thicker as each new dragon was added.

Air dragons, paper dragons, fog dragons, waterfall dragons, rock dragons, some kind of weirdly specific tree dragon—there were even special bonus dragons for all the major holidays, including a special prickly holly dragon for Christmas. The list seemed almost endless. But much to Ayana and Tyler's disappointment, not all of the dragons could be conjured, at least not by the two of them, anyway.

Sometimes they simply lacked the raw materials required. There wasn't a lot of fog in the dusty dry prairies where they lived. And although they were able to find rice paper for the paper dragon, they lacked the other key requirement for the spell, which was to write the Chinese character for dragon in calligraphy using dark ink made from a stalk of black bamboo.

Other times they simply lacked the skill to execute the spell. Sometimes the hand motions were just too complex, and no matter how hard they tried and practised they just couldn't do it and had to wait around another whole month for the next dragon to be revealed.

Winter turned to spring, spring to summer and summer to fall. The seasons passed, as they always do, until the day when the instructions for conjuring a steam dragon magically appeared at the end of *THE BOOK*.

It was a cold and crisp November day, a school day, which meant that Ayana and Tyler had to skip lunch and hurry across town to meet at the halfway point between their schools so they could open *THE BOOK* together and discover the new dragon.

Ayana was late, and Tyler could guess why.

That month it was Ayana's turn to hold on to *THE BOOK*. They'd made an agreement to switch custody of *THE BOOK* back and forth every time a new dragon was revealed. That meant that Ayana was out there somewhere with *THE BOOK* tucked into her jacket or backpack, safeguarding it with her life against anyone who might try to take it from her—someone like Heather van der Sloot.

As Tyler sat there on the concrete orca whale slide, staring across the park in the direction he knew Ayana would come from, he could only imagine what might have happened to make her so late.

"Sorry I'm late," he heard Ayana say from behind him, scaring him half out of his wits.

"Where did you come from?" he asked, spinning around in surprise.

Ayana shrugged her shoulders and slid onto the edge of the orca slide next to him, setting her backpack on the ground and pulling out *THE BOOK*.

"I had to take the long way around," she said simply. That was all the explanation that was required.

Tyler nodded and stared at the ground, kicking the sand with the toes of his shoes.

"I'm sorry," he said.

"It doesn't matter," Ayana said and handed *THE BOOK* to him. "You open it. It's yours to look after for the next month, after all."

Tyler nodded gravely and flipped *THE BOOK* open to the page where they'd left off the month before. The previous month's dragon had been a bamboo dragon, which sounded simple enough on the face of it. All they had to do was find some bamboo, right?

But to their great disappointment, not only did the spell require a very specific and rare type of black bamboo (*phyllostachys nigra aureosulcata*), but Ayana and Tyler could easily see from the step diagrams that even *if* they could find such bamboo, the conjuring hand motions were probably beyond their current abilities anyway.

So, with fingers crossed and breath held in anticipation, Tyler turned the last few pages, hoping that *this* month's dragon would be one that they could actually conjure instead of waiting another whole month for the next one. And what if they couldn't conjure the next one either? Nothing was worse than that.

Fortunately, as soon as they read the title of this month's new dragon, they sighed with relief:

the steam dragon

category: high dragon
difficulty: easy
classification: common

"That sounds promising," Tyler commented as the two of them read further.

the steam dragon is an extremely easy conjuring spell to master and can be performed by even the most basic of amateur conjurers. the spell is not without its difficulties, however. unless it is executed with absolute precision, it can easily reverse itself with potentially grave and unpredictable side effects.

Tyler didn't like the sound of that. Ayana seemed completely unbothered by the warning.

potential conjurers are therefore warned to attempt this spell only if they possess at least a moderate level of experience in dragon conjuring.

That made Tyler feel a bit better. Surely after all the dragons that he and Ayana had attempted to conjure over the previous year had qualified them as being at least moderate in skill and experience.

The only thing standing between them and conjuring a steam dragon was whether they could obtain the materials needed.

Tyler glanced at the bottom of the page.

required material(s): steam

That was easy enough. At least it didn't require something weird like the steam from the brewing of some rare Chinese yellow tea harvested during the third full moon of the year of the dragon or something like that.

Tyler glanced at Ayana. "Sounds easy, but we have to be careful, of course."

"Of course...." Ayana nodded, but Tyler could see that her mind was elsewhere.

"Do you wanna meet up after school—at my house maybe?" Tyler asked.

Ayana stared across the park, her expression blank.

"Why don't we go now?" she said.

Tyler was confused.

"And skip school?" He was surprised at this suggestion. It wasn't like her.

Ayana nodded.

"Yes," she said, staring at the ground again. "I don't feel like going back there today."

"Can we do that?!?" Tyler wondered aloud. "Just skip school, I mean? What if we get caught?"

"So what?" Ayana shrugged. "What can they going to do to us?"

"Suspend us?" Tyler replied nervously. "Expel us?"

Ayana looked up at him as if to say *Seriously?* Instead she said, "Do you really think they'll kick us out of school just for skipping class?"

Now that she put it that way, it didn't seem to make a lot of sense.

"Detention?" he said. "They might stick us in detention for a few weeks."

Ayana shrugged again. "So what? I'll bet they don't even notice. They'll think we went home sick or something."

Tyler still wasn't sure. He'd never done anything like that before. But seeing Ayana sitting there looking so sad and lost made him want to do something heroic for her, anything to make her smile again. Skipping class wasn't exactly heroic, but maybe spending the afternoon playing around with some newly conjured dragons would put a smile on her face.

"Okay," he said. "Let's do it."

Ayana stared at him in disbelief.

"Seriously?" she asked. "I mean, seriously? You? Skipping school?"

Tyler nodded. "Seriously." He tried to sound nonchalant.

Ayana smiled. His heroic gesture was working already.

"Okay," she said, jumping to her feet from the bottom of the orca slide. "Let's go."

Tyler was less convinced than he sounded. What would his mother say if she found out?

She'll probably think Ayana is a bad influence on me, Tyler thought as he pulled himself to his feet and followed Ayana to the edge of the park and across the street.

They stuck to back alleys as much as they could to avoid being spotted by anyone. They didn't talk much. Ayana was clearly upset about something more than whatever might have happened that day between her and Heather van der Sloot.

"I hate it here," she said after they'd walked together in silence for a while. Her voice was strangely distant, and her breath made tiny clouds in the ice-cold air.

"Here in the alley?" Tyler asked, trying to make a not-very-funny joke.

"Here in this city," Ayana clarified. "I hate it here."

"I knew what you meant," Tyler replied.

"I hate that there are no trees or mountains," Ayana continued. "And I hate my school."

"I know," Tyler said quietly.

"No one there likes me," Ayana said, looking desperately sad as she glanced at Tyler for a moment. "You're my only friend."

Tyler blushed but didn't say anything. They walked in silence, both staring at the ground directly in front of them.

"And I hate that my dad left and that me and my mom have to live with my grandparents," Ayana said in almost a whisper before falling silent again.

Tyler didn't know what he could possibly say to make Ayana feel better, so they simply walked the rest of the way to his house without saying another word.

Tyler unlocked the back gate and let Ayana go first. They hurried to the back door, hoping no one would see them, and Tyler unlocked it as fast as he could.

"So how do we make steam for the dragon?" Ayana asked as Tyler closed the door behind them.

"Hot water," Tyler suggested. "Like for making tea. That has steam."

"I'll make us some hot chocolate while we're at it," Ayana said, trying to smile as she opened the cupboard where the hot chocolate packets were kept. "With or without marshmallows?"

"With, of course," Tyler replied as he filled the electric kettle and switched it on. As it heated, the kettle creaked and groaned, a soothing sound on a cold day perfect for skipping school.

"Where are they?" Ayana asked, opening and closing cupboards, trying to find marshmallows.

"Next to the fridge," Tyler replied. He grabbed three big mugs off the rack on the wall and set them on the counter, one for him, one for her and one for conjuring the steam dragon.

While they waited for the water to boil, Ayana watched as Tyler went over the various hand motions of the new spell.

"These are pretty simple," she commented, pointing to the illustrations on the page. The motions were already quite familiar to the two of them.

Tyler nodded. Most of the spell was pretty standard, nothing they hadn't seen before, but it was conjured in a jumbled order. The only thing new to them was how specific the instructions were in terms of the various relative angles and distances of their hands. Complex notes were included for each step in the spell:

step one: starting position

conjurer A: right hand, palm up, fingers between 0.9 and 1.3 centimetres apart at the base of the fingernails. thumb at a 50-60 degree angle, no more, no less. left hand in a fist, palm down, thumb sticking out perpendicular.

conjurer B: left hand out, palm down, right angle to palm of conjurer A, between 3.2 and 4.7 centimetres apart. (the farther apart, the bigger the dragon, but stay within these limits!) right hand, palm down over the right hand of conjurer A at a distance of between 7.9 and 9.4 centimetres, as close as possible while still allowing enough distance to execute a full tourner at the beginning of step two.

And so on, the instructions went. Step after precise step.

"We're gonna need a ruler," Tyler laughed as the kettle began to boil.

"And one of those angle measuring things," Ayana added.

"A protractor," Tyler said. "I have one in my pencil case."

Ayana playfully rumpled Tyler's hair as he filled the three mugs with steaming hot water and put spoonfuls of hot chocolate powder into two of them.

"No one likes a know-it-all," she said, teasing.

Tyler tried not to blush as she tried to straighten his hair again.

"Grab the marshmallows," he said, picking up two mugs in one hand and one in the other.

Ayana followed him upstairs to his bedroom, grabbing a chocolate bar off the kitchen table as she went.

"We need our strength," she explained. "If we're gonna do all this measuring and protractorating."

Ayana giggled at her own joke as she kicked open the door to Tyler's room. As usual, the room was a mess with books all over the place, overflowing from his many bookshelves onto the floor and bed and desk and chairs.

Tossing the chocolate bar and marshmallows onto the brightly coloured bedspread, Ayana flopped down and sat cross-legged. The quilt was decorated with a repeating pattern of small desert islands, each with its own single lonely palm tree, and swimming between each island on a background sea of bright coral reef blue were the grey triangular fins of giant cartoon sharks.

"What's this?" Ayana asked as she pushed some books out of her way to make room for herself.

"Nothing," Tyler said, carefully setting the hot mugs on his bedside table. He grabbed the book nearest to Ayana, a red hardcover book, and moved it out of her reach. It was his diary. It contained his private thoughts, and the last thing he wanted was for Ayana to read any of them.

Ayana ignored him. She knew it was his diary.

"I meant that one," she said, pointing to the other book that she'd just pushed out of the way. It was a pop-up book.

"Just fairy tales," Tyler replied, pushing his diary out of sight behind him.

Ayana flipped through the various pages of the pop-up book, watching in fascination as each scene folded into life in front of her.

"What kind of fairy tales are these?!?" she asked, horrified. "*The Dreadful Story of Harriet and the Matches*?!?"

"That's a good one." Tyler grinned.

Ayana read further.

"What's all this about?!?" she asked, cringing as she read along. "This is terrible! Harriet plays with matches and burns to death until nothing is left of her except her scarlet shoes and a pile of ashes on the ground?!?"

Tyler nodded.

"They're German," he said simply, as if that explained everything.

"They're awful!" Ayana replied, turning to the next page and opening it flat on the bed to reveal a dark forest of tall paper trees and dense bushes.

"This one's even better—*The Story of the Little Thumb-Sucker*," Tyler said, leaning over to examine the scene where a small house was nestled snugly amongst the trees. A small boy with his thumb in his mouth peered out of a window, watching his mother heading off on some errand down a path in the woods. On the other side of the house, hidden nearby in the trees, lurked a terrible looking tall man with a yellow top hat, green tailcoat and bright red knickers. Grasped in the man's hands was a pair of giant scissors.

"What's it about?" Ayana asked, almost afraid to know the answer.

"It's a story about a little boy who always sucks his thumb even though his mother warns him not to," Tyler explained. "And then one day his mother goes out shopping and an evil roving tailor called the *Great Red-Legged Scissor-Man* shows up to teach him a lesson by snipping his thumbs off with a giant pair of scissors."

Ayana made a revolted face.

"That's enough fairy tales," she said, pushing the book away from her in disgust.

"But there's more!" Tyler laughed but Ayana just shook her head.

"Enough," she said. "Can we please just conjure a steam dragon?"

"Okay, fine." Tyler chuckled as he pushed the pop-up book to one side and opened *THE BOOK* between them.

Tyler extracted a small plastic ruler and protractor from his pencil case so they could start working through the steps one at a time, memorising each basic motion and measuring exact distances and angles. It was gruelling work, and it took them more than an hour of repetition after endless repetition and two cups of hot chocolate each before they felt confident enough to try it for real.

The water in the conjuring mug had grown cold, so they ran downstairs and boiled some more water, and hurried back up to Tyler's room where they sat across from each other at the end of his bed.

"Isn't that too hot?" Tyler asked as Ayana positioned the mug between her toes.

She shook her head.

"My feet are cold," she said and placed her hands in their starting position. Tyler sat opposite her and did the same.

"Are you ready?" he asked, staring at her with his big blue eyes through the maze of fingers and arms.

Ayana nodded.

"His name is *Vapor*," she said to no one in particular. "Our steam dragon's name is *Vapor*."

Good name, Tyler thought and began a perfectly executed *tourner* with his right hand.

And so began the dance of hands, each one flowing smoothly between them as they progressed through the spell one step at a time—whirling, spinning and pirouetting the steamy air.

This is it, Ayana thought as she performed the spell's final flourish and watched in amazement as the misty blurry outline of a tiny dragon condensed into form on the palm of her outstretched hand. She leaned close as the little dragon stretched its tiny legs and yawned enormously, its hazy little teeth showing as it opened its mouth wide.

"It's adorable!" she cried as the dragon morphed into shape and unfolded its gossamer wings. It flapped twice, sending little clouds of steam spiralling through the air and filling the little dragon's nose.

"He's going to sneeze," Tyler said, grinning. And he was right. The dragon curled its head to one side and sneezed, sending terse wisps of steam shooting out of his tiny nostrils. What Tyler *didn't* realise, however, was that the little clouds of steam had filled his nose too, and he was about to let out a gigantic sneeze that would have unexpected consequences.

If it had started the same as all sneezes do, coming on slowly and gradually so that you can grab a tissue and prepare for it, maybe things would have been different. But this was one of those sudden surprise sneezes, the kind that come on in the blink of an eye—one second you're fine, the next your whole head explodes in a sneeze.

Maybe even that sudden and unexpected sneeze would have been okay and things would have turned out normally had there not been a mug filled with steaming hot water sitting on the bed between the two of them. But because there was, so began a disastrous chain reaction that would change Ayana and Tyler's lives forever.

Just as the tiny steam dragon was reaching the end of its formation, Tyler sneezed, involuntarily putting his hand up to his face to cover his mouth. Just as he did that, the sneeze finally burst and his whole body convulsed along with it. His legs kicked slightly and knocked against the mug, spilling some of its scalding hot water onto Ayana's toes.

You can probably guess what happened next, or at least part of it, anyway. With her feet suddenly soaked in burning hot liquid, Ayana instinctively pulled her own legs away to protect them and ended up spilling half of the rest of the hot water all over Tyler's feet in turn.

Tyler pulled his feet back, kicking and emptying the remaining water all over the bed and pop-up book. He and Ayana both reflexively jerked their hands out of the spell's final position, but miraculously the steam dragon somehow managed to finish forming, hovering in mid-air for the briefest of moments before everything suddenly went completely wrong.

The next thing that happened was one of those unpredictable side effects that *THE BOOK* had warned them about. Suddenly the steam lingering over the soaking wet pop-up book began to twist and swirl like one of those artificial tornadoes you see when you visit a science centre for kids. It started slowly at first but quickly gained momentum, taking only seconds to reach a feverish pitch that sucked everything nearby into it.

Ayana screamed and grabbed for Tyler's hand, but it was already too late. The two of them (plus *Vapor*) were being sucked toward some kind of weird steamy black vortex that had suddenly opened on the bed beneath them. And like it or not, they were falling into it.

Tyler held on tight to Ayana's hand while clawing desperately with his free hand for anything that might stop them from being sucked in. The only thing within reach was the backpack he'd set on the floor next to the bed, but the weight of that barely even slowed them as the vortex spun faster and stronger than ever.

We can't possibly fit through that tiny vortex, Tyler thought as passed over the threshold and plummeted into the blackness. Tyler wasn't sure, but it felt like their bodies were shrinking as they fell. Either that or the swirling vortex was getting bigger and bigger. He couldn't quite tell which it was.

They plunged blindly through the dark expanse for several long moments, but then there was a sudden crashing cacophony of noise from all around them as they tumbled end-over-end through what felt like wet branches and leaves until finally crashing to earth (or wherever it was) with a heavy resounding thump.

"Ow," Tyler complained, landing painfully on his tailbone and rolling onto his stomach.

Ayana was there too. He could hear her moaning and tossing and turning somewhere nearby.

Tyler pulled himself to his knees and tried to get a look at the world around them. But it was pitch black.

"Where are we?" he asked, his voice sounding strangely faint as his eyes tried to adjust to the dim light.

"I don't think we're in Kansas anymore," he heard Ayana say from somewhere nearby.

Unfortunately, as it turned out, she couldn't have been more right.

chapter six
the pop-up forest

"What *is* this place?" Ayana whispered as she sat up dizzily and stood to her feet, swaying a bit until she regained her balance. The air around them felt steamy and damp, like they'd just missed a sudden thunderous downpour on some oppressively hot summer night.

It took a long time for Ayana's eyes to adjust to the darkness but when they did she realised that they were in some kind of forest. There were trees all around them. At least they *looked* like trees— sort of. There was something decidedly odd about their appearance.

"*Vapor*! Come here boy!" Ayana heard Tyler calling from somewhere close by. There was a sudden rustling of branches and a hiss of steamy breath as the tiny dragon burst out of some nearby bushes and flapped his way past Ayana's face, disappearing out of sight somewhere off to her right.

"Tyler?" Ayana called out. "Is that you? Are you okay?"

All she heard was more rustling and the sound of hissing steam.

"I'm okay," she finally heard Tyler say. "Follow my voice and come toward me."

"Okay," Ayana replied, pushing some branches out of her way as she made her way to Tyler. "Keep talking."

"You're definitely right. We're for sure not in Kansas anymore!" Tyler was laughing, letting his voice lead her on, but Ayana stopped for a moment, frowning as she examined the branches of the tree she was standing next to.

"What's the deal with these trees?" she asked, feeling the branches between her fingers. On the surface, they felt like normal leaves and branches, with rough bark and sticky sap, yet they were different somehow, flat and weird—almost two-dimensional.

"What are you saying?" Tyler asked. Ayana continued toward the sound of his voice, feeling her way to the trunk of the tree.

Just like the branches, the trunk itself also felt very strange.

Ayana leaned over for a closer look. It wasn't round like normal tree trunks are supposed to be. Instead, it was V-shaped, with two thick, flat sides joined together at the base of the V like someone had joined them together to give the appearance of a normal tree.

There was something very familiar about it and Ayana gasped when she realised what it was.

"These are pop-up trees!" she cried, running her hands along the course bark of one of the tree trunk's flat sides. "Just like the paper ones in your pop-up book, except these are real!"

"I know! Isn't it cool?" Tyler exclaimed. He was closer now. Just a few steps farther and she would be able to see him.

Ayana pushed the last of the strange, flat branches out of her way and stepped into a small clearing. Tyler was standing there rubbing his butt painfully but grinning. *Vapor* was there too, rooting around steamily in the dirt, digging for something.

"What's that?" Ayana asked, squinting in the darkness toward the far side of the clearing. There seemed to be some kind of small manmade structure there.

Tyler turned his head.

"It's a book," he said, "the one from my bed. It must have got pulled down in here just like we were."

Ayana took a few steps closer. Tyler was right. It *was* a book, his diary, to be exact, the one with the red cover, except now it was the size of a large automobile, and was propped face down in the bushes like some giant hands had just set it there for a moment and didn't want to lose their page.

"Why is it so big?" Ayana whispered.

Tyler shrugged. "I don't know," he replied. "But I think it's more like we're now very small and it's still normal size."

"Then how did we get so small?" Ayana asked.

Tyler shrugged again.

"Unpredictable side effects of the spell maybe."

"Oh, boy," Ayana said, feeling weak in the knees.

"Here, let me help you," Tyler said, seeing Ayana struggling to stay on her feet. He took her by the elbow and led her to a puffy white beanbag stool that was sitting nearby.

Ayana sank into the soft chair and leaned back, rubbing her forehead as she tried to get a grip on the absolutely insane thing that had apparently happened to them. Somehow they had been sucked into Tyler's pop-up book.

"What's that smell?" Ayana asked, suddenly noticing the strangely familiar sticky sweet powdery aroma lingering in the air around her.

Tyler was grinning.

"Marshmallow!" he cried excitedly. "It's marshmallow."

"Marshmallow?!?" Ayana repeated, confused. She sniffed again and finally understood. The big white beanbag stool she was sitting on was, in fact, a giant marshmallow. Or, more accurately, it was a normal sized marshmallow, and she had somehow shrunk small enough to sit in it like a chair.

Ayana jumped to her feet.

"Isn't it cool?!?" Tyler exclaimed. "And look over here! It's the chocolate bar you grabbed earlier!"

Ayana saw a gigantic plank of chocolate leaning against a nearby tree. It was cracked and bitten off in a few places but was still unmistakably the same bar of chocolate that she'd grabbed from Tyler's kitchen table just an hour earlier. She could even see her huge oversized teeth marks along the edge where she'd been snacking on it.

"This is impossible," Ayana protested, plopping down onto the marshmallow chair again to steady herself. "How is any of this possible?"

"I don't know," Tyler said, and he dragged another marshmallow over to sit next to Ayana. *Vapor* curled up on the ground between them.

"I don't know," he said.

Ayana looked over at him, worried.

"And how do we get back again?" she asked. "To the real world?"

Tyler hadn't thought about that. He'd been too excited about being in the pop-up book world.

"I'm not sure," he admitted with a sigh.

Ayana leaned back and stared up at the trees.

"At least we have the book," she said, holding up *THE BOOK*, which she somehow managed to grab before she fell into the vortex. "And at least it's normal size, instead of like that thing."

Ayana pointed toward Tyler's huge red diary.

"And I have my backpack," Tyler added, lifting it off the ground by one strap to show her.

"What about the protractor?" Ayana teased. "And the ruler?"

"I'm not sure what happened to those," Tyler said.

"I'm just kidding," Ayana replied, laughing nervously. She stared up through the trees again, watching the wind sway the flat branches back and forth.

Somewhere high above them a pale green light was shining. It was the moon, Ayana assumed, and she tried to peer through the breaks in the leaves to see it. Somehow, it didn't look quite right.

"Tyler, look at this," Ayana said, frowning and tilting her head to one side to better see through the trees.

"What is it?" Tyler leaned over to look up into the tree at the same angle that Ayana was.

"It's the moon," she replied. "But look at it!"

Tyler squinted his eyes and tried to see what Ayana was seeing.

"I don't get it," he said. "It's just the moon."

"LOOK at it," Ayana repeated impatiently. "It's not just the moon."

Tyler leaned farther over and looked again. He still couldn't see what Ayana was talking about.

"I don't see...." Tyler began, but then he saw it. It *was* the moon—a plain old normal full moon in a sky full of stars with all the various familiar pock marks and craters scarring its lunar surface—but what was weird about it were the clock hands that appeared to be mounted on top of that.

"Isn't that the clock from your bedroom?" Ayana asked.

Tyler blinked and looked again. It *was* his moon clock—or one exactly like it anyway.

"I think so," he replied hesitantly, straining for a better look. "But what's it doing up there in the sky?"

Tyler blinked again and thought about this for a second. He felt like he was on the verge of figuring out something very important.

"What is it?" Ayana asked, frowning as she noticed the expression on Tyler's face.

"Wait a minute...." Tyler replied, looking off into space as he struggled to understand what his brain was trying to tell him.

Ayana pulled herself up straight in her marshmallow chair and stared at him.

"What is it, Tyler?" she asked, her voice growing concerned. "What's wrong?"

Tyler looked at her for a second as a smile stretched across his face. He pulled himself up out of his chair.

"*Vapor*?" he called, waking up the tiny dragon who'd been sleeping on the grass between them. "*Vapor*? Can you understand me?"

The little steam dragon stared at Tyler looming over top of him.

"Can you fly up above the trees, *Vapor*?" Tyler continued. "Can you find us the tallest tree around here and show us which one it is?"

The little dragon stared a moment longer then suddenly seemed to understand, craning its neck upward and unfolding its wings.

"He understands you," Ayana whispered in amazement as the dragon flapped furiously and lifted itself off the ground, rising through the branches of the trees and disappearing into the sky.

"I hope he does, anyway," Tyler said as they watched and waited for *Vapor* to return.

"He does," Ayana assured him, and soon *Vapor* reappeared at the treetops and soared down toward them again, leading them across the clearing toward a break in the trees.

"Come on, *Vapor*," Tyler encouraged him. "Show us the way."

Vapor seemed to nod his tiny head and flapped over the tops of the bushes while Ayana and Tyler struggled to keep up.

They didn't have far to go until *Vapor* stopped and hovered clumsily in mid-air next to a massive triangular tree trunk that towered high above them.

"Good boy, *Vapor*!" Ayana cried as she stared up at the enormous tree. It was so tall that she couldn't even see the top of it.

"Now we climb," Tyler said, grabbing the nearest sturdy branch and pulling himself up.

"Race you to the top," Ayana said, grinning as she pulled herself onto another branch.

"Not fair!" Tyler cried as Ayana scaled up the side of the tree like a monkey. She was always a much better tree-climber than he was.

"Come on, slowpoke," Ayana called over her shoulder. "What's taking so long?"

Tyler gritted his teeth and clambered up the remaining branches as if he were climbing a ladder.

"Maybe I'm slow because I'm careful," he called out.

"Then don't be so careful," Ayana replied.

"That's easy for you to say," Tyler muttered under his breath as he tried to climb faster. "You're fearless."

"I can't hear what you're saying," Ayana laughed from somewhere high above. "You're too far away."

Tyler poured on the speed and raced up the next ten or twenty feet of tree until he finally caught sight of Ayana again, perched casually on a branch just below the surface of the tree canopy waiting for him. *Vapor* was sitting nearby on another branch just above her shoulder.

"Thanks for waiting," Tyler said as he scrambled up to meet her.

"Of course," Ayana replied. "What else was I supposed to do since I have no idea why we're up here in the first place. Are we trying to get a closer look at your clock?"

Tyler smiled mysteriously and pushed back the last few branches that separated them from the open sky.

"If I'm right...." Tyler said as the view was revealed to them.

Ayana gasped. Nothing could have prepared her for what she was seeing. The view was absolutely incredible.

High above them was a pitch-black velvet sky full of a billion stars that extended from one horizon to the other. Shining in the midst of that starry expanse was the moon, complete with minute, hour and second hands just like the moon clock on the wall in Tyler's bedroom. The clock was stopped at six minutes past two, the exact time that Ayana and Tyler had been sucked into the pop-up world.

Ayana had never seen such a beautiful sky, but what really took her breath away was the landscape stretched out down below them. From their vantage point, they could see for dozens and dozens of miles in all directions, across forests and rivers, oceans and deserts, distant twinkling cities and soaring mountain ranges.

Tyler was nodding knowingly as he looked out across the various worlds. Apparently, he'd been right about whatever it was he'd expected to see from up there.

"I don't get it," Ayana said. "What are you staring at?"

"That," Tyler replied, pointing his finger into the very farthest distance.

Ayana stared past the edge of the forest to a shallow sea dotted with dozens of tiny islands and palm trees. Beyond the enormous waterfall at the boundary of the sea was a vast sandy desert far below. Beyond that, she saw Chinese pagodas at the base of the cliffs, and past the top of the cliff, lights sparkled from what looked like a miniature version of London, complete with a replica of Big Ben. All the way past all of that to a rocky crag beyond was an enormous metal-domed clock tower looming high above the surrounding landscape.

That tower was what Tyler was pointing at.

"I still don't get it," Ayana said, turning to face Tyler. "What's so special about that tower?"

Tyler grinned.

"That's where Professor Möbius lives," he said simply. "He's the one who's going to help us get back home again."

chapter seven
professor möbius

"Who's Professor Möbius?" Ayana asked.

The name sounded familiar to her somehow, but she couldn't quite place it.

"You know," Tyler said, settling on a branch across from Ayana. "Professor Möbius of the *Science Is for Everyone* books?"

Ayana shook her head.

"You mean those nerdy science books you're always reading?" she asked.

Tyler sighed.

"Yes," he said. "Those nerdy science books."

"Okay," Ayana replied. "So what does that mean? What makes you so sure that he can help us?"

"He's a scientist!" Tyler said. "Of course he'll be able to help us."

"And how do you know that he's all the way over there?" she asked, turning her head to stare into the distance again. "Or better yet, how did you know that tower would be there in the first place?"

Tyler grinned.

"Take a look around," he said, gesturing across the breathtaking view in front of them. "Does any of this look familiar to you?"

Ayana frowned as she scanned the varied landscape spread out below them.

"Not really, no," she replied finally. "Is it supposed to?"

"Those islands down there don't look familiar to you?" Tyler asked, pointing to the shallow sea and islands that surrounded the dense pop-up forest on all sides.

Ayana looked again. Now that Tyler mentioned it, there was something slightly familiar about the repeating pattern of small islands strewn across the shallow blue waters. All the islands seemed to be copies of one another—each one completely deserted except for a single solitary palm tree.

"The quilt from your bed!" she cried.

"Exactly!" Tyler replied. "And those cliffs over there?"

Tyler pointed across the chasm at the edge of the sea toward the jagged rock formations in the distance. At first glance, they seemed completely random and natural looking, but the closer Ayana looked, the more regular the various shapes and angles seemed to be.

"Is that a... a chair?!?" she asked in surprise.

"Yes!!" Tyler cried. "It's my desk chair! Here, let me show you." Tyler took her by the hand and pointed all around them.

"This forest we're in now is the same forest in the pop-up book of German fairy tales lying on my bed, remember?"

"I remember. It does look the same," Ayana agreed cautiously.

"And the moon here looks just like the clock on the wall of my bedroom, right?" Tyler asked.

"Right," Ayana agreed again.

"And see those ocean and islands far below?" Tyler continued. "That's my bed. Can you see it?"

Ayana took in the vaguely rectangular-shaped ocean surrounding them.

"I guess so," she said hesitantly.

"And see how the water drops over the edge and forms a waterfall?" Tyler said. That's the edges of the bed, and the desert down below is the floor of my bedroom."

"Okay..." Ayana said.

"And the cliffs on the far side?" Tyler said. "That's my desk and chair. And the mountains beyond? Those are my bookshelves!"

"But that means..." Ayana began to say.

"It's my bedroom!" Tyler said triumphantly. "This whole world we ended up in is laid out just like my bedroom!"

Ayana almost couldn't believe what she was hearing. And yet the proof of it was stretched out right in front of her.

"And Professor Möbius?" she asked. "You know he's over there on your desk because...?"

"Because that's where I left his book," Tyler finished the sentence and climbed up to sit on the branch next to her. "And right now he's doing whatever it is he does with his spare time, just waiting for us to show up and ask for his help."

Ayana looked around again. It was completely crazy, but there was no denying Tyler's logic. The world surrounding them certainly *did* look very much like it was based on Tyler's messy bedroom.

"So all we have to do is go over there and ask him," Ayana said.

"Exactly," Tyler said.

"And how do we do that?" Ayana asked.

But Tyler didn't have an answer for that, at least not yet anyway.

"We can start by walking out to the edge of the forest tomorrow morning," he suggested. "We'll figure things out from there."

Ayana nodded in agreement. Tyler's plan seemed like a pretty good one in light of their current crazy situation.

"Okay," she said, and shivered involuntarily. It was getting cold up there in the wind at the tops of the trees.

"Why don't we head back down?" Tyler suggested.

Ayana nodded and started climbing down the tree, moving more carefully than she had on the way up. *Vapor* followed them down as well, flapping from branch to branch as they slowly descended.

By the time they reached the ground, Ayana was nearly freezing.

"Maybe we can start a campfire and roast some marshmallows?" she suggested, rubbing her arms in a futile effort to keep warm.

"Do you know how to start a fire without matches?" Tyler asked.

Ayana shook her head.

"Not really," she admitted. "Like, rub two sticks together or something?"

Tyler suddenly stopped dead in his tracks and stared at the ground in front of him.

"What is it?" Ayana asked, turning around to see what he was looking at.

Ayana nearly screamed when she saw it. Right on the ground in front of Tyler was a small box of wooden matches. But that wasn't the horrifying part. It was the pair of scarlet red shoes and the pile of ashes lying next to them that made Ayana's stomach heave and her blood run cold.

"What was the name of that fairy tale again?" she asked quietly, biting her lip to keep from screaming.

"*The Dreadful Story of Harriet and the Matches*," Tyler answered.

"And remind me what happened to Harriet in the end?"

Tyler took a deep breath.

"She played with matches and burned herself to death," Tyler replied. "Until nothing was left except her scarlet shoes and a pile of ashes on the ground."

Ayana shivered again, but this time not from the cold.

Tyler reached down and delicately picked up the box of matches from the ground.

"Be careful," Ayana whispered.

"They're just matches," Tyler replied, but he still held the tiny paper box at arm's length like it was a dangerous time bomb.

He carefully put the matches in his pocket and helped Ayana gather some firewood and kindling. When they had chosen a good campsite, he set the matches gently on the ground, and the two of them made a circle of stones and piled the wood together into a small teepee shape to build a campfire.

"Are you sure about this?" Ayana asked as they finished building the base for the campfire and Tyler took out a single match from the tiny paper box.

Tyler nodded, but in truth, he wasn't quite sure about it at all.

What if I light the match and it burns me to ashes? Tyler panicked as he held the match in one shaky hand. He glanced at Ayana, who was shivering worse than ever.

"We don't have to do this," she said. He could tell from her eyes that she was as frightened as he was.

"They're just matches," Tyler said again, more for his benefit than hers, and he mentally braced himself as he dragged the match across the side of the matchbox. At the teeniest hint of trouble, he was ready to throw the match into the woods and roll around on the ground to put the fire out, but the match just flared to life like all normal wooden matches always do, sparking at first, sputtering a bit then blazing strongly.

The two of them stared at the burning match for a moment, not yet sure whether something awful might still happen. They stared at it so long, in fact, that the match had almost burned down to nothing in Tyler's fingers before he remembered why he'd actually lit it in the first place.

"Owww!" he cried as he tried to light the pile of kindling before the match went out. He tossed the match away and pulled out another one, this time successfully getting the small bits of dried leaves and bark at the base of the fire to ignite.

"Come on, fire, burn," Ayana said as she blew encouragingly on the glowing embers, trying to coax them into flame. Slowly the larger twigs and branches caught fire, and soon they had a very respectable little campfire burning in front of them.

Ayana pulled herself in close, rubbing her arms to stay warm. *Vapor* liked the warmth too and curled himself next to the crackling fire near Ayana's feet.

"You stay here and keep warm," Tyler said. "I'll go get some sticks to roast marshmallows."

"Good, I'm starving," Ayana replied. "But how do you plan to roast those giant things over this tiny little fire?"

Tyler rolled his eyes.

"We have to cut them into smaller pieces, obviously," he said. "Like this."

Tyler demonstrated by pulling out his penknife and carving off some small cubes from the nearest marshmallow then spearing them on the ends of some sticks he had sharpened. He then hacked off a couple of fist-sized chunks of chocolate from the giant chocolate bar and brought everything back to the campfire where Ayana was waiting for him.

"Too bad we don't have graham crackers," Ayana remarked as Tyler handed her one of the marshmallow sticks and sat down beside her. "We could have made s'mores."

"I have some oatmeal cookies in my bag," Tyler replied.

Ayana shook her head. "It's not the same," she said.

The two friends sat for a while in silence, roasting their marshmallows and struggling to gnaw off bits of chocolate from the massive bar. Still sleeping at their feet, *Vapor* was dreaming little dragon dreams, his wings twitching as he dreamt of flying.

Tyler was a very careful marshmallow roaster, taking his time to rotate them until they were a perfect golden brown. But Ayana was from a completely different school of thought when it came to roasting marshmallows. She just stuck each marshmallow straight into the fire, pulling it out again and letting it burn for a few seconds before patting it out and pulling the blackened gooey mess off with her fingers.

Ayana suddenly felt a cold drop of water splash on her forehead.

"Oh, no," she said, holding out her palm and turning her face to the sky.

Another raindrop splattered across Ayana's cheek.

" It's starting to rain," Tyler said

"Come on," Ayana said, grabbing his hand. "This way."

The two of them ran over to Tyler's giant red diary that was still lying face down amongst the trees. It was parted open in the middle, forming a perfect shelter underneath its pages.

"Let me grab a marshmallow and some chocolate before they get soaking wet," Tyler said.

"I'll get the marshmallow, you get the chocolate," Ayana replied as she dashed over to the nearest giant marshmallow and dragged it to their book tent. Tyler ran to the huge plank of chocolate and sawed off a square big enough to feed them for a month, which he lugged over to where Ayana was waiting.

The rain was really coming down now, and the two of them held their hands out in it for a few seconds to wash off the sugary stickiness.

"What about *Vapor*?" Tyler asked, suddenly remembering their little dragon.

Ayana peered out through the pouring rain.

"*Vapor*!" she called. "Come here boy! Come here!"

Vapor's tiny head suddenly popped up over one of the logs they'd been sitting on near the fire. He looked around sleepily, his steamy body completely undisturbed by the falling rain.

"Come on, *Vapor*!" Ayana called again. "Over here, boy!"

The cute little dragon crawled onto the log and leapt into the air with a drippy whipping of his wings that sent droplets of water flying everywhere. He flapped clumsily toward the book tent and sent Ayana and Tyler ducking to stay dry as he settled down inside.

"Good boy," Ayana cried once the flying water droplets subsided. "Good boy, *Vapor*."

"So much for our campfire," Tyler observed, looking out through the rain to where the fire was gradually being soaked into non-existence.

Ayana yawned and shrugged.

"I guess we're stuck in here until the rain stops," she said.

Tyler looked around the inside of the tent to see how they could make themselves more comfortable.

"We'll probably have to spend the night in here," he said. "But maybe we can roll ourselves up in the pages for warmth."

Ayana watched as Tyler tugged on the oversized pages of the book, pulling one page free on each side and carefully folding them into makeshift sleeping bags.

"*Voila*!" he said proudly once he finished. "What do you think?"

"Perfect," Ayana said, smiling sleepily as she climbed into one of the sleeping bags to try it out. Once she was inside, *Vapor* crawled on top of her, his steamy little body warming her.

Tyler crawled into his sleeping bag on the other side of the tent and shuffled around until he was comfortable. The sound of the falling rain outside was soothing as the two of them lay there staring at the ceiling.

"Do you really think Professor Möbius can help us?" Ayana's voice floated in the darkness.

"I *know* he can," Tyler replied. "I'm sure of it."

"I hope so...." her voice trailed off into silence.

Tyler stared at the ceiling, and to his horror suddenly realised what was visible there. It was his handwriting—the words of his diary written out in gigantic letters scrawled across the arch of their book tent. Only fragments of the full text could be seen; the rest was obscured by the dark shadows and various folds of the pages, but what Tyler saw there made him cringe with embarrassment.

... I worry sometimes...
... Ayana...
... my best friend ...
... in so much pain ...
... I think I love her...

Tyler could only hope that Ayana wouldn't notice.

"Sometimes I just lie awake at night like this and cry," Ayana said, her voice pale and distant.

"What do you cry about?" Tyler asked, hoping to distract her from the embarrassing revelations scribbled on the ceiling.

"About my father," Ayana replied. "About him leaving us without saying a word."

"Oh," Tyler replied. He already knew what the reason was, but like always, he didn't know what to say to make things better—if there even *was* anything he could say or do, that is.

"My head knows that my mom and I are probably better off without him," she continued, sniffling. "But my heart is stubborn. It wants to understand why it has to feel so broken."

Tyler nodded silently in the darkness. He wanted to say that he understood how she felt but he knew that he actually really didn't.

On the opposite side of the tent, Ayana stared up at Tyler's handwriting on the ceiling. She wanted to say something too, but she didn't. She knew it would embarrass him too much. So they both just lay there, still and quiet, until sleep finally overtook them.

chapter eight
the roving tailor

The next thing Ayana knew she was being sneezed on by a steam dragon. She opened her eyes and found herself staring right at *Vapor*'s tiny face inches away from hers. He'd just sneezed and could obviously feel another one on the way as he slowly twisted his head from side to side in anticipation.

He sneezed again, an adorable steamy little sneeze.

The rain had stopped, and it was getting light outside. Ayana could see the pale blue glow of early morning seeping in through the opening at the end of their book tent.

Vapor stared at her. She couldn't tell if he was smiling or worried.

"What is it, little guy?" she asked. "Is something wrong?"

Just then she heard a sound from somewhere in the distance through the trees, a snapping sound that reminded her of something very familiar.

She tilted her head and listened again, hoping the sound would repeat itself.

A few moments later, she heard it again, a splintery snapping sound that was definitely familiar to her somehow.

It's like the sound of someone trimming the hedges, she thought. Ayana's grandfather was an avid gardener and spent most summer days outdoors tending to his elaborate garden, which included trimming the various trees and hedges into funny shapes that made her laugh sometimes. The sound of his garden shears cutting through the branches sounded exactly like what she was hearing now.

"Is someone outside gardening or something?" Tyler whispered groggily from across the tent. "Those sound like gardening shears."

Ayana looked over and saw Tyler rubbing his eyes drowsily as he sat up in his paper sleeping bag.

"It sounds like it, doesn't it?" Ayana whispered back, her eyebrows arched into a concerned frown. For some reason she didn't like the idea of some unknown person sneaking around in the forest so early in the morning.

"Maybe they can help us?" Tyler suggested, pulling himself fully out of his sleeping bag and stretching his legs.

"Maybe...." Ayana replied uneasily.

The sound came again, only it was closer this time, close enough to hear the tinny scraping sound of the metal blades as they snipped through the tough wood of a tree branch. But there was something slightly off about the sound. It was too high-pitched somehow, too thin and resonant.

"I'm not sure those are gardening shears," Ayana said, pulling her own legs out of the sleeping bag and staring through the opening at the end of the tent, listening intently and seeing nothing unusual.

"What else would it be?" Tyler asked. "What else would you use to snip through tree branches like that?"

Ayana thought about this for a second. Her grandmother was a bit of a gardener as well, but instead of hedges and vegetables, she preferred to grow pretty things like lovely flowers and tiny bonsai trees. And just like Ayana's grandfather, she also occasionally had to prune and trim her various plants, except that they were so small that she didn't have to use gardening shears. A simple pair of scissors always did the trick just fine.

Ayana finally realised what they were hearing.

"They're scissors!" Ayana whispered, her voice edgy with fear. "Giant scissors!"

"Giant scissors?!?" Tyler replied, confused.

Ayana watched as the realisation dawned on Tyler's face as well. The night before they had lit a campfire using leftover matches straight out of one of the pop-up book's horrible fairy tales—*The Dreadful Story of Harriet and the Matches*. But if those matches were real and that story was real, then maybe some of the other stories from the pop-up book were real too, like *The Story of the Little Thumb-Sucker*—the one with the evil roving tailor who cut the boy's thumbs off with a giant pair of scissors.

Tyler's face went completely pale, and he subconsciously tucked his thumbs in under his fingers to protect them.

"It can't be," he said. "It isn't possible."

"Not possible?" Ayana asked as she pulled herself to her feet and crept to the front of the tent to peer outside. "Just look around us. Pop-up trees, giant marshmallows. Is *any* of this possible?"

Somewhere close by they heard the crack of another powerful snip of the giant scissors cutting through a tree branch.

Ayana felt a gentle tugging on her shirtsleeve. She looked down and saw *Vapor* with his tiny teeth clamped onto one of her cuffs, trying to pull her away from the tent opening and the horrible snipping sounds.

"We have to go," Ayana said, noting the panic in *Vapor*'s tiny little eyes.

"Just wait a minute," Tyler said, stepping out of the book tent and into the clearing. "We don't even know if you're right about this or not. Maybe there's a perfectly logical explanation for all of this?"

Ayana didn't want to wait around to find out.

"We really have to go," she said again, more urgently this time. *Vapor* was yanking on her sleeve and flapping his little wings insistently.

From the far edge of the clearing, they heard a drawn-out grinding metallic creak, like the sound of a giant pair of scissors slowly being pulled open. There was a rustling of leaves, and suddenly the tip of a bright yellow top hat emerged from the bushes. The hat was very tall, and it seemed to go on forever, rising out of the underbrush endlessly until the head and face underneath it finally appeared. It was being worn by a man in a green suit and waistcoat with long brown hair, a pointy nose and bright red ruddy cheeks. It was the roving tailor—the same one Ayana had seen hiding in the trees in the pop-up fairy tale book.

The tailor seemed to be smiling pleasantly enough, his thin lips stretched tightly across his teeth, but something disagreeable in his face set Ayana on edge.

"Hello, children," he said, extracting himself even further from the bushes. His lanky long legs reminded Ayana of a spider wearing bright red knickers.

"Who are you?" Tyler asked, looking slightly terrified. "What do you want with us?"

The tailor smiled repulsively and pulled the rest of his body out of the bushes. As his right arm came into view, Ayana could see that the tailor was grasping something in it, holding it tightly with a set of long bony fingers.

It was a colossally huge pair of scissors.

Ayana gasped as she watched the tailor thread the enormously long blades out from behind the leaves and branches.

"I think you know who I am," the tailor said, smiling even more widely now. "I haven't seen any children around here for quite a long time. And I'll just bet that the two of you have been sucking your thumbs, haven't you?"

"No we haven't!" Ayana snapped as she took a few slow steps backward, letting *Vapor* pull her toward the edge of the clearing. She tried to sound as brave as possible, but her insides were churning in fright.

"Yeah!" Tyler said, sidestepping along with Ayana, keeping his distance from the gangly thin figure approaching them menacingly. "Leave us alone!"

The tailor stopped for a moment and lifted his huge scissors in the air, leisurely dragging them open with a prolonged creaky rasp.

"Oh, well," he said, eyeing the blades of his scissors thoughtfully. "I suppose I'll just have to cut off your thumbs anyway."

The tailor turned to look at Ayana and Tyler. His smile was vanishing rapidly now as his mouth stretched open to reveal rows of crooked teeth shaped like tiny fangs. He pulled himself up to his full towering height and glared down at them with eyes that seemed to grow darker and blacker with every vapid blink.

With one quick motion, the tailor reached up with his scissors and snipped the thick branch directly over his head completely in half, sending it plunging to the ground in a flutter of leaves.

Ayana and Tyler jumped out of the way just in time as the heavy branch fell. *Vapor* was pulling on Ayana's sleeve in an absolute panic, trying to get her as far away from the ominous roving tailor as possible. But Ayana didn't need a lot of convincing any more. She was terrified.

"Run!" she screamed at Tyler, grabbing his arm and nearly yanking him off his feet as she pulled him into the bushes behind them.

The two of them crashed and hacked their way through a barrier of thick underbrush until they reached some open space on the other side. Pulling their clothes free of the clingy bushes they broke into a full-out run, dodging left and right around the various trees in the forest as they went.

Too close behind them for comfort, they could hear the sound of the Roving Tailor crashing through the forest, his giant scissors snapping open and shut as he clipped his way through the trees.

"This way!" Ayana yelled, hauling Tyler off to one side and ducking as she followed *Vapor* under a fallen tree and out the other side.

"Don't worry, children!" called the voice of the tailor, taunting and laughing at them through the trees. "Just one snip is all it takes!"

Ayana pushed through some more tree branches, still pulling

Tyler along behind her, and was startled to see a pair of striped grey tabby cats sitting casually next to a tree on the other side. Their whiskers and fur were scorched and burned.

"Meow, meow!" The cats scratched and hissed at Ayana as she hurtled past them.

"What in the world are those?!?" She called back over her shoulder, catching one final glimpse of the two cats before they disappeared into the trees again as quickly as they'd appeared.

"Harriet's cats," Tyler explained as he dodged a branch that Ayana had just sent flying into his face.

"Sorry!" Ayana cried out as she sent yet another branch flying backward.

Tyler darted left to avoid getting a mouthful of leaves and watched as Ayana sprang into the air to jump over a large log. She planted her palms on it and vaulted over it, disappearing down the opposite side.

A moment later, Tyler heard her screaming.

"Ayana!!?!" he shouted as he hurtled over the log after her. "I'm coming!"

Just as he passed over the top of the log, Tyler saw what had caused Ayana to scream. It wasn't the Roving Tailor or any other frightening individual waiting for them on the other side, as he had feared. It was simply that there actually *was* no other side of the log. Once you jumped over the top, the ground simply dropped away, sending the two of them tumbling head over heels down a steep slope covered with more trees and prickly bushes.

"Ow! Ow! Ow!" Ayana complained as she rolled and stumbled and tripped her way through the underbrush until she came crashing to a halt at the bottom, right smack in the middle of a mess of unruly shrubs.

"Watch out!" Tyler cried as he came smashing down on top of her, managing to avoid hitting her at the very last second and colliding with a nearby tree instead. "Ow! My tailbone!"

The two of them sat there dazed for a moment, bruised and aching. It was Tyler who first realised that they had to keep running.

"Come on," he said, somehow dragging himself to his feet. "We have to keep going."

Ayana put a finger to her lips.

"Shhh," she whispered. "Listen."

Tyler stopped and tilted his head to one side, listening intently.

"I don't hear anything," he whispered in reply after a few seconds.

"Exactly," Ayana replied, still listening carefully. "I think we might have lost him."

Tyler was understandably skeptical about this and had to listen to the silence of the forest for a few more very long moments before he even dared to believe it.

"Is it possible?" he whispered softly.

They both listened again, straining their ears, but the only sound they could hear was the gentle rustling of wind in the trees—that and an oddly similar sound like a scratchy papery white noise.

"Shhhhh," Ayana whispered. "What *is* that?!?"

Tyler shook his head. "I don't know." He pointed to a break in the trees that led to a small clearing on the other side. "But it's coming from right over there."

chapter nine
the wishing tree

"What is it?" Ayana breathed, her voice barely a whisper over the whispering of the trees.

"I... don't... know...." Tyler replied, pausing hesitantly between every syllable.

Ayana pushed the remaining branches out of her face with one hand and stepped fully into the clearing. Standing in front of them was a very strange, gnarly, ancient tree with branches so twisted that there seemed to be no visible difference between them and the tree's roots. The branches were bent in all directions in their effort to find the sky; the roots were a mirror image and looked confused as they tried to find the earth. The only difference between the two was that the branches had leaves that were pale grey green in colour, like dusty leaves waiting for a summer rain shower to wash them vibrant again.

But all that wasn't what made the tree so unusual. It wasn't what made both Ayana and Tyler inch slowly and cautiously toward it. What made this particular tree so odd was the fact that its branches were not only covered in leaves, but also in small rectangular paper cards hanging from rough bits of string tied to every branch. There were hundreds of them, at least as many of them as the tree had leaves. All of them were blowing in the gentle breeze, scratching and rustling together, their sound a different voice from the chorus of wind-rustled leaves in all the trees surrounding them.

"Are they luggage tags?" Tyler asked, inching his way forward. He looked slightly frightened, as if this paper-decorated tree might suddenly jump toward him and grab him.

"Or train tickets?" Ayana said, finishing his thought.

Somewhere in the bushes nearby, *Vapor* was rummaging through the undergrowth. They could see little wisps of steam emerging from the dense foliage.

A sudden gust of wind breezed through the clearing and lifted the leaves and cards hanging from the unusual tree, sending them cascading against each other like a kind of paper windchime.

"They're wishes!" Ayana said, staring wide-eyed as she took two steps closer to the tree, craning her head forward get a closer look.

Each of the cards contained a short handwritten message scrawled and scribbled and apparently addressed to no one in particular by whoever had tied them to the tree.

7/12/14

I wish for a healthy baby

... one of the cards read.

15/11/14
I wish for a new pony

... another read.

Tyler took one quick closer look then quickly pulled his head back.

"I'm not sure you should be reading those," Tyler said, keeping his distance.

"Why not?" Ayana asked, pushing some leaves and branches out of her way to continue reading.

"They're other people's wishes!" Tyler said. "If you read them, they'll never come true."

Ayana tilted her head back and stared at Tyler.

"That's not how it works," she said, arching her eyebrows. "They left their wishes hanging out here for everyone to see. How could they possibly assume that no one would look at them?"

Tyler was frowning now.

"That's the whole point," Tyler replied. "That's how the magic works. They leave a wish out here that everyone can see if they want to, except the wish only comes true if no one actually looks at it. That's why we can't look at them. We'd be taking those people's wishes away from them."

Ayana thought about this for a second then shook her head emphatically.

"No," she said, wrinkling her nose adorably. "That's not how it works."

"Of course it is!" Tyler insisted. "How else would it work?"

Ayana shrugged her shoulders.

"The tree grants the wishes," she said. "It's a magical tree."

Tyler was about to laugh in response to this when they both suddenly heard a laughing grunting sound coming from somewhere behind them.

"Actually, you're both wrong," a voice matching the grunting laugh suddenly spoke, scaring them half out of their wits.

Ayana spun around, her heel twisting sharply in the rocky grass underfoot, cutting a divit in the ground and revealing the moist, dark brown soil underneath.

Sitting on a log at the edge of the clearing was an old man. He had one leg folded casually over the other as he sat smoking a long clay pipe and stared at them with cool hazel eyes underneath thick bushy grey eyebrows.

"Who are you?" Ayana cried, clutching one hand to her chest in surprise.

"Who are you?" the old man responded, slowly inhaling a long breath of smoke from his pipe as he deliberately unfolded one leg and draped it over the other, carefully reversing his sitting position.

"Who are *you*?" Tyler said, frowning as he took one protective step forward and placed himself between Ayana and the old man.

The old man sighed heavily.

"We could play this game all day," he snapped gruffly as he again reversed his folded legs. "But that still won't answer the question of who *you* are and what you are doing here in my front yard letting your little beast dig around in my plants and flowers."

The old man took the pipe from his mouth and jabbed with annoyance toward the bushes where *Vapor* was still exploring and tending to his steam dragon business.

His front yard?!? Ayana looked around the empty clearing. *Where's his house?*

"Vapor! Come here boy!" Tyler cried out, slapping his knees lightly to call him over.

The little dragon didn't listen.

"We are trying to get away from the man with the scissors," Ayana explained. "He was chasing us."

The old man nodded slowly, looking wise.

"The roving tailor," he said sympathetically. "You don't want to get on *his* bad side."

"I think we already are," Ayana replied wistfully, squinching her forehead adorably and making Tyler's heart skip a beat. Two or three beats, actually, to be fair.

The old man shook his head disapprovingly, making a *tsk tsk* sound with his dry cracked lips.

"Well, don't worry," he said finally. "You're perfectly safe here for the moment."

Ayana didn't think to ask why. She wanted to know what the old man had meant about the tree.

"You said we were both wrong," Ayana said, pointing toward the tree with the handwritten wishes hanging all over it. "About the wishes."

"That's right," the old man answered, watching her suspiciously.

"But why?" Ayana asked, leaning forward and squinting her eyes adorably.

Tyler was close behind her, keeping one careful eye on the old man as he tried to keep himself between the two of them.

The old man sighed impatiently.

"Why do you think?" he grumbled. "It's a wishing tree."

"A wishing tree?" Ayana replied, her eyebrows raised like two exclamation points.

"Yes, a wishing tree, didn't I just say that?" the old man continued grumbling. "What else would it be?"

Ayana couldn't take her eyes off it. She took a few steps back so she could see the whole tree better.

"But what exactly *is* a wishing tree?" she asked, still hypnotised by the hundreds of paper cards flapping and fluttering in the breeze.

"Oh, for crying out loud...." the old man muttered irritably. "You make a wish. You write it on a card. You tie the card to the tree, and voila! It's a wishing tree!"

"And then the tree grants the wishes?" Ayana asked, still wanting to know how it really worked.

"No, the tree doesn't grant the wishes," the old man said. "It only channels the magic."

Tyler's ears perked up.

"What magic?" he asked.

"The wishing magic," the old man said with an air of annoyance. "You make a wish and write it, leaving it on the tree for any passer-by to see. And then, if some other stranger happens by and sees it, perhaps they will think your wish is worthy of wishing on themselves as well. If they do, they stop for a moment and close their eyes and wish your wish again for you. That's the magic. And your wish will come true."

Tyler frowned. He didn't like the way the old man was speaking so grumpily to Ayana, but she didn't seem to mind. She simply smiled at the old man.

"Like blowing out the candles on a birthday cake?" she asked.

The old man scoffed, grunting derisively.

"Hardly," he said. "Have you ever made a wish on some silly birthday candles and actually had it come true?"

Ayana thought about this for a second and glanced at Tyler. He shrugged his shoulders.

"Not really," she replied.

"Exactly!" the old man cried cantankerously. "Bunch of silly superstitions, if you ask me, blowing out birthday candles, wishing on falling stars, blowing your eyelashes around. A bunch of bollocks if you ask me!"

"How is this any different?" Tyler snapped at the old man, tired of his grumpy attitude.

The old man grunted again and leaned forward on one knee, pointing the stem of his clay pipe firmly in Tyler's direction.

"This," he said, stabbing the air as if to prove his point. "Is real."

Tyler and Ayana looked at each other again, not believing a word of it.

"How is this any more real than those other things?" Ayana asked, smirking.

The old man was taken aback, his bushels of eyebrow hair rising in surprise like he didn't even understand the question.

"Because these wishes come true," he said simply.

Ayana made an adorable face as she glanced sideways at Tyler.

"Okay, then I want to try," she said, planting her hands on her hips. "I want to make a wish."

"Be my guest," the old man chuckled, leaning back again and looking her up and down contemplatively.

"Okay. How?" Ayana replied. "I mean, where can I get one of these cards?"

The old man laughed again.

"Right there in that bucket," he said, pointing with his pipe to a small tin pail sitting at the base of the tree, nestled in a gaggle of gnarled roots that seemed to be embracing it like the tentacled arms of some great wooden octopus.

Ayana charged over determinedly, ducking her head under the

tree's lowest branches as she went.

"It's empty," she said as she peered into the bucket.

"Of course it's empty," the old man said. "You didn't think I was giving away the cards for free, did you?"

Ayana snorted.

"How much?" she asked, pushing her way out of the branches and digging in the pockets of her jeans to pull out a handful of lint and coins.

The old man shrugged his shoulders.

"The price is different for everyone," he said. "Just try it and see."

"Just try it?" Ayana asked.

The old man nodded toward the bucket and Ayana stalked over again. She held out her hand, a single quarter gripped between her thumb and index finger. She released the coin, and they watched it tumble end over end through the air before clattering on the bottom with a satisfying metallic clink.

Ayana leaned forward and stared into the bucket. She frowned and reached for another quarter.

Again the coin fell through the air, spinning and glinting brightly in the flickers of bright sunshine knifing through the canopy of trees. Again, the coin clinked and clattered around on the bottom of the bucket, metal on metal, but Ayana was still frowning.

"How much more do I need?" she asked, flipping another quarter through the air with her thumb.

This time the coin almost didn't make it. It glanced off the rim of the bucket, ricocheting a few inches into the air before falling again squarely inside. But this time, as the coin passed the threshold of the bucket, a dim flash of blue filled the bucket and seemed to swallow the coin mid-air.

"Six bits," the old man commented, nodding sagely. "You're lucky."

Ayana bent down and peered into the centre of the bucket. This time it was no longer empty. Lying on the bottom was a blank paper wish card and a short length of string coiled neatly beside it. She reached down and extracted both of them.

"Me too," Tyler cried, hurrying over, standing closer to Ayana than he knew he should but unable to help himself in his excitement.

He pulled the coins from his lint-free pockets and carefully sorted them into their various denominations. He didn't have any quarters, but a vast collection of dimes had been weighing him down for several days now, and he would be glad to be rid of them.

Tyler counted off seven dimes and a nickel and took a step forward. He held out his hand and dropped the first dime into the bucket.

To his and Ayana's surprise, the dime tumbled down and promptly disappeared into a flash of purple, leaving his own card and string sitting on the bottom.

"Not fair!" Ayana cried as she spun toward the old man. "Why was his only ten cents?"

"He could have dropped a penny and it would have been enough," the old man replied. "The tree already knows what everyone will wish for and adjusts the price accordingly."

"If the tree already knows, then why do we even have to buy a card in the first place?" Ayana asked, still annoyed that she'd had to pay so much for her wish card.

The old man laughed. Ayana was still sulking.

"That still doesn't explain why I had to pay so much and he didn't," she said.

The old man shrugged again.

"The tree knows," he replied cryptically. "And different wishes have different values."

"Stupid tree," Ayana mumbled, pouting.

But Tyler was quite pleased with himself. For the bargain price of just ten cents, he had his wish card, and he knew exactly what he was going to wish for.

I wish that Ayana would kiss me, he thought to himself, stealing a glance at her out of the corner of his eye. His heart swelled inside his chest as she chewed her lip with a sulky frown on her face.

Tyler dropped to one knee and pulled off his backpack, rummaging around inside it for a pen. His fingers finally wrapped around the familiar shape and he pulled it out, a roller-gel glitter pen that he'd bought at the craft store the week before. He pulled off the cap to write his wish.

I wish that Ayana

... he began to write. But then he stopped.

I can't wish for that, he thought. *I mean, I want that more than anything, but I can't wish for it.*

Tyler knew that making this wish was very important and not something to be taken lightly. He knew that the Wishing Tree also knew this. Why else would it have given him his wish card so cheaply if not for him to use his wish for a better purpose?

I wish that Ayana could be whole again.

...Tyler finally wrote, finishing the sentence. His wish was a little vague, but somehow he knew that the Wishing Tree understood what he meant and would pass that information along to any future passers-by. Ayana was holding on to a lot of pain, and Tyler wanted nothing more than for some small fraction of that pain to just go away forever.

Tyler wrote the date at the top and held the card close to his chest, like a poker player keeping his hand secret from the other players. He looked at Ayana and smiled. She tried to smile as he got to his feet and held out the pen to her. Tyler couldn't help but think of how much he wanted to kiss that smile, but he tried to push the thought out of his head.

"Your turn," he said, handing the pen over.

"Thank you," she replied, kneeling down and scribbling her own wish on her wish card.

"Do we just tie them to the tree like this?" Tyler asked, threading the string through the reinforced cardboard hole at the top of the stiff paper card.

The old man nodded, and Tyler fixed his to one of the branches over his head, carefully tying it off with two half hitches like he'd learned in Cub Scouts. He stood on tiptoe, tying it to one of the higher branches—the farthest that he could reach—hoping that it was high enough so that Ayana wouldn't see it.

Ayana finished her wish and stood up to do the same, tying a series of messy granny knots to secure her card to the tree. When she was finished, she looked at Tyler.

"What was your wish?" she asked.

Tyler shook his head.

"I can't tell you," he replied. "The rule is that the wish maker has to keep it a secret."

Ayana frowned.

"That's not one of the rules," she said, turning to the old man for confirmation. "Didn't you say that this was *not* the same as wishing on falling stars or birthday candles?"

The old man just grunted and shrugged his shoulders, not really giving a clear answer.

Ayana was about to ask again when *Vapor* suddenly burst out of the nearby bushes, his steamy outline disturbed and blurring for a second as he passed through the barrier of leaves before reforming again on the other side.

He flapped his misty wings urgently to regain his balance and then hurtled toward them. He was opening and closing his miniature mouth anxiously as he flapped in a clumsy panic, tendrils of steam shooting out of his tiny nostrils.

Something was wrong.

From somewhere deep in the forest came the sound of crashing tree branches. The sounds were still far off, but whoever was making them was closing in fast. The grainy snaps, one after the other, of a pair of giant scissors snipping through the wood echoed through the trees.

It was the Roving Tailor again, and he was coming for them.

The old man chuckled.

"The two of you had best run along," he said. "I wouldn't want to see what happens if the tailor finds you here."

"I thought you said we were safe here!" Tyler protested.

"For the moment," the old man replied. "I said you were perfectly safe here *for the moment.*"

"What does *that* mean?" Ayana cried, glancing nervously over her shoulder toward the source of the muffled crashes and snipping sounds.

The old man leaned forward, planting one wrinkled and musty hand on his knee as he peered at the two of them. The expression on his face was grim and serious.

"It means," the old man. "That at that particular moment you were perfectly safe."

Ayana shot Tyler a worried look.

"And now?" Tyler asked. "What about at *this* particular moment?"

"At this moment you're not," the old man replied, laughing heartily through his teeth, which remained firmly clamped on the stem of his pipe.

chapter ten
the pearangorine tree dragon

"Thanks a lot," Ayana said to the old man as she clamped her hand around Tyler's arm and dragged him into the forest at a full-out run.

"You're welcome!" the old man yelled after them, apparently not catching Ayana's sarcasm. "And stay out of my fruit orchard!"

"His fruit what?" Tyler mumbled.

Vapor was racing ahead of them, leading the way through a thick grove of small, thin trees. In the distance, they could hear the incessant snipping sounds of the Roving Tailor following close behind.

They were going faster now. Everything seemed to be downhill with the path so steep in some places that they had to take it slow to avoid falling over the jumbles of tangled roots that littered their way.

It was also getting lighter in the forest as well. At first Tyler wasn't sure if he was just seeing things or not, but after blinking a few times, he realised that it wasn't just an illusion. It was *definitely* lighter in the forest now, and getting brighter by the second.

Up ahead they could see bright sunlight streaming in through the canopy of trees, and a blinding radiance filled the world just beyond the edge of the treeline.

It's the edge of the forest, Ayana thought to herself as they hurtled toward the light. *This is where the forest ends and....*

She didn't have time to finish the thought. Her feet caught on the roots of a nearby tree and sent her rocketing through the air, crashing through the last barrier of low bushes and out into the blinding sunlight.

"Ooof!" Ayana grunted as she plunged headfirst into the soft sand, her arms sinking in up to the elbows.

"Ow!" Tyler cried as he stumbled over her feet and fell backwards onto the sand. "My tailbone!"

Vapor was hovering over them making tiny clucking noises almost as if he was laughing.

The sudden transition into the brilliant light was painful, and it took a lot of squinting and gradual eye opening before they were able to get a proper look at the world around them.

They were on a long sandy beach at the barrier between the trees and the water that stretched off into infinity in both directions from where they were standing. Something about it reminded Ayana of the beaches her father used to take them to on Vancouver Island during summer vacation. The scene was a never-ending wall of green trees, golden sand and blue ocean beyond.

The waves were lapping at the shore a short distance from where the two of them had landed. Crystal clear water stretched out to the distant horizon, dotted here and there by the tiny deserted islands that they'd seen the night before. It was Tyler's bedspread brought to life.

"It's beautiful," Ayana breathed as she shielded her eyes against the glare of the exquisite blue water.

"What do we do now?" Tyler asked, looking left and right along the seemingly endless expanse of beach on either side of them.

As if to emphasise Tyler's point, they both suddenly heard the far-off snipping of the tailor's giant scissors descending through the forest above them.

"I don't know," Ayana said, looking up and down the shoreline.

Maybe the beach isn't the answer, Ayana thought, turning her eyes once again to gaze out across the sapphire sea. *Maybe we need to get out to one of those islands, but how?*

The closest island to them was quite a long way off. They could try to swim for it, but she wasn't sure that either she or Tyler was capable of such a long distance swim.

Maybe there's another way? she thought.

"What kind of tree is that?" Ayana asked, grabbing Tyler by the arm and pointing a short distance up the beach to where some smaller, more cultivated trees were arranged nicely along the edge of the forest.

Tyler stared.

"I don't know. A cedar?" he replied. "Or a Douglas Fir?"

Ayana tugged on his arm again.

"Not *those* trees," she said, pointing farther down the beach. "Those ones there. The fruit trees!"

Tyler looked again and shrugged his shoulders. The few trees closest to them were heavy with mottled green pear-shaped fruit hanging low from their branches.

"A pear tree?" he said.

"And those ones?" Ayana asked, pointing beyond the pear trees.

Tyler squinted and took a few steps closer.

"I don't know," he said. "Some apple trees... oranges... peaches. No, wait, nectarines... cherry trees...."

"And mango," Ayana said. "Can you see the mango tree at the far end?"

Tyler looked down toward the far end of the row of fruit trees.

"It looks like it," he said. "It must be that old guy's fruit orchard."

"Exactly," Ayana said. She was grinning from ear to ear.

Tyler didn't get it.

"So what?" he asked. "Shouldn't we be worrying about how we're going to get out of here instead of making a list of the old guy's trees?"

"Don't you see?" she said, still smiling like crazy.

Tyler didn't see.

"Pear trees, nectarine trees, mango trees!"

Something about the combination of those three fruits *did* sound vaguely familiar to Tyler somehow. But he still didn't get it.

"I don't...." Tyler said, shaking his head.

"Gaahhhh!" Ayana cried out in frustration, pulling *THE BOOK* out of her back pocket and flipping furiously through it. She found the page she was looking for and held it up for Tyler to see.

the pearangorine tree dragon

category: collector's dragon
difficulty: moderate
classification: rare

the pearangorine tree dragon is one of the more rare and eccentric types of dragons that conjurers will encounter and requires a very specific combination of wood from a trio of fruit trees in order to make the spell work successfully. despite the fact that only a small sample of each type of wood is required to conjure even a medium-sized dragon, for some the difficulty in obtaining these raw materials may outweigh the possible benefits. however, this creature's friendly nature and striking appearance makes the pearangorine tree dragon a must-have for any true dragon connoisseur.

required material(s): nectarine tree wood, mango tree wood, pear tree wood

It was coming back to Tyler now. The pearangorine tree dragon was one that the two of them hadn't been able to conjure because they hadn't had any of the exotic woods the spell required. They'd tried to conjure it using the fruits themselves—a nectarine, a mango and a pear that Tyler's mom had brought home from the store—but the spell hadn't worked. Obviously, the spell required the actual tree wood itself.

"Okay," Tyler said. "So now what?"

Ayana groaned in aggravation.

"So we can conjure it now!" she replied. "We have the wood right here!"

Tyler glanced toward the forest where the distant snipping sounds of the Roving Tailor were drawing closer and closer.

"I don't think this is really the time for...."

"Tyler!" Ayana snapped, pointing out across the sea toward the closest deserted island. "We can use the dragon to get out there—to escape!"

Tyler arched his eyebrows and stared out across the water, trying to judge the distance.

"Can we conjure such a big dragon?" he asked.

Ayana nodded excitedly and pointed to the third step in the conjuring instructions.

"See?" she said, reading the directions off the page. "It says the size of the dragon depends on how many fingers you extend in this step—one finger for a super small dragon and up to eight fingers for a medium-sized one."

"Will a medium-sized dragon be big enough to fly us over there?" Tyler wasn't convinced that it would carry their weight.

Ayana gave Tyler a funny look.

"Fly us?" she asked. "It doesn't have to fly. It just has to float."

It took Tyler a second to register this idea.

Of course! he thought. *It's a tree dragon! It's made of wood! And wood floats!*

"You're a genius!" Tyler cried. "I never would have thought of that!"

Ayana blushed.

"We have to hurry," she replied, dragging him toward the orchard of fruit trees.

Tyler nodded and pulled his penknife out of his pocket. The previous Christmas he'd written to Santa (Santa Claus, North Pole, Canada, postal code HoH-oHo) to ask for the fancy little Swiss Army knife he'd seen at one of the stores in the mall. And right now he was glad he had, because the knife's saw tool was the perfect thing for the job at hand.

"Okay," he said, pulling down one of the low branches of the pear tree. "Pear first."

Tyler used the saw to cut off a small branch from the tree. His knife was a good one, and it only took a few seconds to hack all the way through.

"Now nectarine," Ayana said, grabbing the pear branch and leading Tyler further down the beach. *Vapor* flapped nervously behind them, staying close.

Tyler sawed off a nectarine branch and handed it to Ayana before rushing to the very end of the row of trees and starting on one of the mango branches.

"And mango," he said as he cut through the last of the branch and turned toward Ayana.

Ayana plopped down onto the sand, stacking the three freshly cut branches in front of her. Tyler knelt opposite her and explained the spell instructions.

It was all very nerve-wracking. The spell's motions and gestures were fairly complex, and the constant snipping and crashing through the trees above them didn't help their concentration much.

"Okay, got it," Ayana cried, finishing her fourth reading of the steps. Tyler wasn't far behind and soon finished as well.

"Are you ready?" he asked, leaning toward her.

Ayana nodded in reply, forming her starting position with her hands. Tyler did the same, and the two of them took one last look at the instructions before starting.

"Wait!" Tyler cried. "What do we name it?"

Ayana groaned. She'd completely forgotten about that step.

"*Mongo*," she said, the name suddenly coming to her from out of nowhere.

"*Mongo*?" Tyler replied but quickly shrugged his shoulders.

"We name this dragon *Mongo*," Ayana announced to the universe and looked across at Tyler with her fierce blue eyes.

Tyler's heart skipped a beat.

"Are you ready?" she asked.

Tyler nodded.

"Okay, go," Ayana said, and she executed the spell's very first motion.

"Don't forget, eight fingers on step three," Tyler said as he followed Ayana's lead and wove his own half of the spell.

The entire conjuring took about half a minute to complete, and to their surprise, they executed it perfectly the first time around. As Tyler completed the final moves, they watched as the branches on the sand between them suddenly came to life, twisting and churning like strange wooden tentacles. The branches were growing so fast as they threaded their way around each other that Tyler and Ayana had to crawl to their feet and step out of the way.

As the branches grew, they slowly began to take on the familiar shape of a pear-shaped pot-bellied dragon. Bits of twigs and leaves poked out here and there from the dragon's body and tail, and its colour gradually changed as the creature grew larger. The three types of wood seemed to have fused together to form a strange red-green-yellow bark with the texture something like that of an avocado.

As the dragon approached full size, it lifted its head and spread its wings, sending *Vapor* tumbling backwards through the air and the two kids scrambling out of its way.

"You're so beautiful," Ayana whispered as she cautiously approached the dragon to pet him on his wooden nose.

"But will he help us?" Tyler wondered aloud, staying two steps back from Ayana. Even though this was only a medium-sized dragon, it was by far the biggest dragon they'd ever conjured, and its size made him a bit nervous. The instructions had said it was a very friendly dragon, but its powerful wings and claws looked like they could really hurt someone.

"Of course he'll help us, won't you *Mongo*?" Ayana said, nuzzling her face against the rough bark of the dragon's snout.

The dragon reared its head and seemed to nod in reply.

"You see?" Ayana said.

At that point, Tyler didn't see that they had much choice. The cracking and snapping sounds of the branches behind them in the forest were nearly on top of them now.

Ayana led *Mongo* gently to the edge of the water where he clumsily waded in until it was deep enough for him to float. He extended his tail behind him, laying it flat toward the shoreline so Ayana and Tyler could climb across it and onto his back without even getting their feet wet. *Vapor* had no such difficulties, of course, and simply flapped his way onto the arch of one of *Mongo*'s strong wings.

Mongo raised his head and let out a dry raspy call as Ayana and Tyler settled down around his neck. With one powerful heave of his back legs they pushed off out into open water.

"Wait! Wait!" Ayana cried suddenly, jumping to her feet.

Mongo dug his feet in and brought them to a quick halt. He twisted his head back and stared at her with a quizzical expression.

"Where are you going?!??" Tyler shouted tail and onto the beach.

Ayana didn't seem to hear him and dashed up the beach toward the tree line.

"Ayana!!! Are you crazy?!? The tailor is coming as Ayana unexpectedly grabbed his backpack and ran down *Mongo*'s!!" Tyler shrieked. The sound of his giant scissors were extremely loud and incredibly close now. He could emerge from the trees at any second. Even *Mongo* and *Vapor* were freaking out at Ayana's sudden return to the beach.

Ayana didn't seem to hear them as she raced straight up the beach toward the sounds of the approaching tailor.

"What is she doing?!?" Tyler muttered in frustration as he pulled himself to his feet and prepared to go after her.

Mongo and *Vapor*'s facial expressions said it all. *Beats me*, they seemed to say. But in another two seconds, the answer became clear. Ayana finally reached the edge of the trees and grabbed fruit as quickly as she could. Apples, oranges, pears, nectarines, mangoes—she stuffed everything she could get her hands on into Tyler's backpack.

"Is she out of her mind?!?" Tyler mumbled. "Ayana!!!! Hurry!!!"

"I'm hurrying!!" Ayana yelled back, grabbing a few last handfuls of cherries before sprinting back down the beach again toward Tyler and the others.

"Ayana!!!!" Tyler screamed as he saw a flash of bright yellow through the trees beyond her. "Run!!!"

The Roving Tailor was suddenly upon them, bursting out of the trees, his awkward legs and long arms flailing about like some kind of maniacal monster.

"Go, go, go!" Ayana shouted as she clambered up *Mongo*'s tail and onto his back.

"Are you crazy?!?" Tyler shouted as he grabbed the backpack from her and took hold of her wrist to pull her all the way on board.

"We have to eat properly!" Ayana shouted back, sounding

suspiciously like Tyler's mother. "We can't just eat chocolate and marshmallows!"

Mongo looked back and kept a careful eye on them as they scrambled down and wrapped their arms firmly around his neck. Satisfied that they were holding on tight, *Mongo* gave a mighty push with his legs and not a second too soon he sent them plowing through the breakers and out past the waves toward the open water beyond.

Behind them on the beach the Roving Tailor reached the water's edge just a moment too late and could do nothing more than stand there, angrily snapping his scissors open and closed while he gnashed his pointy teeth together.

"You filthy dirty little children!" he screeched after them. For a moment it looked like he might actually wade into the water after them, but he took one look at his fancy two-tone leather wing-tip shoes and apparently thought better of it.

"See ya later!" Ayana cackled triumphantly as *Mongo* swam them farther and farther from shore and out into the safety of open water.

"Yeah! See ya later!" Tyler shouted too, giggling nervously in complete and utter relief at their narrow escape.

Mongo gave another happy raspy cry and lifted his wings from his sides and used them like sails, catching the wind and sending them flashing over the surface of the water toward the tiny islands in the distance.

As they cut through the waves and whitecaps Ayana and Tyler watched the Roving Tailor getting smaller and smaller in the distance behind them and began to laugh like crazy. Their laughter only angered the tailor, and he stamped his feet and furiously threw his bright yellow top hat onto the sand. But there was nothing he could do. They were long gone, sailing across the bright blue sea with the wind in their hair and the warm sun on their backs.

"Well, I guess we're safe now," Tyler chuckled as a gust of wind launched them up and over the next swell. The Roving Tailor was far behind them now, barely even visible, but Tyler still spoke too soon. As they crested the wave, they saw the unmistakable shape of a shark fin slicing through the water just ahead of them.

"Tyler? I remember your bedspread having a pattern of islands and palm trees on it," Ayana said, frowning. "But please tell me there weren't sharks on it too."

Tyler gulped. Unfortunately, there *were* sharks on the pattern of his bedspread.

"Ummmmm.... " Tyler said, not sure how to answer the question.

"Oh, that's just great," Ayana muttered as they watched the ominous grey fin cut the surface of the water and make a sharp and deliberate turn in their direction.

chapter eleven
the palm tree island

"Go, *Mongo*, go!" Ayana cried, patting him on his thick wooden neck. "Head for the nearest island!"

Mongo gave a frightened cry and flapped his feet and wings urgently, swimming as fast as he possibly could.

"There's nothing to worry about," Tyler said, not understanding why Ayana was so anxious. "We're perfectly safe up here."

Ayana looked at him and frowned.

"*We* are safe," she replied sternly. "But *Mongo* isn't!"

Tyler looked back at the shark fin trailing behind them and thought this over.

"But *Mongo* is made of wood," Tyler protested. "Would a shark be interested in eating wood?"

They didn't have to wait long for an answer. They watched the grey fin carve through the water like a blade, closing fast on them until the pointy nose of the beast suddenly burst out of the water, mouth open and rows of terrible teeth flashing wet in the sunlight. The shark leapt for one of *Mongo*'s back legs, clamping down tightly on it with its razor-sharp incisors.

Mongo shrieked in pain and jerked the awful creature loose with one violent kick of his leg, swinging his tail and knocking the shark off to one side.

"See?!?" Ayana screamed, tears forming in her eyes at the sound of *Mongo*'s pained cries.

Tyler felt terrible. *How could I be so stupid!* he thought to himself, fighting back tears of his own.

"Swim, *Mongo*!!" Tyler cried. "Faster!"

Ayana glanced ahead of them to see how close they were to making landfall. They were close, but she quickly realised it wasn't close enough when she saw the shark's ugly grey fin turning back to make another run at them.

"Give me your backpack!" she shouted at Tyler.

Tyler obeyed immediately and handed the pack to her.

"What are you doing?" he asked as Ayana unzipped the top of the pack and quickly stood to her feet, clutching Tyler's arm for balance.

"Don't let go of me!" she said as she locked her left hand around his wrist. He grabbed her wrist in return and watched as she pulled a big red apple out of the backpack, cocking her free arm back and getting ready to throw it.

Tyler glanced back at the shark fin. It was so close now, and *Mongo* knew it. He was thrashing and kicking wildly with his back legs and tail trying to scare it off. But the shark was undeterred and continued knifing forward, closer and closer.

"Take, *THAT*, you stupid shark!!!" Ayana screamed, hurling the apple like a professional baseball pitcher. Tyler crossed his fingers as he watched it spin through the air and strike the shark fin dead on with a satisfying thump.

The shark was startled by the sudden painful impact on his dorsal fin and veered off to the side, wobbling confusedly.

"You did it!" Tyler cried. *Vapor* flapped and squeaked approvingly as they watched the shark break off his attack.

Ayana shook her head and watched the shark circling around again for another go. She narrowed her eyes and took out another big apple from Tyler's backpack. The shark was making another pass at them now, cutting menacingly through the water as it went in for the kill.

Ayana took a deep breath and focussed. Everything else in the world seemed to fade away as she concentrated every bit of her mental strength on the nasty grey fin that was quickly closing the gap between them. Her father had taught her this trick before he left so suddenly. They would sometimes go out to the park together in the summer and hit baseballs. For her birthday one year he bought her a giant bag full of brand new baseballs—dozens and dozens of them—so they could go out and hit balls over and over again without having to chase after the same ball every time. It was supposed to be one of her fondest memories, but after he left, she threw the whole bag into the garbage along with every other tiny little thing that reminded her of him.

"You should have stayed," Ayana muttered bitterly under her breath as the shark closed in on them.

With a ferocity that startled her, Ayana launched another apple, sending it rocketing through the air in a flash of bright red that smashed into the shark fin with a thick resounding punch.

"Yah!!" Tyler cried as the shark split off again, giving up the chase for a second time.

"You just don't know when to give up, do you?" Ayana mumbled as the shark regrouped and came back for another pass. She grabbed a bigger fruit this time, a nice, big mango.

"We're almost there," Tyler said from somewhere beside her. "Just a few more seconds and we'll be at the beach."

But Ayana didn't hear a word he said. Her energy and concentration were focussed completely on the horrible grey fin that was stubbornly coming up behind them.

Ayana thought of her father and how angry she was that he had disappeared from her life like that. And yet, not a day went by when she didn't look for him. Maybe he would send a letter or an email.... something... anything. Ayana hated herself for always looking at the faces in every crowd, hoping one would be her father, but she missed him far too much to do anything else.

"I miss you," she whispered and sent the big fat mango flying like a missile through the air. It flew straight and true and collided dead on with the leading edge of the shark's exposed fin. The sound of the impact was much heavier and louder than the previous two had been. This time it sounded like it *really* hurt, and Ayana wasn't the least bit surprised. Every ounce of her pain and anger had been behind that last throw.

"You did it!" Tyler shouted as the shark swerved off to one side and back again, confused and stunned. "We made it!"

Ayana felt *Mongo*'s body lurch beneath her as his feet reached the solid sand of the island and he pulled himself onto dry land. She wiped a tear from her eye with the corner of her palm and breathed a sigh of relief.

A short distance from the shore, the shark circled again and again, stalking them, looking to make another attack, but for the moment they were safe on the white beach of the tiny deserted island.

"Over here," Tyler called out as he slid off *Mongo*'s back and down to the hot sand. Ayana followed him down, and they hurried around to assess at the damage the shark had caused to *Mongo*'s back leg.

Ayana winced at the sight of it. The rough bark of *Mongo*'s hock was lacerated in a semi-circle of teeth marks. The wounds weren't deep, but they looked painful, and *Mongo* immediately set about licking them.

"It could have been much worse," Tyler said, patting Ayana on the back. "You were awesome back there! Where'd you learn to throw like that?"

Ayana smirked.

"You expected me to throw like a girl?" she asked.

Tyler shrugged his shoulders.

"What does that even mean?" he asked.

"Good answer," Ayana mumbled in reply.

Mongo licked his wounds while *Vapor* flapped a short distance up the beach and into the shade of the solitary palm tree.

"Come on," Ayana said, hefting Tyler's backpack over one shoulder and trudging up the beach. She paused for a moment to gently pat *Mongo* on the neck then continued on to join *Vapor* in the shade.

Ayana tossed the backpack onto the sand and collapsed, exhausted, at the shady base of the palm tree next to where *Vapor* had curled himself up. She grabbed a pear out of the pack and took a bite of it as she leaned against the tree's smooth trunk. Tyler flopped down beside her and grabbed an apple.

"So what's the plan now?" Ayana asked, taking another bite of her pear. They'd successfully escaped the clutches of the Roving Tailor, but they obviously couldn't stay on that tiny little island for long, nor could they leave it if there were sharks infesting the waters surrounding it.

Tyler stared out across the water and chewed on his apple.

"We have to get to Professor Möbius," he said, thinking aloud. "And that means getting off this sea of islands, then off the edge of my bed, across the floor and onto my desktop where Professor Möbius's book was before we got sucked into all this."

"Okay," Ayana replied, grabbing another pear from the backpack. It seemed like a straightforward plan.

"So somehow we have to sail over to the edge of the bed," Tyler continued. "Then down the waterfall to the floor of my bedroom."

"And how are we supposed to do that?" Ayana asked.

Tyler paused for a moment.

"I've been thinking about the waterfall," he said, reaching for *THE BOOK* and flipping it open. "Do you remember that one of the dragons we got a few months ago was a waterfall dragon?"

"Yeah," Ayana said, nodding. "I remember. But we couldn't do it because we didn't have a proper waterfall to conjure it from."

"Right," Tyler replied. "But now we do. Over there where this ocean pours off the edge of my bed is the biggest waterfall anyone's ever seen."

Ayana stared off toward the other side of the horizon. She wasn't sure how this helped them in their current situation.

"I don't get it," she said. "How does a waterfall dragon help us actually get *down* the waterfall to the bottom?"

Tyler slid over next to her and showed her:

the waterfall dragon

category: thrill dragon
difficulty: moderate
classification: legendary

grab your swimsuits and towels for this one! conjuring a waterfall dragon and riding it down the face of a real life waterfall (the bigger, the better) will definitely be one of the highlights of your entire life, but also an experience where you are guaranteed to get hopelessly soaking wet. simply conjure the dragon, hop on its back, and hold on tight. after this experience, waterslides and water parks will never feel the same ever again.

note: unlike most other dragon spells, the waterfall dragon does not need to be named. this is because the dragon only exists long enough to complete a single thrilling ride down the face of a waterfall, after which it naturally dissipates.

required material(s): a medium size waterfall or larger, swimsuits (optional), towels (optional)

As soon as she read it, Ayana immediately remembered how she and Tyler had been so disappointed that they couldn't find a proper waterfall the first time they read the spell. There simply weren't any waterfalls in the flat prairies where they lived. They'd thought about trying to use the waterfall fountains in front of City Hall, but those hardly seemed to qualify as even a small waterfall, much less a medium sized one or larger. But Tyler was right; the waterfall they'd seen the night before, far off in the distance where the water plummeted off the edge of Tyler's bed, was enormous— frighteningly so.

"Will it be safe?" Ayana asked. "What if this waterfall is too big?"

"It says the bigger the better," Tyler replied, pointing to the page. "I assume that means that it's safe."

Ayana nodded and flipped to the next pages of *THE BOOK* to examine the actual spell itself.

"Okay," she agreed after reading through the steps a few times. "But that still doesn't answer the question of how we get to the waterfall in the first place."

Tyler frowned and grabbed another apple. He was starving.

"No, it doesn't," he replied with a sigh. But he didn't have any other ideas.

The two sat silently, lost in thought as they watched *Mongo* crawl along the beach toward them. The wound on his leg looked much better now, as if licking it had somehow magically healed it.

Mongo nuzzled Ayana's shoe then tilted his neck back and nodded toward the water, his eyes gazing into the distance.

"What does he want?" Tyler asked, frowning.

"I think he's trying to tell us that he wants us to sail on him out to the edge of the sea," Ayana said.

Mongo nodded his head vigorously.

"No way," Ayana replied, shaking her head emphatically. "We're not going back in the water as long as those sharks are out there."

Mongo bleated and nosed Ayana's shoe again.

"I said no!" Ayana scolded. "It's too dangerous!"

Mongo looked disappointed.

"What if we could protect ourselves from sharks?" Tyler asked.

Ayana and *Mongo* just looked at him with blank expressions.

"How would we do that?" Ayana asked.

Tyler sat up straight, his brain formulating a plan.

"Obviously throwing fruit at them worked pretty good," he said. "So what if we built a kind of slingshot or something so I could fire things at them too? Between the two of us we should be able to scare off any sharks that come after us."

"A slingshot?" Ayana asked.

Tyler grabbed his backpack and flipped it around so Ayana could see the criss-crossing bungee cords pulled taut across the back of it.

"With these," he said, snapping the thick elastic cords with his fingers. "I can stretch these between some of those palm branches to make a slingshot."

Ayana tried to imagine what Tyler was dreaming up.

"That *might* work," she replied, pulling open the top of the backpack to look inside. "But we don't have much fruit left for ammunition."

"How much do we have?" Tyler asked.

Ayana quickly counted.

"Two mangos, two apples, four nectarines, two oranges, one pear and some cherries," Ayana replied.

Tyler's heart sank. The nectarines and cherries were too small to be of much use. That left only seven pieces of ammunition between the two of them.

"If only there was something around here that we could use," he said.

Just then, almost as if the world was trying to tell them something, they heard a faint crack from high up in the palm tree. Half a second later, a bright green coconut fruit smacked onto the ground between them. The force of the impact sent a splatter of sand in all directions, briefly waking *Vapor* from his nap.

Ayana craned her neck and stared into the tree towering overhead. Nestled at the base of the branches high above them were several bunches of raw coconuts, dozens and dozens of them.

"Something like those?" Ayana asked, grinning ear to ear.

chapter twelve
the last island

"What do you think? Watch this!" Tyler said. He braced his legs, pulled back the big slingshot he'd built and fired a coconut across the island, hitting the solid trunk of the palm tree dead on.

"Bulls-eye!" Ayana cried, thoroughly impressed. "You're getting really good with that thing!"

Tyler had always been good at building things. For as long as he could remember, he wanted to be an engineer when he grew up. When he was just eight years old, he constructed an elaborate tree fort in his back yard, built to look like the deck an old-fashioned sailing ship, complete with a big steering wheel and a large bucket on hinges mounted overhead that could be filled with water and poured down to simulate giant waves crashing over the deck.

With such advanced construction experience behind him, it was pretty easy for Tyler to come up with the idea to build a functioning slingshot made of palm branches and bungee cords.

As the sun passed overhead through the hottest part of the day, he sat in the shade with Ayana and the two dragons watching in fascination as he tried out different slingshot designs before settling on one that he thought would work the best. The resulting slingshot was a big one—so big that Tyler had to use his knees and legs to hold it in place as he test-fired the heavy coconuts.

"Let me try it," Ayana said, taking the slingshot from Tyler and firing a few coconuts of her own while Tyler ran back and forth to recover them so she could fire all over again.

"You're pretty good with that too," Tyler said.

Ayana shrugged.

"Not as good as you," she said, handing the slingshot back to Tyler.

"You throw better than me, anyway," Tyler said.

"I guess we're a perfect team," Ayan said, smiling at Tyler and making him blush. "But we're definitely gonna need more coconuts."

The two of them turned their heads up and stared at the bunches of green coconut fruit hanging far out of reach above them.

"How are we gonna get the rest of them?" Tyler asked as they peered up into the palm tree.

They'd already tried shaking the tree as hard as they could to loosen the coconuts, but that had only succeeded in making five or six of the heavy fruits break free and plummet to the sand, barely missing them by inches. *Mongo* had also tried flapping clumsily up to the clusters of coconuts and knocking them with his tail, but that had actually made more branches fall than coconuts.

"Give me your knife," Ayana said.

"What do you need it for?" Tyler asked, handing the knife over.

"We need more ammunition, right?" she replied, not waiting for an answer before hurrying to the base of the tree and shimmying up it.

"Wait!" Tyler cried, chasing after her. "You can't climb all the way up there!"

"Why not?" Ayana called over her shoulder as she demonstrated her remarkable tree-climbing skills.

"It's too high!" Tyler protested. "It's not safe!"

Ayana laughed.

"*Mongo* will catch me if I fall, won't you boy?" she said as she raced up the tree trunk. She was halfway to the top already.

"Be careful!" Tyler cried, looking at *Mongo* to see if he actually *could* catch her if he wanted to. He and *Vapor* looked just as worried as Tyler felt.

"I will," Ayana said. "Don't worry. I'm almost there."

As hard as it was to believe, Ayana was right. She was almost all the way to the top and was already pulling out Tyler's trusty Swiss Army knife to saw some coconuts off.

"Look out below!" Ayana cried as coconuts rained down all over the beach while Tyler and the dragons ran for cover.

Ayana shimmied back down the tree again.

"See?" she said, planting her feet on solid ground again. "Nothing to worry about."

Tyler breathed a sigh of relief. They now had everything they needed to defend themselves against sharks as they sailed from island to island, leap-frogging across the shallow sea until they reached the last island before the waterfall. But he was still nervous. What if something went wrong? What if they couldn't scare the sharks off?

"Are we absolutely sure that *Mongo* can't fly with us on his back?" Tyler asked hopefully. "Because if he could, we could avoid all of this."

"We're too heavy," Ayana replied. "You said so yourself this morning."

"Maybe I was wrong?" Tyler suggested.

They both looked at *Mongo*, who shook his head no, and confirmed what Tyler had already thought. They were too heavy for him to carry.

"Maybe he could do it if there was just one of us on his back?" Tyler suggested. "Like, he could fly us to the island one at a time?"

They looked at *Mongo* again. He flapped his wings, slowly at first then faster and faster, sending sand and bits of palm branches flying all over the place with every mighty down stroke. His wings were generating a lot of wind and power, but unfortunately his body was quite large and made of heavy wood, so even with just his own body weight to deal with he could still barely lift himself off the ground, much less anyone else.

Mongo settled into the sand and folded his great wings under his sides, shaking his head with a look of deep sadness.

"So much for that," Tyler shrugged.

"It was worth a try," Ayana said, patting him on the back.

After they finished collecting all the coconuts, Ayana sorted them into two stacks and loaded them into a pair of baskets she'd woven from palm leaves while Tyler had been experimenting with slingshot designs—smaller ones for her to throw at the sharks and larger ones for Tyler's slingshot.

Mongo knelt in the sand so that the two of them (plus *Vapor*) could climb onto his back and get everything strapped down and secure. Tyler double-checked everything then gave *Mongo* the thumbs-up sign to signal that they were ready to go.

"All set," he said then he and Ayana grabbed hold of the makeshift palm branch harness they'd looped around *Mongo*'s neck.

Mongo lifted his head and gave an excited cry as he pushed himself to his feet, waddled to the water's edge and waded in.

"Keep a sharp lookout for sharks," Ayana reminded everyone as *Mongo* floated off the beach and began swimming for deeper water.

Tyler nodded and kept his eyes trained on the seemingly endless water on his side of the boat, looking for any sign of fins cutting across the surface. Ayana did the same on her side of the boat as well and saw nothing.

Once they reached open water *Mongo* bleated happily and lifted his wings into the brisk ocean breeze to let the wind push them along even faster.

"So far, so good," Tyler said, echoing what Ayana had been thinking at the exact same moment. "Maybe you scared off that shark we saw earlier."

Ayana pulled her baseball cap over her eyes to shield them from the sun and scanned the horizon.

"Just keep your eyes peeled," she said, not letting her guard down for even one second.

Unfortunately for them, it was difficult to stay focussed. The sea and sun were blinding and endlessly the same no matter what direction they looked as they continued sailing, minute after minute after minute, until the minutes turned into half hours, then finally hours.

The original plan had been to stop at every island along the way, but since there were no signs of sharks anywhere, they decided to keep going without stopping.

"We're gonna get sunburned," Tyler complained, rolling up his shirt sleeves to inspect the pale white skin underneath. The real world that the two of them had left behind was cold and wintry. They were hardly dressed appropriately for the blistering sun.

"Too late," Ayana replied, showing Tyler her raw, red forearms. Unlike Tyler, Ayana's shirt had short sleeves. But at least she had her baseball cap to shield her face. Tyler's face was already bright red.

"We're pretty close now," Tyler said, pointing to where a pale misty haze obscured the horizon in the distance. It reminded him of when his parents had taken him to visit Niagara Falls a couple of years earlier. Even if you were too far away to see the falls, you knew they were there because you could always see the mist rising up from them.

"Just one more island to go," Ayana reported. "Do you think we'll get there before sunset?"

Tyler looked up over the sun which was now getting low on the horizon off to their left.

"We should be okay," Tyler replied.

The heat of the sun diminished as it sank toward the horizon. This was a welcome relief to their baking skin, but the lower the sun dipped, the more difficult it was for Tyler to see. Its blinding rays were shining directly into his eyes.

That's when the sharks decided to strike.

It was almost as though they'd been stalking them all day, waiting for the perfect moment to make their move. With the sun low and Tyler and Ayana's guard down from an uneventful and tiring afternoon, the timing couldn't have been better for a surprise attack.

The first shark came in fast, cruising like a torpedo through the dazzling sunset-tinted water along the left side. Tyler almost didn't see it in time.

"Shark!!!" he screamed, scrambling to load his slingshot as fast as he could. But the shark was too fast. Tyler wouldn't be able to get his complicated contraption loaded in time. Thankfully, Ayana unleashed a blistering coconut fastball that smacked satisfyingly into the shark's fin, causing him to break his pursuit and circle out toward the sunset.

"There's another one!" Ayana cried, pointing to the opposite side where another forbidding grey fin was slicing toward them. "Swim, *Mongo,* swim!"

"Got it," Tyler replied coolly, firing a perfectly aimed coconut that bounced off the fin and sent the shark veering away.

"How many of them are there?!?" Ayana shouted, pointing past *Mongo*'s tail where yet another shark was heading for them.

Tyler grabbed another coconut from the basket nearest him and fired it off. But the instant it left the slingshot, he knew he should have waited a bit longer. The shark was still too far off, and the coconut splashed uselessly in the water.

"Sorry!" Tyler cried, embarrassed by his terrible aim.

"I've got him," Ayana said, narrowing her eyes in concentration.

Wait for it... wait for it, she told herself as she watched the shark's fin cutting closer and closer to them. *Mongo* was swimming as fast as he could with his wings up to catch as much of the wind as possible. He was almost fast enough to outrun the shark, but slowly and surely the fin drew closer.

"Now!" Ayana cried, twirling her arms and flinging a small coconut through the air that smacked the shark right on the top of his fin. The shark thrashed around angrily, his head poking out of the water as he gnashed the air with his teeth.

"Nice one," Tyler said, grinning.

"There's one coming back again," Ayana cried, pointing toward Tyler's side of the boat.

Tyler fired again but missed. His coconut glanced off the water just inches away from the oncoming fin. Ayana stepped up and pitched one perfectly straight down the line; it struck the shark's fin hard enough to scare him off.

"How much farther?!?" Tyler cried as he grabbed another

coconut and loaded his slingshot again as another two sharks started in on them from directly behind.

Ayana spun her head around to look, flipping her ponytail across the back of her neck as she did so. *Mongo* had his head down and was swimming fast. They were almost there. The final island between them and the waterfall was just a hundred feet ahead.

"Almost there!" Ayana cried, turning back and letting loose another fastball at the first fin she saw.

The sharks were getting more aggressive now, the four of them zeroing in on *Mongo* from all sides. Ayana and Tyler had to race to keep firing off coconuts fast enough to keep them at bay, littering the water with floating green coconuts. The sharks were getting braver now too. Sometimes it took two or even three hits from a coconut to scare them off.

Just when Ayana thought they couldn't possibly keep the sharks away any longer, she finally felt *Mongo*'s feet touch ground and pull his clumsy body onto the sand.

"Take THAT!" Ayana yelled, and she hurled one last coconut at the nearest shark that was still twenty or thirty feet off. The shark veered to one side as the coconut splashed down, dodging it before curling around and heading toward them again, but now they were home free.

"We made it," Tyler gasped as *Mongo* crawled up the beach to safety.

Ayana seemed not to hear him. She grabbed a handful of coconuts, jumped down to the sand and ran to the water's edge where she hurled one coconut after another at the four dark fins patrolling back and forth in the deeper water.

"I hate you!!!" she shrieked, and as she threw the last coconut, her legs folded underneath her and she collapsed onto the sand in tears.

Mongo, *Vapor* and Tyler looked at one another for a second then carefully plodded down the beach toward Ayana.

Tyler sat in the sand next to her, wishing he was brave enough to put an arm around her to give her a hug.

"They're leaving now," Tyler said, nodding out toward the open water where the shark fins were swimming toward the setting sun. "You must have scared them off."

Ayana laughed, but just barely.

The two dragons came over and sat next to Ayana as well. *Vapor* curled up by her toes while *Mongo* flopped down in the sand behind and rested his head affectionately on her knee.

Ayana laughed again, but more genuinely this time.

No one said anything—there wasn't much to be said, anyway—and they all just watched the sun sink slowly into the sea, lighting the sky and clouds ablaze in a hundred shades of red and orange.

"It's beautiful," Ayana whispered, leaning back on the sand as the light gradually bled away and sank their world into darkness.

Up above their heads a million stars soon poked their way through the black canopy of sky. It reminded Ayana of the summers when her family went house boating on a lake in the mountains. They had spent their days swimming and water skiing until the sun faded away, bringing campfires and barbecues, and night skies filled with more stars than she had ever seen in her entire life.

On the opposite end of the heavens, the moon clock slowly crept into the sky, bathing the world below in an icy white light.

"Our parents must be freaking out wondering where we are," Ayana said in a quiet, sad voice.

Tyler thought about this for a second before answering.

"I'm not so sure," he said, propping himself up on his elbows so he could see the face of the moon clock better.

"What do you mean?" Ayana asked. "We've been gone for so long."

Tyler nodded. "I know, but look at the moon. The clock hands have barely moved since we got here."

Ayana lifted herself up and craned her neck to look at the moon. The hands of the clock face had stopped at seven minutes past two, not much more than a minute later than the time they had been showing the night before.

"How is that possible?" Ayana asked. "We've been here for almost an entire day."

Tyler shrugged.

"I think what we're seeing is what time it is in the real world," Tyler said, lying back in the sand again. "Time must move differently here."

Ayana thought about this. If Tyler was right, then probably no one even noticed they were missing yet.

"I hope you're right," Ayana replied and lay down again next to Tyler, their heads almost touching as their legs stretched out at an angle away from each other. *Vapor* sighed a dreamy dragon sigh and rolled over into a more comfortable position. *Mongo* lifted his head for a moment while Ayana got more comfortable then lay down again across her knees.

"Can you hear that?" Ayana heard Tyler say as she drifted off to sleep. With the warm sand at her back, she felt like she was floating on a sea of fluffy white clouds.

"Hear what?" Ayana asked sleepily.

"The waterfall," Tyler replied. "It's faint, but you can hear it out there."

Ayana held her breath for a moment and listened. Somewhere behind the quiet lapping of the waves on the beach she could hear the dim and distant thunderous roar of water like some throbbing white noise.

I can't believe we're actually gonna ride down that thing tomorrow, she mused as her mind went blank and crazy dreams of dragons and waterfalls took flight inside her head.

chapter thirteen
the waterfall dragon

"We have to be absolutely sure about this one," Tyler said as he spread *THE BOOK* out between them, opened to the instructions of the waterfall dragon spell. "We're only going to get one shot at it."

"Okay," Ayana replied. "We'll practise it as many times as we need to."

They were sitting across from each other in the shade of the island's lone palm tree, eating a breakfast of nectarines and cherries as the sun started its climb toward the top of the sky.

"Step one," Tyler said, his tone serious as he moved his hands into starting position and double-checked himself against the instructions. "Now you."

Ayana nodded and positioned her hands opposite Tyler's just as the instructions showed.

"Step two," Ayana said, moving her hands one at a time through the next step of the spell.

"Now step three," Tyler took over, each of them watching carefully as their magical dance of hands continued.

"And four," Ayana said, spinning and twirling awkwardly through the most difficult step of the spell.

"And five," Tyler continued. They were both stumbling a little more now, but they weren't worried. The motions were always clumsy the first time around. By the time they were finished practising, their hand movements would be as graceful as a ballerina's dance.

"And... we're finished," Ayana said, moving her hands through the spell's final motion.

"What do you think?" Tyler asked uncertainly.

"I think we have to try again," Ayana answered honestly. "And then again and again and again. But we'll get it. I'm sure."

Ayana moved her hands into starting position and nudged Tyler with her elbow. Again and again and again they worked their way through the steps of the spell backwards and forwards, stopping to double-check each other as they went.

They continued practising for more than an hour longer until they were both satisfied that they knew the spell by heart and were absolutely sure that when the time came they would be able to execute the spell with one hundred percent accuracy. Only then did they stop for a short rest before getting everything ready to head out into the water again for the final dash to the edge of the world. Ayana scrambled up the tree to cut down some more coconuts for ammunition, and Tyler made a few repairs to his slingshot to make sure it was ready to go.

Ayana got the attention of *Mongo* and *Vapor*.

"Once Tyler and me jump on the waterfall dragon, it's up to you guys to fly down to the bottom to meet us, okay?" Ayana explained to the two dragons as they made their final preparations.

Mongo and *Vapor* nodded enthusiastically.

"Can you carry Tyler's backpack down?" Ayana asked *Mongo*.

Mongo nodded again as Ayana strapped the backpack around *Mongo*'s thick neck. She stepped back to assess her work, and had to stop herself from laughing. He looked ridiculous—a big wooden dragon wearing a tiny little backpack.

"Are we ready?" Tyler asked, business-like as usual. The others nodded, and everyone climbed onto *Mongo*'s back to get settled.

"Okay *Mongo*!" Ayana called out once she and Tyler were secure. "Let's go!"

Mongo pushed himself to his feet and lumbered down toward the water. Ayana and Tyler kept a lookout for sharks, balancing themselves against his wings as they entered the water.

"Keep your eyes peeled," Ayana warned *Mongo* as he quickly moved out into open water.

Unfortunately they didn't have to wait very long before the distinctive dark fins appeared on the horizon. There were more of them this time, five or six at least, and they were closing fast.

"Get ready!" Tyler shouted as the closest shark swooped in.

"Leave us alone!" Ayana screamed as she sent the first coconut sailing through the air on a collision course with the rapidly approaching fin. Tyler fired too, hitting the shark with a quick one-two punch that made him spin away to have a bit of a think about the wisdom of trying to come after them.

"Here comes another one!" Tyler yelled, turning himself around to fire off another coconut at the next shark.

"And another!" Ayana cried, spinning around to send the next coconut sailing across the water.

The next few minutes were a frenzy of flying coconuts as Ayana and Tyler fought off shark attacks from all directions. They simply wouldn't stop. And with every pass they got smarter and braver, venturing closer and closer to *Mongo* as he paddled furiously toward the drop-off.

The roar of the waterfall was drawing closer. The noise was terrifying, but neither Ayana nor Tyler had time to worry about it. They were too busy trying to keep the sharks away.

How are we supposed to do the spell with all these sharks around?!? Ayana thought, trying not to panic.

As it turned out, she didn't have to worry. As the world around them seemed to shake loose of its foundations and the mist of the plunging water enveloped them, the sharks suddenly stopped and circled back to a safe distance.

"They're running away!" Ayana cried as she watched the sharks swimming desperately away from the overpowering suction of the waterfall—the same suction that was now pulling them forward, faster and faster every second.

"We have to start the spell!" Tyler yelled, pulling frantically on Ayana's sleeve.

Ayana whipped her head around and saw the swirling maelstrom of snarling white foam where the ocean plummeted over the edge of the world coming up fast—much faster than they ever could have anticipated. The air around them seemed to quake like an enormous rolling wave of thunder passing over their heads.

Vapor squealed and lit off, flying as hard as he could to escape the choking curtain of mist engulfing them. *Mongo* stretched his wings and turned his head to look back at Ayana and Tyler, screeching at them to hurry.

"We're not going to make it!" Ayana screamed.

Tyler grabbed her by the arm and pulled her down hard. If he and Ayana were going to do this, they had to do it *quick*.

"We can still do it," he said, grabbing her hands and forcing them into starting position. "Just concentrate."

Ayana closed her eyes for a moment and took a very deep breath. The world around them was shaking like an earthquake. The noise of it was deafening.

"Okay, go," she said, staring across at Tyler as droplets of wet spray condensed on their cheeks and foreheads, running down their faces in a hundred tiny little rivers. "Step two."

Ayana moved her hands, gracefully twisting them through the first of the spell's motions. Tyler followed suit, his hands ducking and weaving in a beautiful ballet of movement.

"Careful, careful," Tyler warned as they rushed a bit through a few of the steps.

"We've got this," Ayana reassured him, spinning her hands through the final step.

As she completed the final movement they glanced nervously at the rim of the waterfall. They were almost on top of it now, and *Mongo* was flapping crazily, trying to lift himself into the air to escape the plunge, but they were too heavy.

Suddenly, out of nowhere, a sound like the tearing of fabric ripped through the mist, and the ethereal shape of a gigantic dragon formed right in front of them. With its wings outstretched, it filled their entire view as it coalesced into existence. The dragon was absolutely enormous, its skin a pale cloudy blue that spun and rippled in constant motion exactly like water pouring down the face of a waterfall.

Mongo was about to go over the edge. It was now or never. They had to jump.

"We forgot to change into our swimming suits!!!!" Tyler cried as Ayana grabbed him by the hand.

"Jump!!!!" she screamed, and pulled Tyler straight up onto the back of the immense waterfall dragon.

Jumping onto the waterfall dragon was like stepping into a cold wet hurricane. The water was screaming past their ears like a jet engine as they hung suspended at the precipice, holding on for dear life to the dragon's broad shoulders.

Just underneath them *Mongo* flapped his wings and leapt out over the edge of the world, kicking off into a graceful spiral through the clouds of mist and soaring down to the floor below. Just ahead of him, *Vapor* was doing the same, both of them twisting their heads back to see what would become of Ayana and Tyler.

Ayana looked past her feet to where the vast ocean was pouring off the edge of the world in an unimaginably powerful torrent of water. The waterfall dragon was hovering there, tucking its wings close to its body.

"What's going on?!?" Tyler screamed, straining to be heard over the shriek of wind and water. "Why is nothing happening?!??"

But Ayana couldn't hear a word Tyler was saying. The noise was just too overpowering.

"Here we go!!!!" she screamed as the dragon nosed forward, tilting her and Tyler headfirst over the edge of the waterfall.

"Ahhhhhhhhhhhhhhhhhhhhhhhhhhhhhhhh!!!!" they both howled as

the dragon pushed off the edge and dove straight down.

"Ahhhhh! Tyler!!!!" Ayana shrieked as they rocketed down the face of the waterfall. Her stomach dropped straight into her feet as they accelerated faster and faster until reaching complete free fall. They were falling as fast as the waterfall beside them now, and everything seemed to be moving in slow motion.

"Ayana!!!!" Tyler screamed. He was clutching her hand in his so hard that her fingertips were turning blue.

"Tyler!!!!" Ayana shrieked as they plummeted endlessly toward a billowing white cloud of mist below.

The dragon tucked its wings in even closer now, making them fall even faster as they plunged into the mist and their entire world went white. Slowly but surely they felt the dragon pulling out of its headfirst dive, gradually levelling off as they shot out of the mist just inches from the surface of the enormous lake at the foot of the waterfall. Skimming the surface of the water, they had just enough time to look over their shoulders at the endless wall of water towering above them.

The dragon was slowing down now. Up ahead, Ayana could see *Mongo* and *Vapor* standing on the shore of the great lake, staring at them and looking worried.

What now? Ayana thought. *How do we get off this thing?*

She didn't have to wait long for an answer because at that exact moment the waterfall dragon dissipated, almost instantly disappearing into thin air and leaving her and Tyler skimming across the surface of the water for a moment before smacking straight into it in a massive splashing wipe-out of epic proportions.

Water flew everywhere, jetting into the air and blinding everyone as Ayana and Tyler came grinding to a sudden halt just a few feet shy of the shoreline.

Ayana blinked and wiped the water from her eyes, planting her feet in the shallow water and standing precariously on a pair of wobbly legs.

"That was so AWESOME!!!" she cried.

Tyler was having a hard time getting to his feet. Every time he got himself half-upright, he got dizzy and fell back down again.

"I know!!!" he replied, giving up on standing and just sitting back in the shallows, laughing his head off.

Ayana splashed the rest of the way out of the water and ran over to where *Mongo* and *Vapor* were waiting anxiously.

"Don't look so frightened!" Ayana told them as she flung her arms around *Mongo*'s neck to hug him. "We're perfectly fine!"

"I was so scared!!!" Tyler cried, trying to get to his feet again.

"Me too!!!" Ayana agreed. "I totally thought we were going to die!!"

Tyler tottered as he pulled himself upright but somehow managed to wade to the shore and onto dry land. They were both soaking wet and still laughing.

"That was the coolest thing I've ever done in my life!" Tyler said, kicking his shoes off and plopping into the sand next to Ayana.

"We are so soaking wet!" Ayana said. She couldn't stop laughing.

"Don't worry, our clothes will dry in this heat in no time," Tyler replied.

Ayana looked around them at the strange new world in which they found themselves. On one side was the massive lake with the waterfall pouring down on them from far above. On the other side was an endless ocean of sand, rippling golden dunes and waves of desert as far as the eye could see.

Tyler was right. The air was extremely hot and dry. Their clothes would be dry in no time flat. And so would they, if they weren't careful.

"What is this place?" Ayana asked in wonder as she took a few tentative steps out into the sea of sand.

"I'm not sure," Tyler replied. "But I think I might have some idea."

chapter fourteen
the sandworm

"So where do you *think* we are?" Ayana asked, leaning against *Mongo*'s side in the shade of his wing to take her shoes and socks off.

Tyler scanned the endless dunes as if he was looking for someone or something.

"I'm not sure," he said, lost in thought.

Ayana reached for the backpack to pull out Tyler's bottle of water. Tyler's mother always made sure every morning that he had enough water to drink. "You have to drink two litres every day, Tyler!" she always said. But Tyler never did. He could never remember. And so the big bottles of water his mom sent off to school with him always came home nearly full. And thank goodness for that, because Ayana and he had been sharing the same bottle of water for two days now, but there wasn't much left.

Maybe we can fill it from the lake, Ayana thought, momentarily forgetting that the lake was made of salt water from the ocean they'd just left far above. Her hands were wet from pulling her socks off, so just to be sure, she gently tasted the tip of her finger with her tongue. *Nope*, she thought, making a sour face. *It's salty. So much for that idea.*

Tyler was still wandering around the dunes, cresting one sandy hill after another, searching for something. Ayana was about to call out to him to see if he wanted some water, but she thought better of it and put the water bottle away and got up to dust off her shoes and socks so they could dry properly.

"I'm sorry, *Mongo*," Ayana said, grinning as she neatly laid out her socks across the arc of his wing in the sun. "I know you're not a clothesline."

Mongo bleated happily. He didn't mind.

The sun didn't seem to bother *Mongo* at all. He seemed content to lie there basking in the harsh sunlight. *Vapor* had already found a nice cool spot in the shade beneath *Mongo*'s wing.

Ayana smiled to herself as she took a few steps out into the desert to brush the sand off her shoes. She didn't want sand blowing into anyone's faces, after all.

She spotted Tyler moving along the crest of a large dune, scanning the horizon and shuffling along in a very peculiar way, like a zombie.

"What are you doing?!?" she yelled out to him.

Tyler didn't seem to hear her and continued to zombie along, down into the trough of the next sandy wave.

Ayana shrugged and pulled her shoes out from under her elbows.

"Maybe he's looking for water or something?" Ayana mumbled to herself as she swung her arms and began beating her shoes together to knock the sand off.

For some reason the sound of Ayana rhythmically smacking her shoes caught Tyler's attention, and he suddenly started running down the face of the dunes in her direction, waving his arms over his head and screaming frantically.

"I can't hear you!" Ayana shouted back, tilting her head toward him to hear better.

"Stop! Stop!!" Tyler was shouting. "Stop!!!!"

"Stop what?" Ayana muttered in confusion as she looked down at the shoes that she was holding in her hands.

An instant later, she felt a low vibration passing through her body. It felt like the earth was moving beneath her feet, trembling and quivering and getting stronger with every second.

"What's happening, Tyler?!??" she cried as the ground began to shake violently. The two dragons were startled awake and were already flapping their way into the air to escape the quaking earth. *Mongo* was headed in Ayana's direction, but Tyler waved him off.

"No, *Mongo*, no!" he shouted. "She's fine as long as she doesn't move.

Tyler stopped a short distance away from Ayana and pounded his feet in the sand over and over and over again.

"What are you doing?!?" Ayana screamed.

"Don't move!" Tyler yelled. "No matter what happens, *don't move!*"

"What's happening?!?!?" Ayana screamed again.

But Tyler didn't answer. He suddenly stopped pounding his feet and shuffled awkwardly off to one side like a zombie. He then stopped and turned around to look back at Ayana, putting one finger to his lips and holding up his palm to remind her to stay still.

What is happening?!??? Ayana cried to herself as the shaking all around her reached a breaking point. Suddenly the surface of the earth cracked open right in from of them leaving a giant gaping hole that sent dust and sand spiralling down into it.

Or at least it *looked* like a hole. It took Ayana a moment or two longer to realise that it was, in fact, the gigantic gaping mouth of some horrifically enormous creature exploding out of the sand right in front of them at the exact spot where Tyler had been stomping his feet.

Ayana glanced at Tyler, resisting the urge to run away screaming. Tyler was standing there perfectly calm and still as the huge worm-like creature moved over the top of the sand, its enormous head swinging left and right.

As the creature passed close to Ayana it opened its mouth again, its lips curling back to reveal sharp, dagger-like teeth. It's hot, dry breath smelled like some kind of revolting cinnamon, and Ayana had to stop herself from gagging as the gigantic worm slithered past and reared its head to dive back under the sand again.

The creature was moving off now, plunging deep under the sand once again, but its body was very, very long, so it took a great deal of time before it had passed completely by and its tail disappeared under the endless waves of sand.

As soon as the worm disappeared, the quaking of the earth gradually subsided, slowly lessening until the entire world around them was still and quiet again. Ayana didn't dare to move a muscle. Out of the corner of her eye, she could see the two dragons circling toward them from the safety of the sky.

Tyler zombie-shuffled over to Ayana as the two dragons flapped toward them.

"Why are you walking like that?" Ayana whispered out of the side of her mouth, still too afraid to move.

"Walking rhythmically attracts the sandworms," Tyler explained. "You have to walk with as random a pattern to your footsteps as possible."

Ayana had absolutely no idea what Tyler was talking about.

"The sandworms?"

Tyler nodded.

"The sandworms!" he said. "They live here! On *Arrakis.*"

Ayana *still* had absolutely no idea what he was talking about.

"You're lucky that I'm too terrified to move," she said. "Because unless you start making sense, I'm gonna punch you."

Tyler laughed and flopped onto the sand, pulling Ayana down with him. The two dragons landed beside them, *Mongo* using his wings to shade them from the sun.

"It's *Arrakis*," Tyler explained. "At first I wasn't sure because I couldn't remember where I'd left the book lying around. It was right here on the floor of my bedroom the last time I saw it, but I thought maybe my mom had moved it or something. But that sandworm we just saw proves it. We're on *Arrakis*."

Ayana raised her eyebrows and stared at Tyler.

"And what is *Arrakis*?" she asked.

"*Dune!*" Tyler replied. "You know? The book? *Dune*?"

Ayana shook her head.

"Never heard of it," she said.

Tyler rolled his eyes.

"How can you never have heard of it!" he exclaimed. "It's like the best-selling book of all time!"

"I thought that was the Bible," Ayana said.

Tyler rolled his eyes again.

"The best-selling science fiction book," he clarified.

"I still haven't heard of it," Ayana said. "What's it about?"

Tyler stopped and thought this over for a while.

"Ummmm...." he said.

"Yes?" Ayana prompted him.

"It's a bit complicated," Tyler explained. "Like... there are these different houses run by dukes and barons... and there's this emperor... and he tells this one duke to take over *Arrakis*, where the spice comes from... and...."

"And...?" Ayana prompted him again.

"Okay, I admit it," Tyler snapped. "I didn't actually read the whole thing. It was too long and weird."

"Okay," Ayana replied, secretly smiling to herself.

"But the point is that we're there... on the planet *Arrakis*, I mean. And *Arrakis* is just one big desert with no water...."

"No water?" Ayana said, suddenly feeling very thirsty.

Tyler nodded his head vigorously.

"No water," he repeated. "And somehow you and I have to get from here over to my desk, which is probably going to take us several days if we walk it...."

"We can't walk that far without water!" Ayana cried. "Even if we walked at night we'd still die of thirst!"

"I know, I know," Tyler replied. "That's why we need help. And that's what I was looking for before you accidentally summoned that sandworm by smacking your shoes together."

Ayana blushed.

"I didn't mean to," she said.

Tyler grinned.

"I know," he said. "I mean, how could you possibly have known that would happen?"

"You knew," Ayana replied.

Tyler shrugged.

"So let me get this straight," she said. "This big desert in front of us right now is *Arrakis*, right?"

Tyler nodded.

"And all of this, the sandworms and everything, comes from some book you left lying around on the floor called *Dune*?" Ayana asked.

Tyler nodded again.

"Yes," he replied.

Ayana thought about this.

"Tailors with giant scissors and gigantic sandworms," she muttered as she slowly shook her head. "Don't you have any books *without* villains in them?"

"All books have villains, Ayana," Tyler replied. "Besides, the sandworms aren't really villains."

"Oh yeah?" Ayana asked. "That one we just saw looked pretty villainous to me."

"It was just defending its territory out of instinct," Tyler said.

Ayana thought about this. Maybe Tyler was right?

"So what were you looking for out there?" Ayana asked, nodding her head toward the endless dunes. "You said you were looking for help to get across the desert."

Tyler nodded.

"I was looking for the *Fremen*," Tyler replied. "They're the people who live on *Arrakis*. They know how to survive the desert, and they can travel easily through it from years and years of experience."

"And did you see them?" Ayana asked. "From the tops of the dunes?"

Tyler shook his head.

"Nothing," he replied. "I couldn't see any sign of them at all."

"Oh," Ayana said.

"But I have an idea that might work," Tyler continued.

"I thought you might!" Ayana grinned.

Tyler reached into the backpack and extracted *THE BOOK*.

"Remember a few months ago when the dragon of the month was the sand dragon?" Tyler asked.

Ayana nodded. She remembered it well. They'd gone out to the sandbox in Tyler's back yard, which was still there from when he was younger, and they'd conjured the dragon there. The result was an incredibly cute, soft, squishy dragon that looked a little bit like a sandy Twinkie.

Tyler was flipping pages quickly now.

"And remember how good it was at smelling things?" he said as he found the page he was looking for and held it up for Ayana.

the sand dragon

category: utility dragon
difficulty: easy
classification: common

there are few dragons who are as fun to play with as the sand dragon. this squashy little fellow will have you laughing all day long with his boundless excitement and energy. sand dragons also love the ocean, and thanks to their notoriously powerful sense of smell, they have been known to sense the smell of the ocean from many miles off. so if you're ever lost and need to find the ocean, just conjure a sand dragon and let him lead the way.

note: just like when you spend a day at the beach, conjuring a sand dragon will result in finding sand in the strangest places for many days afterward. be sure to have a vacuum cleaner and floor brush handy if you plan on taking him indoors.

required material(s): sand, vacuum cleaner (optional)

Ayana finished reading and stared at Tyler.

"I don't get it," she said. "So what if they can smell the ocean? Why do we need that? We already know where the ocean is. It's right over there."

Ayana pointed in the direction of the waterfall and the massive salt-water lake.

"Yeah, but remember how he could also smell other things as well?" Tyler asked. "Remember how he went straight for our iced tea and sandwiches that we left on the back deck?"

"I could use some iced tea right now," Ayana admitted with a sigh. "Iced tea in the desert sounds divine."

"Oh, and remember how he dug up all the dog poo in my back yard?" Tyler continued.

Ayana made a face.

"I was trying to forget about that, actually," she said.

Tyler frowned impatiently. "The point is that he had a really good sense of smell!"

"Okay," Ayana agreed. "But what does that mean for us? Is he going to smell his way to these vermin people or whatever you call them?"

"*Fremen*," Tyler corrected her.

"Whatever," Ayana continued. "Do these *Fremen* guys smell really bad or something? Is that how he's going to help us find them?"

"Actually, that's exactly right," Tyler said, flashing Ayana a knowing smile. "I'm willing to bet that the *Fremen* DO smell really bad."

chapter fifteen
tea in the sahara

"Do the *Fremen* really stink so bad that a sand dragon can smell them from miles away?" Ayana asked, raising her eyebrows sceptically.

Tyler nodded.

"I think they *have* to stink a lot," he explained. "They have these special suits called *stillsuits* that they wear to keep from dehydrating in the desert. The suits catch all their sweat and pee and then somehow filter it into water that they can drink. That's how they survive for weeks on end out in the desert."

Ayana stared at Tyler in disbelief.

"You're kidding," she said.

Tyler shook his head. "Totally serious," he said.

Ayana couldn't believe her ears. "What kind of stupid book is this, anyway?" she asked.

Tyler shrugged. "I told you it was long and weird," he said defensively.

"It sounds *totally* weird," Ayana replied. "And totally gross."

"But don't you think that someone wearing a suit like that would smell really bad?" Tyler said.

Ayana cringed.

"Of course they would!" she said. "How could they possibly *not* smell really bad?!?"

"Exactly!" Tyler agreed enthusiastically. "You see? And they would have such a strong smell that a sand dragon would be able to smell them and track them down, right? So my idea wasn't so stupid after all!"

"I didn't say your idea was stupid," Ayana teased. "I said this *Dune* book sounded stupid."

Tyler ignored her and flipped to the next page of *THE BOOK* to scan the conjuring instructions for making a sand dragon.

"I remember this spell," Tyler said, nodding in recognition.

Ayana slid next to him and watched over his shoulder, checking her own parts of the spell. Soon she was nodding too. It was a spell that she remembered well.

"Okay," Ayana said after she'd read the steps a couple of times to refresh her memory. "If we're gonna do this, I'm ready whenever you are."

Tyler took one last look then shuffled over until he was sitting directly opposite Ayana.

"What do we name him?" he asked. Ayana was always better at naming the dragons than he was.

"This one's your idea," Ayana replied, smiling. "You name him."

Tyler thought about this for a second then made his choice.

"*Dune Buggy*," he said. "We name this dragon *Dune Buggy*."

Ayana nodded in approval and waited for Tyler to move his hands into position. *Mongo* and *Vapor* watched in fascination as the two of them worked their way through the graceful series of motions.

When Ayana executed the final flourish, the sand under their toes suddenly came to life, snapping together into the shape of a pudgy little sand-coloured dragon like someone releasing a taut elastic band. As dragons go he was a small one—hardly bigger than a medium-sized dog—but he had the energy of twenty dragons (or dogs for that matter) and immediately began sniffing the air and ground and legs and toes and arms and anything else he could get his nose into.

"Stop him!" Ayana cried, pulling the backpack away before he sniffed out the last of their fruit.

Tyler tried to grab him, but he was too slow. *Dune Buggy* was off and running, maniacally sniffing *Mongo*'s wings and tail. *Mongo* made a funny noise and wriggled uneasily as the smaller dragon stuck his nose into every nook and cranny.

"*Dune Buggy*! Come back, boy! Come here!" Ayana cried, and she circled around *Mongo* in the opposite direction to cut Dune Buggy off at the pass.

Dune Buggy didn't listen very well. He was lost in his own world of sniffing and exploring. Ayana tried to get his attention as she came around *Mongo*'s front side, but the little sand dragon playfully dodged left and right then left again and left Ayana and Tyler in his dust as he sniffed the entire perimeter.

Flapping above them and watching all of this was *Vapor* who apparently found the whole thing terribly amusing.

Dragons don't laugh, do they? Ayana thought as she watched *Vapor* giggling at their futile attempts to catch up with *Dune Buggy*.

"Maybe we just need to let him sniff himself out," Tyler suggested, weary from trying to keep up with the little sand dragon. "There's not much around here anyway. Eventually he'll have smelled everything."

"Maybe," Ayana replied uncertainly as *Dune Buggy* headed down the dunes toward the edge of the lake to sniff around there for a while.

Tyler was panting and out of breath from chasing the little dragon around. Ayana was too. It was easy to get winded out there in the hot, dry desert.

The two of them stood there for a while watching *Dune Buggy* sniff along the edge of the water. They almost lost sight of him at some points. He ventured quite far along the shoreline in both directions, his sand-coloured body camouflaged against the endless beach. Eventually he gave up sniffing and headed back up the face of the dune where they stood waiting.

"You see?" Tyler said, grinning proudly. "He's all sniffed out."

Ayana wasn't so sure.

"Not yet," she replied as they watched *Dune Buggy* sniffing all around *Mongo* again.

"He's not gonna go through all that again, is he?" Tyler asked as *Mongo* shifted uncomfortably in place as the sandy nose of the smaller dragon poked and prodded him.

Finally, *Dune Buggy* seemed to reach the end of his sniffing explorations. He stopped suddenly, sniffed the air for a moment, then came padding happily toward Ayana and Tyler.

"Good boy! Good *Dune Buggy*!" Ayana cried, smiling as she petted the cute little dragon's head and dusted her hands off on her pants afterward.

"Good boy?" Tyler replied cynically. "He just ignored us and sniffed around for half an hour when he should have been helping us!"

Ayana frowned at Tyler.

"He's not our slave, Tyler!" she said as *Dune Buggy* climbed into her lap, scattering sand all over her. "He had some little dragon errands to deal with first, but he'll help us now, won't you, boy?"

The sandy little dragon nodded enthusiastically.

"You see?" Ayana said. "Just tell him what he needs to do."

Tyler stared at Ayana for a second then leaned down to speak directly to *Dune Buggy*.

"We need to find the *Fremen*," Tyler told him. "They are a band of humans living somewhere in this desert."

"And they smell really bad," Ayana interjected. "Tell him about the sweat suits."

"*Stillsuits*," Tyler corrected her.

"Whatever," Ayana giggled. "Peesuits."

Tyler rolled his eyes before continuing his explanation.

"Anyway, she's right," Tyler said, leaning down again nose-to-nose with the little dragon. "We think these *Fremen* probably don't smell very good because of the special suits they wear. And we thought maybe you could help us find them."

Ayana and Tyler watched *Dune Buggy* sniff the air. His head moved from side to side, slowly at first as he carefully tested each new smell and sensation then more confidently as he crawled off Ayana's lap and headed out across the open sand.

Dune Buggy stopped suddenly and looked back expectantly at Ayana and Tyler. If ever there were such a thing as a dragon smile, then *Dune Buggy* was definitely smiling.

"He's got it!" Ayana said excitedly. "He's found the scent!"

Before they could say another word, *Dune Buggy* raced off across the sand and disappeared over the top of the next dune.

"Come on!" Ayana cried, gesturing for the others to follow her as she galloped over the top of the dune chasing after *Dune Buggy*.

Tyler and the other dragons stood dazed for a few seconds before realising that if they didn't get moving, they were going to be left far behind. Tyler grabbed his backpack and broke into a run while *Mongo* and *Vapor* flapped their wings and lifted off the ground to follow the others from the air.

"Don't forget to run un-rhythmically!!" Tyler shouted after Ayana and *Dune Buggy*. "You don't want to attract the Sandworms!!"

Ayana glanced back and nodded vigorously, suddenly remembering and breaking into a gawky zombie-run. The last thing she wanted to do was come face-to-face with another one of *those* things.

Dune Buggy took the advice too and spread his wings, leaping off the crest of the next dune and soaring into the air on a straight run across the desert floor.

The five of them made quite a sight as they continued across the desert. Taking the lead was *Dune Buggy*, gracefully soaring up the face of one dune and down the next, stopping occasionally at the summit of the higher dunes to wait impatiently for the others to catch up. High above them, *Mongo* and *Vapor* circled around and around, keeping a watchful eye on Ayana and Tyler who were clearly the slow ones of the bunch as they shambled over the sand.

We must look SO stupid, Ayana thought as she and Tyler lurched and plodded up one dune and down the next, desperately trying not to make any kind of rhythmic sounds that might attract the attention of a passing sandworm.

Not only did their zombie running look ridiculous, it was also ridiculously tiring. Running on soft sand is hard enough as it is. Running on sand like a bizarre lurching zombie is ten times more difficult.

Ayana wasn't sure how much longer she could do it and was about to call out to *Dune Buggy* with what little breath she had left to tell him that they had to stop and rest for a while. But then she saw him standing at the top of the next dune, staring ahead with an alert and proud expression on his face.

"What is it, boy?" Ayana gasped as she and Tyler clambered up the side of the dune and collapsed breathlessly into the searing hot sand next to him.

It was the *Fremen*. *Dune Buggy* had found them.

Staring down over the crest of the dune Ayana and Tyler saw a group of five human figures walking up the rise toward them. They were dressed in strange snug-fitting black suits that covered their entire bodies. Draped over the suits were long capes and hoods that they soon pulled back to reveal their faces, with goggles covering their eyes and masks over their noses and mouths.

The lead figure approached cautiously, her body tense and ready to strike as she pushed her goggles onto her forehead to reveal a pair of deep and radiant blue eyes. As she moved, Ayana noticed that every motion she and her companions made was without rhythm. But unlike Ayana and Tyler's ungainly zombie lurching, the movements of these strange black-suited *Fremen* were subtle and fluid and graceful, as if they'd been moving that way their entire lives.

"Who are you? What are you doing here so far out in the desert?" the woman asked, pulling the mask from her mouth and nose. Her face and eyes were hypnotically beautiful, and as far as Ayana could tell, there was absolutely nothing particularly smelly about her or any of her companions.

The woman eyed *Dune Buggy* and the two other dragons circling above them suspiciously.

"We need your help!" Tyler sputtered nervously as he tried to scramble to his feet.

The woman's eyes narrowed, and for the first time Ayana noticed that the heel of her right gloved hand was balanced on the pommel of some kind of knife that was sheathed at her side. The hands of her companions were also poised threateningly over the handles of similar knives at their sides.

"I asked who you were," the woman repeated, her fingers closing around the grip of her knife.

"My name is Ayana!" Ayana dropped to her knees and held out her arms to show that she was unarmed. "And this is Tyler."

Tyler nodded in agreement, and he stretched his empty hands and arms out as well. Even *Dune Buggy* mimicked Ayana's subjugated posture and folded in his wings to make himself as small and nonthreatening as possible.

This seemed to make the woman and her companions relax. Her fingers loosened their grip as she took another couple of steps closer.

"And how is it that you are so far out here in the desert?" she asked.

"We came down the waterfall," Ayana explained, nodding in the direction of the enormous waterfall in the distance.

Ayana wasn't sure if the woman understood this answer or not.

"And what of these strange creatures?" the woman asked, nodding toward *Dune Buggy* and the other dragons. "Are they under your command?"

Ayana nodded slowly. "They're friends of ours, yes," she replied.

The woman examined *Dune Buggy* closely.

"I've never seen such a creature," she said. "Is he some kind of pet?"

"They're called dragons," Ayana answered. "This one's name is *Dune Buggy*. And flying up above us, the big one is *Mongo* and the smaller one is *Vapor*."

"The smaller one?" the woman asked in surprise as she and her companions turned to stare into the blazing bright sunlight.

"Right there," Ayana replied, pointing out the almost invisible shape of the steam dragon. "That's *Vapor*. He's our friend too."

The woman stared at the sky for a moment as though she couldn't believe her eyes, and then she turned to face Ayana again.

"I am Chara," the woman said. "And these are *my* companions."

"You are *Fremen*," Tyler blurted out.

Chara smiled. "Yes," she replied. "That we are."

"We've come to seek your help," Tyler said, pushing himself to his feet. "We need to get across the desert."

Chara looked them up and down.

"You are not dressed for life in the dunes. Without the proper protection you must be exhausted and thirsty," she said.

"We are almost out of water," Ayana said, reaching for Tyler's backpack to show them their nearly empty water bottle.

Chara looked back at one of her companions. He nodded and pushed his goggles up to reveal eyes as deeply blue as Chara's. He pulled out a small flask from a pack he was wearing at his side.

"Water is precious," Chara said, stripping off her gloves and reaching for the flask. "But we can offer you each two sips of a special tea to quench your thirst."

Chara took out a small cup and brushed the sand from it with her fingers. She poured a small amount of a pale amber-coloured liquid into the cup and handed it to Tyler who drank it gratefully. Chara then poured the same for Ayana and handed the cup to her.

"What kind of tea is it?" Ayana asked, smelling the strange liquid.

"It's a special *Fremen* melange," Chara replied cryptically. "It will protect you from thirst and sun."

Ayana drank the tea in one gulp, allowing the nearly tasteless liquid to slide down her throat and cool her stomach. There was something a bit cinnamony about it with a hint of spearmint.

Like cinnamint. Ayana smiled to herself.

Ayana handed the cup back to Chara.

"Now tell me," Chara said as her companion whisked the cup and flask away again into his pack. "You say you've come for our help. What can we do for you and your strange pets?"

Ayana looked at Tyler.

"We are on a long journey," Tyler explained. "And we must get to the far side of the desert. It is too far for us to walk, so we were hoping you could take us there."

Chara looked at Tyler and smiled.

"Is that all?" She laughed, looking back at the companion who had handed her the flask of tea. "Such a thing is easily done! Namret and I will summon a sandworm, and we'll ride it together to the farthest edges of the desert."

A sandworm?!? Ayana suddenly felt rather anxious. *Did she just say we're going to ride a sandworm?*

chapter sixteen
ideray ethay ormway

"Wait a minute," Ayana cried in disbelief. "Did you just say we're gonna ride a sandworm?!?"

Chara stared at Ayana, not understanding the question.

"Of course," she replied.

Ayana looked at Tyler questioningly.

"Did you know about this?!?"

Tyler shrugged. "Of course," he said. "How do you think the *Fremen* would get around when their whole planet is a desert?"

Ayana couldn't believe her ears.

"Oh, I don't know...." she said. "Like in sand cars or something, or dune buggies?!?"

"The vibrations from the engines would attract the sandworms," Chara said, frowning. She seemed befuddled that Ayana hadn't thought of this.

Ayana stared off into space to think for a minute, trying to make sense of it all.

"How does that even work?" she finally asked. "The sandworm we saw was huge. How exactly are we supposed to ride something like that?"

"Actually, the sandworm we saw was a pretty small one," Tyler interjected.

Ayana glared at him.

"You're missing my point," she replied.

Chara laughed heartily and clapped them both on the back jovially.

"Our people have been riding the worms for centuries," she assured Ayana with a grin. "We're happy to take you and your friend where you need to go, but in order to do that, you'll just have to trust us."

Ayana glanced at Tyler. He was clearly very excited about the idea of riding a giant sandworm.

"Okay," she said finally. "I trust you."

"Splendid," Chara replied, smiling broadly. She turned to her companion, Namret, and gave him a quick nod.

Namret turned to their other three companions and spoke to them in some strange language. Two of them nodded curtly and headed off along the crest of the dune away from the rest of the group. The third man knelt in the sand and reached over his shoulder to un-strap a long bundle from his back. He removed several large tools. The first two were long poles with elaborate curving hooks fashioned onto each end. The third tool was smaller, like a kind of pointed mechanical spike with some sort of device attached to the blunt end.

The large man handed the hooked poles to Chara and Namret and set off down the dune with the mechanical spike in his hands.

"Are these Maker Hooks?" Tyler asked, tentatively reaching out to touch the long hooked pole.

"That's right," Chara replied.

"What are Maker Hooks?" Ayana asked, curious about exactly how they expected to ride such an enormous creature as a sandworm.

Chara knelt in the sand next to her.

"First we plant Thumpers in the sand to attract a worm," Chara explained, pointing first to the two distant figures at the far end of the dune, then to the larger man who was now positioned just a few hundred feet below them. Each of them planted one of the strange mechanical spikes firmly into the sand and switched them on before quickly moving off to a safe distance.

"And those are Thumpers?" Ayana asked. At the top of each of the mechanical spikes, some kind of machine was oscillating up and down to create a deep rhythmic pulse that resonated through the sand.

Chara nodded.

"It won't be long before a worm surfaces," she said. "And when it does, we must remain perfectly still until the head passes by us."

Ayana and Tyler nodded solemnly.

"Once the head is past, we can safely approach the worm and run up alongside it," Chara continued. "Me first, then both of you, and Namret will bring up the rear. Understood?"

Ayana and Tyler nodded again.

"Once we're close enough, that's when the Maker Hooks come into play," Chara said. "I will use mine to pry open a gap between two of the worm's outer ring segments."

"Does that hurt him?" Ayana asked. As frightening as the sandworms were, she couldn't bear the thought of hurting one.

"No, no." Chara smiled. "It only causes a bit of an itching sensation when the sand gets into the soft skin underneath. But that's the magical part, because of course the worm has no arms and can't scratch itself, so what it does instead is rotate its body so the exposed skin is as far away from the sand as possible."

Ayana and Tyler stared at Chara, not understanding.

"It rolls over!" She laughed. "And then it carries you and me and all of us right up to the very top of it."

"I'm not sure I understand," Ayana said.

Chara tilted her head to the side, listening.

"The worm will be here soon," she said. "Your dragon pets should keep their distance."

Ayana nodded and turned to *Dune Buggy* to lift him and help him flap into the air. Once airborne he quickly flew up to join *Mongo* and *Vapor* so the three of them could move off to a safe distance.

"The worm is here," Chara said. "Watch for lightning when he surfaces."

"I don't hear anything," Ayana said, but suddenly the sand underneath her palms began to vibrate, only slightly at first, but building to a frightening intensity that made the entire ground shake.

"Be ready!" Chara cried as a bolt of lightning split the sky and struck the ground a short distance away.

Ayana was startled and tried to pull away.

"Stay perfectly still," Chara reminded her as she placed her arm gently around Ayana's shoulders.

Another bolt of lightning crackled through the air, and another and another until the entire sky was teeming with electricity.

"He comes," Chara whispered as the face of the opposite dune exploded with the force of a powerful bomb. An instant later, the head of a gigantic sandworm burst into the air, its mouth gaping open as a deluge of sand rained down around it.

The worm was enormous, much larger than the one they'd seen just a couple of hours before. If it wasn't for Chara's reassuring arm around her, Ayana might have actually broken down and run for her life. But Chara was pretty much the coolest girl that Ayana had ever met in her entire life, and there was no way she was going to run away like a big scaredy-cat in front of her.

As the worm passed by, Ayana looked at Chara and imagined what it would be like to be as cool and strong as she was.

Heather van der Sloot would be in a lot of trouble if I was as tough as Chara, she thought.

"Be ready," Chara shouted as the worm quickly slid past them along the trough between two high dunes. "Now!!"

Chara sprang to her feet in a flash and sprinted toward the worm. She was off so fast that the others had to struggle to keep up with her.

Wasting no time Chara ran alongside the worm, brandishing her Maker Hook, and expertly pierced the gap between two of the worm's hardened outer rings.

"Grab on to me!" she cried as Tyler and Ayana finally caught up with her. "And whatever you do, don't let go!"

They did as they were told, each of them grabbing on to a side of Chara's utility belt.

"Here we go!" Chara laughed as she twisted the Maker Hook and split open the worm's rings to reveal the soft pink flesh underneath. The worm reacted immediately, emitting an almost imperceptible low groan as it slowly turned over. With the Maker Hook firmly planted between the worm's rings, all Chara had to do was hold on to it and the worm did all the work, gradually rotating so that the three of them were now at the top of the worm, its huge body providing a wide, flat surface for them to stand on . Just below, Namret ran up to the worm and planted his Maker Hook into its skin, and within seconds, he was pulled along for the ride just as they were.

"Now, on our feet!" Chara shouted as she pulled her Maker Hook free and scrambled to her feet. Ayana and Tyler followed suit but kept their hands firmly wrapped around Chara's utility belt until they found their balance.

Namret also pulled his Maker Hook free, and the worm almost stopped turning over. He and Chara quickly redeployed their hooks along the seam between two of the worm's hard rings and drove the sandworm forward as if they were driving a team of horses.

"This is how we can steer the worm and keep him from diving back under the sand," Chara explained as she pressed on her hook and forced the worm to make a long slow turn to the left.

Tyler stayed close to Chara and watched how she skilfully manipulated her Maker Hook to make the worm do her bidding. She looked at him and smiled, making him blush and look away. Something about her reminded him of Ayana.

Meanwhile, Ayana was looking around at the landscape and couldn't believe her eyes. There they were, standing on top of a gigantic worm thirty storeys tall, gliding effortlessly across the desert sand.

Ayana caught a sudden glimpse of movement and looked up just in time to see the three dragons soaring in for an easy landing on the wide-open surface at the top of the worm. It was a bit shaky up there for all of them, but after a lot of flapping and squawking, they were able to brace themselves and hunker down for the ride. Ayana thought about crawling back to join them, but she and Tyler were both still keeping a firm hand on Chara's belt so they wouldn't fall off.

"This is unbelievable!" Ayana shouted over to Tyler.

"I know!!" he shouted back, all smiles and laughing. "And it sure beats walking!"

You can say that again, Ayana thought to herself, and she pulled off her baseball cap and let the cool dusty air blow through her hair. When she closed her eyes, it felt like she was flying.

Opening her eyes again, Ayana turned to have a look around. From the top of the worm she could see for miles, but there was nothing but desert as far as the eye could see.

There's no way we could have walked all this way, she thought as they traversed mile after endless mile of sand. The desert was so relentless that Ayana wondered if there was nothing left in the entire universe except this never-ending sea of sand.

"Look ahead!" Chara cried after they'd been travelling for more than an hour. "It's the edge of the desert!"

Ayana squinted against the sun and sand and saw that Chara was right. On the far horizon ahead of them, a dark band of greenish grey-black was forming against the backdrop of unbroken golden yellow.

"My desk!" Tyler said to Ayana, shouting to be heard over the sound of the wind and sand.

Ayana nodded vigorously. As they made their approach, the outline of a dense jungle began to take shape at the edge of the desert. Beyond the jungle and farther in the distance a series of sheer grey cliffs climbed precariously into the sky. Ayana couldn't help but smile when she saw that the base of those cliffs was shaped like the spindly rolling wheels on Tyler's desk chair.

How in the world are we going to climb up all that?!? Ayana thought as the jagged, broken cliffs came into view. She couldn't imagine even the most skilled mountain climber in the world being able to scale up anything so precipitously sheer as what was looming ahead of them.

But before they could even think about climbing the cliffs, they had to reach them first. And that meant navigating the dense tangle of bamboo and banyan trees that was quickly coming up to meet them as the great sandworm finally reached the edge of the desert.

"Hold on tight!" Chara cried out as she skilfully twisted her Maker Hook and used it to put the worm into another roll, this time slowly lowering them to the ground while the dragons flapped their way down. Ayana and Tyler held on tightly to Chara's belt and watched the ground come up to meet them as their feet dangled beneath them. At first, Tyler felt his head spinning when he realised just how high up they were, but then his feet were back on solid ground again, and the exhilaration kicked in.

"That was so awesome!" he cried as Chara and Namret pulled their hooks free and stepped back to watch the sandworm dive under the desert sand and disappear from sight, like a gigantic dusty whale heading back into the safe depths of a sandy ocean.

It seemed to take forever for the enormous worm to disappear, but once he did, the world was quiet and still again. It was *so* quiet and still, in fact, that Ayana actually missed the noise and dust and excitement of riding the great sandworm.

"This is where we leave you," Chara said as the four of them walked to the very edge of the desert where the dragons were already waiting for them. One step further, and they would enter the world of the steamy thick jungle that stretched out as far as the eye could see in either direction.

"Thank you so much!" Ayana cried, wrapping her arms around Chara in an unexpected hug.

"Yes, thank you," Tyler agreed, hesitating for a moment before giving Chara a hug as well. "I don't know how we can ever repay you!"

Chara glanced at Namret and chuckled.

"You don't think we brought you all this way for free, do you?" Namret laughed, speaking for the first time since they'd met him.

"What do you mean?" Tyler asked apprehensively.

Ayana patted the pockets of her jeans nervously. She had already spent most of her change on the stupid Wishing Tree.

"We don't have much money," she said. "But you're welcome to everything we have."

Chara and Namret laughed again.

"It's not money we want," Chara said.

"What do you want, then?" Ayana was scared to know what the answer might be.

Chara pointed a single gloved finger at *Dune Buggy*.

"Your little pet there," she said simply. "What do you call it? A sand dragon?"

Ayana spun around to look at *Dune Buggy*. He and the other dragons were sitting behind them looking worried and afraid, but *Dune Buggy* looked the most frightened of all. He was nervously backing up in an effort to hide underneath one of *Mongo*'s wings.

"No!" Ayana cried, rushing over to put herself between Chara and the dragons. "You can't take him!"

"What else, then?" Chara asked. "How else do you propose to repay us?"

"We thought you were just being nice!" Ayana cried tearfully as she held her arms out to stop them. "We thought you were giving us a ride for free!"

Chara smiled sympathetically.

"Nothing is free in the desert," she said, taking another step toward Ayana and the dragons, her hand perched on the hilt of her knife.

"No!!!" Ayana shrieked. "Stay back!!!"

Tyler put up hands and tried to calm the situation.

"Maybe we can just conjure another Sand Dragon just for them," Tyler whispered to Ayana.

"You know that doesn't work," Ayana hissed back. "There's a limit of one dragon at a time, remember?"

Tyler glanced nervously over his shoulder at Chara and Namret.

"What, then?" he asked. "What are we supposed to do?"

Ayana had an idea.

"Okay, okay!" Ayana said, stepping around Tyler. Tears were running from her eyes as she held up her palms in surrender.

"Ayana! What are you doing?!?" Tyler asked, scrambling to keep up with her.

"You can have the dragon," Ayana continued, ignoring Tyler. "But can we at least say goodbye to him first and explain what's happening?"

Chara eyed Ayana suspiciously but slowly nodded her agreement.

"Of course," Chara replied. "But no funny stuff."

Ayana nodded her head in a silent promise and grabbed Tyler by the hand, dragging him back to where the dragons were sitting. She knelt in the sand in front of *Dune Buggy* and tried to coax him out from behind *Mongo*'s wing.

"Come on, little guy," she said, choking on her tears. "Please come out."

Reluctantly, *Dune Buggy* came crawling out toward her, looking desperately sad and dragging his nose in the sand.

"Don't be scared, little guy," Ayana said as she let the little dragon climb into her lap. "Everything is going to be okay. Just trust me."

Ayana continued petting him gently and did her best to calm him, but she was a complete wreck herself. She and Tyler were both sobbing uncontrollably.

"Enough!" Namret shouted from somewhere behind them. "No more stalling."

"I really don't like this guy," Ayana muttered under her breath.

"Me either," Tyler agreed. "It was better when he didn't say anything."

Dune Buggy crawled down off her, and she led him out into the open to where Chara and Namret stood waiting.

Ayana led *Dune Buggy* forward and presented him to Chara. His little sandy dragon eyes looked completely terrified.

"There you go. He's all yours," Ayana announced as she took a few small steps backward toward the jungle. She surreptitiously slid her hand into Tyler's and squeezed it.

Chara and Namret watched them distrustfully as they continued backing up toward the cover of the bamboo trees. *Dune Buggy* just sat there watching Tyler and Ayana with sadness in his eyes.

"Good boy, *Dune Buggy*," Ayana called to him, her voice cracking with emotion. "You're a good boy. Stay with them."

"What are we doing?!?" Tyler muttered out of the corner of his mouth as they kept walking backward.

"Etgay eadyray otay unray," Ayana replied under her breath.

"Huh?" Tyler looked at her like she was crazy. "What did you say?!?"

"Etgay eadyray otay unray," Ayana repeated.

She was speaking Pig Latin. Tyler had to sort out the syllables in his head to decipher it.

"Get...." Tyler sounded each word out one at a time.

"Ready...."

"To...."

"RUN!!!!" Ayana screamed, pulling Tyler by the hand and dashing for the safety of the trees. As she ran, she pushed *Mongo* by the butt, forcing him and *Vapor* to take flight and run away as well.

Ayana glanced over her shoulder and saw Chara and Namret watching them in confusion. They weren't coming after them. Why should they, after all? They had what they wanted.

After a few seconds, *Mongo* and *Vapor* had successfully flapped into the air and were now flying off, soaring quickly to a safe altitude. Ayana stopped just at the edge of the bamboo jungle and looked back toward *Dune Buggy* and the two *Fremen*.

"Now get ready to *REALLY* run," she said to Tyler.

"What are you going to do?" he asked apprehensively.

Ayana just gave him a grin.

"Yggubenud!!!" she screamed, and yanked Tyler out of sight and into the deep dark jungle. Tyler didn't see it, but Ayana did. Back on the sand behind them *Dune Buggy* instantly winked out of existence the instant that Ayana said his name backward, leaving Chara and Namret scratching their heads in bewilderment.

chapter seventeen
the re-conjuring

"Run, Tyler, run!" Ayana yelled as they plunged into the darkness of the jungle.

It took their eyes a moment to adjust to the sudden change in light, but they didn't have a second to lose so for the first few seconds they simply stumbled and tripped over the chaotic jumble of tree trunks and tentacle-like roots in their hurry to put as much distance between them and the *Fremen* as possible.

"Wait, Ayana!" Tyler complained as he fell over a tangle of vines that overgrew the path.

"There's no time!" Ayana cried, pulling Tyler up and forcing him to run against his will. "They're coming after us!"

Ayana was right. On the other side of the tree line, they could hear the soft padded footsteps of Chara and Namret running toward them.

"Come on, Tyler!" Ayana whispered as she yanked Tyler to his feet again and dragged him along behind her as she dashed forward, ducking from tree to tree and jumping over anything that got in her way.

In the distance behind them they could hear Chara and Namret noisily pushing their way through the plants and trees. They moved slowly and loudly at first, but they were picking up speed and getting quieter as they closed in.

"In here," Ayana whispered, pointing toward a dense thicket of bushes.

"Are you sure?" Tyler asked, looking at the prickly clump doubtfully.

"Hurry!" Ayana hissed, and gave him a shove.

Tyler gritted his teeth and pushed his way through the thick barrier as the branches and thorns bit at his clothing and scratched his exposed skin. Ayana was right behind him, forcing her way into the tightly woven undergrowth.

"Are you sure they won't find us in here?" Tyler whispered.

"Positive," Ayana replied.

At least I hope not, she thought to herself as she strained her ears to listen.

For a moment, they couldn't hear anything except the buzz of insects and the gentle clonking of bamboo stalks knocking against one another in the breeze.

Ayana put a finger to her lips. She could hear the faint sound of footsteps approaching through the thick trees. Tyler could hear it too. Someone was definitely approaching. And it wasn't difficult to guess who.

Through the heavy foliage, Ayana saw the unmistakeable figure of Chara carefully padding her way through the jungle, moving as stealthily as a cat as she scanned all around her for any sign of Ayana and Tyler.

If that's Chara, Ayana thought, turning her head ever so slightly when she heard another set of footsteps coming up behind them, *then that must be Namret.*

Ayana and Tyler sat with their arms around each other and watched as Chara inched forward, scanning the jungle for anything suspicious.

What if she sees us?!?? Tyler panicked. But she didn't. She went right past them and out of sight again.

The sound of both pairs of footsteps slowly faded until all they could hear were the insects, bamboo and the sound of their own pounding hearts.

Five minutes passed... then ten... then twenty. But they still didn't move a muscle.

Ayana was wondering how long they should sit there when suddenly they heard footsteps again, louder this time.

She and Tyler clung to each other anxiously as the sound of footsteps got closer and closer until they saw Chara and Namret emerge from the trees. They both looked annoyed and were walking quickly back in the direction of the desert, obviously no longer even trying to be stealthy.

They're giving up! Ayana thought, her heart jumping for joy as she watched them disappear into the jungle again. She looked at Tyler and smiled happily.

But still they waited, listening to the sound of footsteps fading then sitting silently, minute after minute, just to be sure.

Somewhere in the direction of the desert, they heard the sound of thunderclaps and caught faint glimpses of lightning flashes through the tops of the tree canopy above them.

"Another sandworm," Tyler whispered.

Ayana nodded. It was definitely another sandworm. But were Chara and Namret giving up and leaving, or were they just bringing in reinforcements to help in the search? There was no way to tell, so they had no choice but to sit there and wait.

Ten more minutes passed.... then twenty... then thirty.

Ayana's heart sank when she heard the sound of footsteps approaching through the jungle, only they were much louder this time than they had been before.

There must be a dozen of them! Ayana thought as the noise of breaking branches and snapping twigs got closer.

"It's *Mongo*!!" Tyler cried as he spotted the familiar shape of the wooden dragon clumsily pushing his way through the trees.

"And *Vapor*!" Ayana replied as she excitedly jumped to her feet and painfully fought her way out of the thorny bushes. She ran over to the two dragons and gave them both a big hug.

"I can't believe it!!" Tyler cried as he pulled himself free of the bushes right behind Ayana. After sitting motionless for so long he was happy to be able to stretch his legs again.

"Are the *Fremen* gone?" Ayana asked *Mongo*, looking him straight in the eyes as she snuggled with his long, spiky nose.

Mongo nodded his head happily.

"You saw them go?" Tyler asked. "On a sandworm?"

Vapor answered this time, nodding enthusiastically.

Tyler looked at Ayana admiringly.

"You did it!" he said proudly. "We escaped!"

"Not quite," Ayana said, frowning.

"What else, then?" Tyler asked as he watched Ayana gesture for everyone to follow her back down through the trees.

Ayana didn't answer. She was already heading determinedly back toward the edge of the jungle where the desert began.

"Where are you going?!?" Tyler cried as he and the dragons stumbled along behind her.

"To get *Dune Buggy*!" Ayana replied resolutely.

"Get him back from where?!?" Tyler asked, grabbing Ayana by the arm and forcing her to stop.

"Do you remember what *THE BOOK* says about re-conjuring dragons?" Ayana replied.

It sounded vaguely familiar, but Tyler couldn't remember exactly, and shook his head no.

"Here," Ayana said, reaching into Tyler's backpack to grab *THE BOOK* and flipping quickly through its pages and reading aloud. "Don't worry—un-conjuring a dragon does not harm them in any way, and they can be re-conjured again at any time."

"But what does that mean?" Tyler asked. "How exactly are we supposed to do that?"

Ayana shrugged her shoulders slightly.

"I don't know," she admitted. "But I'll bet that's why we have to name the dragons in the first place—to summon them again later if we need to."

The importance of this was just sinking in for Tyler.

"That's why you un-conjured *Dune Buggy* the way you did," he said, breathless with respect and admiration. "Because you knew you could bring him back again."

Ayana stared at Tyler for a second.

"Of course," she said. "And that's why I'm heading to the desert again. I want *Dune Buggy* back!"

"Then let's go get him," Tyler said excitedly, grabbing Ayana by the hand and leading all of them out of the jungle and into the blinding world of the desert sands.

Both Ayana and Tyler took a careful look around to make sure that there was no sign anywhere of the *Fremen*, but the coast was clear. There was nothing but sun and sand as far as the eye could see.

"So how do we do this?" Tyler asked, sitting in the sand with *THE BOOK* open in front of him. "Do we have to do the spell backwards or something?"

Ayana waited for *Mongo* to settle into the sand next to them and provide a bit of shade before she flopped down across from Tyler.

"I think we just do it like normal," Ayana said. "And use the same name we used before."

"How will we know the dragon is really *Dune Buggy*, then, and not just some other Sand Dragon?" Tyler asked.

Ayana thought this over.

"We'll just know," she said finally. "And he'll know us too. Besides, we've conjured enough dragons to know that they never turn out the same each time."

Tyler nodded in agreement. Ayana was absolutely right. Every dragon was always slightly different.

"Okay, let's do it then," Tyler said, giving the instructions another quick read to make sure he remembered them correctly. "And then let's get out of this sun."

Ayana totally agreed. She was so sick of sun and sand that she didn't care if she ever saw the beach again as long as she lived.

Moving their hands into starting position, Ayana looked around one last time to make sure they were all alone out there.

"This spell is to bring *Dune Buggy* back to us," she said loud and clear to no one in particular. Her only answer was the ceaseless dry desert wind.

Ayana nodded confidently and the two of them started the spell, quickly weaving through the steps in no time flat until a spongy, sandy little sand dragon snapped into existence right in front of them.

It didn't take very long to realise that it was most definitely *Dune Buggy* they'd re-conjured. From the moment the spell was complete, the little dragon was jumping and pawing gleefully all over Ayana and Tyler, leaping back and forth from one to the other and licking their faces with his abrasive little sandy tongue.

"*Dune Buggy*!!!" Ayana cried joyfully, tears of happiness streaming down her face. "I was so scared that we had lost you forever, boy! I was so scared!!"

Dune Buggy jumped to the sand and spun around crazily in a circle, making little dragon barking noises that sounded almost exactly like a dog.

"You're crazy!" Ayana squealed and laughed as *Dune Buggy* bolted out into the open air and sprinted happily around and around and around in big wide circles.

Ayana and Tyler followed him out and watched as he scrambled up *Mongo*'s back and neck and tried to give him some little sand dragon kisses as well, but *Dune Buggy* was too excited to keep his balance and fell into the sand in front of *Mongo*'s face.

The two dragons snuggled noses together affectionately for a moment, and then *Dune Buggy* was off running again, trying to find *Vapor* to give him some kisses as well.

Through all of this excitement, Ayana and Tyler stood laughing at *Dune Buggy*'s crazy antics. They were so relieved to have their friend back that they didn't notice the vibrations rumbling underneath their feet.

"What is it?" Ayana asked *Mongo* when she saw the worried expression on his face. "What's wrong?"

Suddenly Ayana felt it too. The ground was shaking stronger and stronger with every second. She grabbed Tyler's arm and whipped her head around toward the open desert.

"A sandworm is coming!" Ayana cried, scanning the horizon for the first signs of it.

"What?!??" Tyler replied. "Where?!?"

Ayana pointed out across the dunes to where a flurry of lightning was sizzling through the atmosphere. The worm hadn't surfaced yet, but it would any second now.

"Back in the jungle!!" Ayana cried, leading the charge back to the safety of the thick trees. "Run!!!"

Tyler and the dragons fell in behind her, running as fast as they could through, dodging left and right from one tree to the next.

"Is it the *Fremen*?!?" Ayana shouted back to Tyler as she climbed up and over a maze of banyan tree roots.

"I don't think so," Tyler replied, huffing for breath. "They only ride the worms on the surface, remember? This one was coming up from underneath. It was probably *Dune Buggy*'s rhythmic racing around that attracted him."

That makes sense, I guess, Ayana thought with relief. But she wasn't planning on taking any chances. She just kept running and running and running in a desperate attempt to get as far away from the desert as she possibly could.

"Ayana, wait up!" Tyler cried after her, out of breath and exhausted after running for so long. "We can't keep up with you!"

"We can't stop now!" Ayana called back over her shoulder in alarm. "They're not taking *Dune Buggy* away from us again!"

"Ayana, wait!" Tyler cried again. "Everything is okay! It was just a sandworm! There's no one back there chasing us!"

But Ayana wasn't listening. She was in a complete state of panic, running and ducking through the trees in a mad dash to get away from everything. She was so distraught, in fact, that she didn't realise how exhausted and dizzy she was getting from running so long through the stifling hot and humid jungle. By now, Tyler and the dragons were so far behind that they could no longer do anything to slow her down.

"I have to... get away," she muttered under her breath as she tried to pull herself over the decaying trunk of a fallen tree. But just as she successfully hauled herself on top of it, the whole world began to spin uncontrollably.

"Watch out, my dear!" she heard a voice say from somewhere nearby.

And then everything went black.

chapter eighteen
phyllostachys nigra

Ayana was safe and warm, floating along on a soft cloud without a care in the world. Somewhere nearby she could hear birds singing. She slowly opened her eyes to see them.

"Oww, my eyes," she mumbled as she squinted and tried to block out the bright sunlight with her hands. "Why is it so bright in here?"

But where, exactly, *was* here?

Forcing her eyes open again, Ayana took a moment to let them adjust to the blinding light and saw that she was in some kind of small, sparsely furnished bedroom. The sun was streaming in through some open windows set high along the wall. The windows were covered in some kind of decorative wooden grates that made a pattern of sunlight and shadow on the wooden floor, and she could see some birds singing happily in the tree branches outside.

Ayana was lying on a wonderfully soft mattress set into a low wooden bed, and the wall above her head was painted with an elaborate Chinese style mural showing a long blue dragon snaking its way through the clouds. At the foot of the bed stood an intricately carved wooden chest decorated with rocks and trees and waterfalls.

Ayana closed her eyes again and just lay there for a while. Her head was pounding. She tried to sit up, but every time she did, the room spun woozily around, and she was forced to lie back down again.

"My head," Ayana groaned, and she touched the back of her skull with one hand. She could feel an enormous bump there as she gingerly ran her fingers over her hair.

She tried again to sit up. This time she somehow made it and sat for a while at the edge of the bed while the room finally settled down. There was a basin of water near the corner of the bed, and someone had folded some fresh clothing for her nearby. Ayana was grateful to be able to splash some water on her face and wash away some of the sand and sweat. Next, she unfolded the complicated multi-layered dressing gown and tried to figure out how to put it on, but it was obvious that she was probably going to have to stick with the grubby T-shirt and jeans that she was already wearing.

"Hello?" Ayana called out hesitantly. "Is anyone there?"

The only answer was the birdsong outside her windows.

At the far end of the room, she saw a wood-framed sliding door that was apparently the only way in and out of the room. After pulling herself to her feet and making sure she wasn't going to fall back down again, Ayana shuffled to the door and pulled on one of its wooden handles to slide it open.

The door led out to a covered walkway overlooking a beautiful Chinese garden. At the centre of the garden was a large reflecting pond with rough grey stone and sculpted trees lining the perimeter. The pond was dotted with lily pads of various sizes, their colours bright purples and blues.

At the far end of the pond, perfectly framed by a beautifully carved circular doorway directly in front of Ayana was a small red pagoda with a clay-tiled roof flared at the corners in the traditional Chinese style. Towering above the garden in the distance, she could see the same jagged grey cliffs that she and Tyler had seen earlier when they'd been at the edge of the desert.

Ayana gasped at the view. It was so beautiful and peaceful, and it looked completely deserted.

"Hello? Is anyone there?" she called out again as she made her way through the doorway and along the covered walkway.

There was no answer, but with every step she took her view of the garden changed, each perfectly framed view more beautiful than the one before it. At the end of the walkway, a narrow path wound its way through a stand of green and yellow bamboo.

Ayana cautiously made her way along the path, pushing the bamboo stalks out of her way to reveal the full length of a small bridge leading to a red pagoda. Standing at the centre of the bridge was an old man with a wispy long white beard and moustache. He was dressed in a traditional Chinese robe, red and black with a high collar and sweeping wide sleeves.

"Hello?" she called out to the old man. "Excuse me?"

The old man didn't seem to hear her. He was staring down at the pond.

Ayana took a few steps closer.

"Hello?" she said again, stepping onto the foot of the stone bridge.

"Look at those fish down there," said the old man, without turning his head. His entire attention was focussed on the water below where a number of large spotted goldfish were swimming.

"What about them?" Ayana asked, grasping the railing and pulling herself forward to look down at the fish as well.

"They are so happy!" the old man observed with a toothless smile.

Ayana stared at the fish. They did indeed *look* happy. But they were fish. Could fish really feel happy? Ayana didn't know.

"How do you know they're happy?" she asked. "I mean, you're not a fish. How could you possibly know what they are feeling?"

The old man turned to Ayana and smiled even wider.

"Very true," the old man replied. "On the other hand, you are not me, so you cannot possibly know what I know."

He's got a point there, Ayana thought to herself with a smirk.

The old man turned back to contemplate the fish a while longer. Ayana was reluctant to disturb him, but she was dying of curiosity to know what had happened to her, and how she had ended up there.

"I'm Ayana," she said, extending her hand and smiling her friendliest smile.

"And I am Zheng Xiu," the old man replied, squeezing her hand warmly and bowing his head before turning back to his fishes.

"I am looking for my friends," Ayana continued.

"A young man and three very strange creatures," the old man replied, nodding. "You need not worry. They are here too."

"And where is here?" Ayana asked. "What is this place?"

The old man waved his arms dramatically across the entire garden.

"This is my sanctuary," he said simply, "a place where I can find serenity and contentment."

Ayana nodded.

"It's beautiful here," she replied. "But the last thing I remember was being in the jungle...."

"Yes," said the old man, "and you were running like a furious eastern wind until you collapsed from exhaustion. I tried to catch you, but I'm afraid you hit your head."

Ayana rubbed the back of her head and winced in pain.

"Yeah," she said. "I can feel it."

"You've been resting for a night and a day," the old man continued. "You must be starving."

Ayana's stomach grumbled in reply.

"Why don't I reacquaint you with your friends?" he asked,

gesturing for Ayana to head back toward the low buildings and walkways behind her. "And get you something to eat while we're at it?"

Ayana nodded hungrily and followed the old man through the bamboo and a confusing maze of walkways and arches until they came to an open courtyard where Tyler and the dragons were waiting.

At first, they didn't see her. Tyler was kneeling in the middle of the courtyard with a scattered mess of paper and ink and brushes spread out in front of him. He'd changed clothes since the last time she'd seen him, and now he was wearing a beautiful embroidered silk robe similar to the one the old man was wearing.

The three dragons were lounging in the sun, curled up on padded blankets of varying sizes that they'd formed into makeshift beds.

"Ayana!" Tyler cried, springing up from whatever he was working on and running over to greet her. "You're awake! How do you feel? We were so worried. Does your head hurt?"

Ayana didn't have time to answer his many questions because the dragons were already on top of her. *Mongo* and *Vapor* snuffled their noses into hers while *Dune Buggy* jumped and danced excitedly around her feet and legs.

"Oh, I missed you guys too!" Ayana cried happily as Tyler and the dragons crowded around her affectionately. "So much!"

"Whenever you are ready," the old man announced from the doorway, "my housekeeper has some food waiting for us."

"Oh! You have to try the food here!" Tyler cried, tugging Ayana by the arm and leading her toward a doorway at the opposite end of the courtyard. "It's all vegetarian, but you won't believe how good it is!"

As the old man led them across the yard, she could already smell it. He led them up some wooden stairs, and after taking their shoes off and leaving the dragons outside by the door, he ushered them into a simple room with red-painted walls and three very short stools arranged around a simple wooden table in the middle of the room.

"Please have a seat," the old man said, gesturing for Ayana to take a place at the right side of the table. Tyler took the spot at the left, and the old man finally took his place in the very middle once the other two were seated.

Without the old man saying a word, a panel slid open at the back of the room, and a wizened-looking old woman shuffled into the room hunched over a tray stacked high with teapots, cups and covered bowls. She set the tray on the table and efficiently distributed the various dishes to Ayana and Tyler, pouring tea and lifting the lids off delicious-smelling steaming bowls of vegetables and rice.

"Please, help yourselves." The old man smiled, and the woman bowed then quickly disappeared from the room.

"Thank you!" Ayana called after her, almost forgetting her manners in her excitement to have some real food for a change. She wasn't sure if the old woman even heard or understood her.

"Aren't you eating, Mister....?" Ayana asked, pausing when she realised that she wasn't sure of how to address the old man. He'd said his name was Zheng Ziu, but she vaguely remembered learning at school that in China it was the family names that came first.

"Mister Zheng," the old man replied, confirming Ayana's guesswork.

"Mister Zheng," Ayana repeated his pronunciation carefully.

"And I would love to join in this wonderful meal, but I am fasting at the moment," Mr. Zheng explained. "But please don't let that stop you from enjoying my housekeeper's excellent cooking."

Ayana felt a bit rude eating while her host sat hungrily by, but she was so starved that she couldn't help but dig in immediately. She fumbled at first with her chopsticks but her fingers soon remembered from all the nights that her family had gone out for Chinese at any one of dozens of amazing Chinese restaurants in Vancouver. Her father had been an avid fan of taking her and her mother out to all kinds of different restaurants.

Burying that painful memory for the moment, Ayana snagged some steamed bamboo with her chopsticks and gobbled it down.

"You should see all the cool stuff Mr. Zheng has been teaching me," Tyler said as he slurped some soup. "About making paper kites and calligraphy and this really cool game that looks like *Reversi* but with different rules."

Mr. Zheng smiled as Tyler rattled on excitedly.

"It was a pleasure," he said. "It is so rare that we have visitors here."

"And you know what else is here?" Tyler asked Ayana, leaning over the table conspiratorially as he did so.

"What?" Ayana answered, fumbling with her chopsticks again as she tried to get some rice into her mouth.

"Black bamboo," Tyler replied.

Ayana nodded.

"Yeah, I saw it. Pretty cool, huh?"

"And you know what else?" Tyler continued, obviously trying to make some point that Ayana wasn't getting yet. "Mr. Zheng also happens to know how to write the Japanese symbol for dragon."

Mr. Zheng looked at Ayana and smiled as he nodded his head.

Ayana stared at the two of them over her bowl of steamed rice. It was obvious that Tyler was telling her all of this for a reason, but she had absolutely no idea what that reason could be.

"I don't understand," Ayana replied, confused. "Isn't Mr. Zheng Chinese?"

"Yes, he is," Tyler nodded. "But he's travelled around a lot, including many trips to Japan. And he speaks thirteen languages fluently, including Japanese."

"Okay," Ayana replied. She was still completely lost.

Tyler rolled his eyes.

"Don't you remember?" he asked. "Black bamboo? The Japanese symbol for dragon?"

For a few long seconds Ayana was at a total loss. But then she finally remembered.

"The paper dragon!!" she cried suddenly.

"Yes!" Tyler replied and slid *THE BOOK* across the table to her, his index finger marking the appropriate page.

Ayana picked up the book and opened it.

the paper dragon

category: collector's dragon
difficulty: challenging
classification: rare

following the japanese tradition of paper folding known as origami, the paper dragon is, in essence, a living origami dragon that is a must-have for any serious collector of dragons. as can be expected in conjuring such an unusual dragon, not only is the spell itself highly difficult, but obtaining the required materials may also prove to be fairly challenging as the spell requires a square of rice paper with the japanese symbol for dragon inscribed on it at the very centre in dark ink blended from green tea and the pigment from the outer layer of a stalk of black bamboo (phyllostachys nigra).

note: the larger the paper that you use to conjure the dragon, the bigger the resulting dragon will be.

required material(s): rice paper, a calligraphy brush, black bamboo ink

As Ayana read the instructions, the smile on her face grew bigger and wider. She remembered the spell now. It was one of those dragons of the month that she and Tyler hadn't been able to conjure because they didn't have the raw materials. The rice paper they could have found somewhere, of course, but the black bamboo to make the strange ink was another matter entirely. After all, where were they supposed to find such exotic bamboo in the tiny little city of Medicine Hat, Alberta?

But now they had found some. A major thicket of black bamboo was growing in the garden not more than a hundred feet from where they were sitting. And the rice paper was no problem, either, since it was a pretty good bet that the paper that Tyler had been doing his calligraphy on was probably made of rice. Both of those things plus Mr. Zheng's encyclopaedic knowledge of the Japanese language meant that they only needed one last ingredient to conjure a paper dragon.

Green tea.

Ayana stared down at her half empty teacup and grinned.

chapter nineteen
the ancient art of paper folding

"How long do you think it has to boil, Mr. Zheng?" Tyler asked.

The three of them were in the courtyard huddled around a charcoal stove. Hanging over the hot coals was a small iron pot filled with a mixture of green tea and wooden shavings from the bark of a stalk of black bamboo. The whole mixture was boiling and gradually turning a rich, deep black colour.

"Not much longer," Mr. Zheng replied as he bent down to inspect the inky fluid. "And then we leave it to cool."

Ayana nodded and continued stirring the black concoction with a wooden spoon for a couple more minutes until Mr. Zheng said it was ready, and then he used a wooden pole to lift the pot off the coals and set it onto the paving stones nearby.

While the ink cooled, there was plenty of work for Tyler and Ayana to do. Not only were the materials for the dragon hard to come by, but the spell itself was also incredibly challenging.

Mr. Zheng took his leave of them for a little while to give them some time to wash up and practise their spell. His housekeeper guided Ayana and Tyler back to their bedrooms where fresh hot basins of bathing water were waiting for them. She silently showed Ayana how to tie the complicated dressing gown around herself before disappearing again, sliding the door closed behind her without a word.

Ayana's bath was completely blissful. She felt like an entirely new person after washing the sand and grime and salt water of the past days off her skin and hair. Once clean and dry, she still wasn't sure about wearing the traditional Chinese clothing, but she couldn't bear the thought of climbing back into her filthy T-shirt and jeans, so she forced herself to figure out how to put the strange garment on.

If Tyler can do it, so can I, she told herself as she fumbled with the folds and ties and buttonhooks until she finally seemed to get it right.

Leaving her dirty clothes behind, she stepped out into the walkway and went looking for Tyler. She found him in the courtyard where a light rain had begun to fall, so the two of them (plus dragons) took shelter underneath one of the many covered walkways that connected the various buildings and gardens of Mr. Zheng's estate.

"I'm not sure we can actually do this," Tyler said, scratching his head as he and Ayana sat cross-legged across from each other with *THE BOOK* between them, studying the spell's intricate movements and gestures.

"Of course we can," Ayana replied, flipping the book around so she could see what Tyler was talking about. At first glance, she thought that maybe she had spoken too soon, but as she closed her eyes and visualised every graceful sweep and turn of their hands, she soon realised that the spell wasn't quite as complex as it appeared to be.

"I can't do it!" Tyler cried, throwing up his hands in frustration after he and Ayana had practised a few times and he floundered at the third step of the spell for what felt like the hundredth time.

"You *can* do it," Ayana said patiently. "Let's start again."

"No, Ayana! I can't!" Tyler replied, aggravated. "I'm not as good at this as you are!"

Ayana lowered her hands and let them rest in her lap.

"That's not true," she said in a quiet voice.

"It *IS* true!" Tyler replied, frowning.

Ayana shuffled forward until her knees were almost touching Tyler's.

She looked him in the eyes.

"Hey, Tyler, come on," Ayana said quietly. "We can do this—you and me together. That's how it always is. Okay?"

Tyler looked up at her and smiled weakly. How could he resist?

"Okay," he agreed and moved his hands into starting position.

The two of them practised the spell over and over and over again until they finally got the hang of it. By then the rain had stopped and beautiful bright sunlight was streaming down onto the courtyard again, drying the cobblestones and burning off the clouds that clung to the sheer cliffs rising above them. Ayana could see the vague, craggy outline of Tyler's desk and chair formed by the rock.

Out of nowhere, Mr. Zheng's hunchbacked housekeeper appeared and padded over to them. Without a word, she arranged a beautifully painted teapot and two cups.

"Thank you," Ayana said, again not sure whether the woman

heard her as she vanished out of sight through some sliding doors as quickly as she'd appeared.

"I never really liked green tea before," Tyler said, pouring each of them a small cupful. "I always thought it just tasted like weird hot water. But now I'm kinda liking it."

Ayana laughed and took a sip of her tea. She pushed *THE BOOK* aside and turned so she could stretch her legs out in front of her.

"What do you think this place is?" she wondered aloud, looking around at the astounding natural beauty and architecture surrounding them. She'd never experienced a place as lovely and tranquil before.

Tyler shrugged his shoulders and stretched his legs out as well.

"I had a book of Chinese folk tales and philosophy on the floor next to my desk. My mother gave it to me, but I hadn't read much of it yet."

"And that's where all this came from?" Ayana asked. "I mean, that's how all of this came into existence here in the book world?"

Tyler nodded.

"It must be," he replied, taking another sip of tea.

"It's beautiful," Ayana said softly as she closed her eyes and breathed in the fresh, clean air. The smell reminded her of home, but not her home in Alberta—her *real* home in Vancouver. She wondered if she would ever see either of her parents again.

"It almost makes you wonder what other amazing worlds are out there," Tyler said. "All around my whole bedroom, I mean. I can't imagine how many books are lying around all over the place."

Ayana laughed.

"I can!" she replied. "Your bedroom is always a total mess! There must be a hundred other little book worlds scattered around out there."

Tyler had to laugh too. Ayana was right. His bedroom was always littered from top to bottom with books everywhere. His mother nagged him about it all the time since his bookshelves were only half-full, but he had his own unique system of organisation that just happened to involve storing books in every conceivable bit of free space throughout his entire bedroom.

Suddenly Mr. Zheng appeared, strolling into the courtyard through one of the archways.

"Hello, my friends," he said as he walked sedately toward them. "Have your hours of studying and practising been fruitful?"

"Definitely," Tyler replied, looking at Ayana for confirmation. "I think we're almost ready to give it a try."

Mr. Zheng nodded solemnly and gestured for them to follow him. With the dragons tagging along behind, Ayana and Tyler followed Mr. Zheng across the courtyard and through the archway into the garden. He led them along a maze of paths and through bamboo groves until they emerged at the top of a small hill overlooking the reflecting pond. The red pagoda Ayana had seen earlier was just ahead of them.

"Please," Mr. Zheng said, ushering them into the pagoda where he had already prepared things for them. Stacks of rice paper in various shapes and sizes were piled nearby. A wooden box containing several calligraphy brushes was open on a short table in the middle of the pagoda floor, and an inkpot filled with black bamboo ink stood nearby. Three low stools were arranged in a semi-circle around the centre of the pagoda.

Ayana and Tyler sat on either side of Mr. Zheng.

"How big a dragon should we conjure?" Ayana asked as she tucked her slippered feet underneath her.

"A *big* one!" Tyler grinned.

Ayana frowned.

"The spell is hard enough as it is," she said. "Why don't we try something smaller first?"

"Okay, fine." Tyler sulked as he pulled out a small square of rice paper from the nearby stacks and laid it flat on the wooden floor in front of them. "Now we just need to write the Japanese symbol for dragon on it."

Ayana and Tyler looked to Mr. Zheng, who smiled at them enigmatically.

"In the modern world where the two of you come from, there are several ways to write the word dragon in Japanese," he explained in his soft voice as he selected a calligraphy brush and carefully dipped it into the inkwell. "But in its oldest and most basic form the Japanese character is identical to the one that we use here in China."

Mr. Zheng handed the brush to Tyler and leaned over to help him inscribe the complex symbol onto the square of paper. Ayana watched, completely mesmerised by the quick flowing strokes of the brush.

142

"Ryū," Mr. Zheng said as he and Tyler completed the symbol's final brushstroke. "Dragon."

"I love it," Ayana whispered.

Tyler nodded in silent agreement.

"So what do we name her?" Tyler asked. "The dragon, I mean."

Ayana thought about this.

"What's the Chinese word for paper?" she asked Mr. Zheng.

"Zhĭ," he replied, his voice rising to pronounce the word's strange inflections. But neither Ayana nor Tyler was sure that they could replicate the word's pronunciation.

"How about in Japanese?" Tyler asked.

"*Kami*," Mr. Zheng replied. The pronunciation in Japanese was much simpler.

"Why don't we name her *Kami*?" Ayana asked, looking to Tyler for agreement.

"I like it," Tyler smiled.

"Okay, then," Ayana grinned.

"But now comes the hard part," Tyler said, taking the square of paper and placing it on the floor between them.

"Are you ready?" he asked.

Ayana nodded and took a deep breath before moving her hands into starting position. Tyler did the same, stealing a glance at Mr. Zheng as he did so. This would be the first time they'd ever tried to conjure a dragon while someone was watching.

Tyler began the spell by smoothly opening his palm one finger at a time and rotating his hand face down as he did so. Ayana was next, sweeping the air with her fingers and gracefully segueing into Tyler's next motion.

They worked through the steps slowly and methodically, making sure they were executing every motion with the utmost precision. They knew that they could always try again if it failed the first time, of course, but by the time they reached the third step something happened that convinced them that a second try at the spell wasn't going to be necessary.

As Ayana's hands turned through the air, the paper on the floor between them began to twitch and quiver, folding over on itself as though some invisible hands were manipulating it and fashioning it into an incredibly complex and intricate design.

Ayana and Tyler both gasped at the sight of the paper moving magically all on its own, but somehow they managed to keep going with the spell. As they continued, they suddenly realised that the paper was mimicking their hand motions and folding itself into a perfect *origami* dragon.

As Tyler completed the spell's final flourish, the tiny paper dragon on the floor suddenly came to life, rearing her head back and sneezing violently.

"I can't believe it!" Ayana squealed, pushing her chair out of the way to lie down face-to-face with the amazing little creature. "You are so cute!"

Ayana held out her hand and let *Kami* crawl onto her palm. Ayana held *Kami* up to her face and the little dragon sneezed again, blowing the hair out of Ayana's eyes as she did so.

"Tyler, look!" Ayana cried, holding the adorable little dragon out toward him.

"I know!" Tyler replied excitedly as he leaned in, hoping that *Kami* would sneeze on him as well.

Mr. Zheng sat by quietly, nodding his head and smiling as Ayana and Tyler played with their newly conjured dragon.

"Look at her wings!" Ayana cried as the little dragon spread herself out to her full width and tried to fly for the first time. A series of complex oriental symbols and patterns in stark black ink flashed across the white paper of her wings as she flapped them quickly and lifted into the air. It was like nothing they had ever seen before, and they could hardly believe their eyes.

Kami flapped around the pagoda, flitting from here to there to look at everything she could find. She zipped over to *Mongo* first, dashing around the larger dragon's snout, sniffing and inspecting him thoroughly. She then flashed over to *Vapor* and *Dune Buggy* to have a look at them before returning to the middle of the room to check out Mr. Zheng last of all.

Apparently satisfied that she'd met all of her new companions, *Kami* sailed back toward the others and came in for a perfect landing on Ayana's shoulder. As soon as she was settled, the flashing patterns on her wings quickly faded, and she sneezed one final time before sitting back on her haunches with a rather proud look on her face.

Ayana and Tyler laughed.

"Amazing," Mr. Zheng said. "Congratulations to both of you."

"Thank you," Ayana replied, blushing.

"You will be glad to hear that I have asked my housekeeper to prepare a special meal for you," Mr. Zheng added, "to celebrate this amazing and magical feat of yours."

"Oh, no, please don't worry," Ayana said. "There's no need for her to go to the trouble."

"But my child, it's no trouble at all! The meal is already finished!" Mr. Zheng replied, laughing heartily.

"Already finished?" Tyler asked.

"Of course!" Mr. Zheng replied. "Everything is waiting for us right now at the main house."

"But I don't understand," Ayana said. "How did you know that we'd succeed? How did you know that we'd actually be able to do it?"

Mr. Zheng smiled his enigmatic smile and leaned in close, as if he was planning to impart some deep wisdom to them.

"I just knew," he said simply and sprang to his feet with the agility of a man half his age. He gestured for everyone to follow as he breezed out the door and down the path that led through the garden in the direction of the buildings on the opposite side of the pond. Ayana and Tyler and the dragons scrambled to their feet and hurried after him.

Back at the main house, Mr. Zheng was as good as his word and slid the dining room doors open to reveal an elaborately ornamented table stacked high with bamboo steamer baskets filled with an almost endless variety of small bite-sized morsels of dumplings and pastry.

"Oh, *dim sum!*" Ayana cried, and she sat down and began exploring the contents of the various steamer baskets while *Kami* watched intently from his spot on her shoulder. *Dim Sum* was another favourite of Ayana's from her old life in Vancouver.

Mr. Zheng took a seat between them, and both Tyler and Ayana were surprised when his housekeeper also joined them for dinner. As usual, she didn't say a word, nor did she eat very much, but she clearly enjoyed watching the others delight in the amazing variety of foods that she'd prepared.

"I don't know how we will *ever* repay you for all of this," Ayana said as she finished one too many dumplings and leaned back to give her full stomach a bit of breathing room.

A sudden chill ran down Tyler's spine, and his body tensed when he realised what had happened the last time that one of them had said those very same words. They had almost lost *Dune Buggy* to Chara and Namret.

"Don't worry, my child," Mr. Zheng assured them. "I believe that if a stranger comes to you in need, you must always welcome them with open arms, because you never know when you might be a stranger yourself."

Tyler relaxed when he heard this.

"Well, we can never thank you enough," Ayana said, "for everything, especially for helping us conjure the latest addition to our little dragon family." Ayana turned her head to nuzzle noses with *Kami*, who'd stayed on her shoulder through the entire meal.

"I do have one final surprise for you this evening, however," Mr. Zheng announced. "I spent most of the afternoon meditating about it and folding it in preparation for this moment."

Tyler felt himself tense up again.

"What kind of surprise?" he asked apprehensively, glancing nervously at Ayana.

"Please, follow me and I will show you," Mr. Zheng said. He rose to his feet and walked to the sliding doors. He waited for everyone to join him before sliding them open and revealing one of the most beautiful sights that Ayana had ever seen.

Their meal had taken so long that by now, night time had fallen, and the courtyard and gardens were completely dark. The only illumination came from an array of dozens upon dozens of brightly coloured paper lanterns that were burning brightly and floating on strings throughout the courtyard.

Ayana gasped in astonishment and scurried down the steps. Each lantern was a meticulously folded masterpiece of paper, each with a different Chinese symbol painstakingly inscribed on its side. At the base of each lantern was an opening with a small flame burning to heat the air inside. Like restless wild horses, the lanterns were tugging and pulling on the strings that tied them to earth, trying to get away and fly freely into the night sky.

"This is absolutely incredible," Tyler breathed.

Ayana was completely speechless and could only wander silently through the forest of light and colour, her eyes wide open and mouth agape.

"I was inspired by your plan to conjure your little folded paper *origami* dragon," Mr. Zheng explained. "In China we also have a tradition for paper folding, but unlike in Japan where the designs often involve various animals and flowers, the designs here in China are usually much simpler and pragmatic, like these sky lanterns."

"It's amazing, Mr. Zheng," Ayana cried. "I can't believe how beautiful they are."

"Ah, but the best is yet to come," Mr. Zheng said cryptically and gave his housekeeper a quick nod.

Ayana and Tyler smiled and watched in anticipation as they walked to the edge of the courtyard and deftly untied a knot in one of the strings that was anchoring the fiery lanterns to the ground. The knot fell away effortlessly, and all of the strings throughout the courtyard went slack. The entire collection of lanterns broke free and glided magically into the sky.

Ayana put her hands to her mouth and gasped in wonder. All those dozens of lanterns—a vibrant canvas of colour and light—adrift on the warm evening breeze as they ascended to heaven.

Ayana and Tyler craned their necks to watch the lanterns rise, each one twirling and spinning as it climbed along the face of the sheer cliffs, setting sail for the endless river of stars high above. Even the dragons seemed to be completely hypnotised by the sight of it.

"It's so beautiful!" Ayana whispered as the light from the lanterns slowly faded away in the distance. Tears filled the corners of her eyes at the sheer splendour of it.

Ayana glanced at Tyler. She didn't want him to see her crying. But Tyler was lost in his own little world. She could almost see the cogs and wheels in his brain spinning furiously.

"What is it, Tyler?" Ayana asked. "What are you thinking about?"

Tyler just stood there, silently smiling and nodding to himself.

"I think we just figured out how we're going to get up those cliffs to the top of my desk," he said simply.

chapter twenty
the sky lantern

Ayana really had to hand it to Tyler. When he got an idea in his head, he was relentless in pursuing it. The sight of all those glorious fiery lanterns sailing into the heavens the night before was all it took to set his imagination in motion.

"All we need to do," he explained excitedly as he spread paper, glue and bamboo sticks around the courtyard, "is build a sky lantern big enough to lift us all the way to the top of the cliffs."

Ayana was skeptical.

"It would have to be *huge* to be able to lift all of us off the ground."

Tyler shook his head, undeterred.

"It doesn't have to lift *ALL* of us; just you and me. The dragons can fly on their own."

Oh right, Ayana thought. *I forgot about that.*

"Still," Ayana said. "It's gonna have to be pretty big."

Clearly, Tyler was well aware of this, judging from the scale of the construction he was laying out in front of them. He put everyone to work, including Mr. Zheng and his housekeeper, although in Mr. Zheng's case, his contributions consisted more of wise observation and brainwork than anything hands-on. But his housekeeper (her name was Qiaohui, Mr. Zheng told them) more than made up for that by proving herself to be an incredibly resourceful builder, despite the fact that she never spoke a single word to anyone.

"Qiaohui prefers the silence that comes with hard work and contemplation," Mr. Zheng explained as they watched her skilfully weaving a large basket from strips of bamboo.

The basket was for Ayana and Tyler to ride in. They would attach it to the bottom of the enormous sky lantern and stand in it as they floated up the face of the cliffs.

The only problem was steering. Tyler knew well from reading books and watching television shows that it was notoriously difficult to steer things like hot air balloons, which is essentially what their giant sky lantern was going to be.

The way around that problem, Tyler realised, was to take advantage of their own flying friends, the dragons—*Mongo* in particular.

"If we attach some kind of harness to *Mongo*," Tyler explained, sketching his ideas on paper with a small piece of charcoal, "not only can he help provide us with some lift, but he can also pull us in whatever direction we want to go. That way, we won't be blown here and there in whatever direction the wind happens to be blowing.

"Makes sense," Ayana agreed, nodding her head. Truth be told, all of these designs and plans and schematics that Tyler was drawing up made Ayana's head spin. As far as she was concerned, whatever Tyler thought was best was fine with her.

"You see," Tyler explained, leaning over his drawings like some kind of crazed genius. "If we only build an enlarged version of Mr. Zheng's paper lanterns, it will be too heavy and we'll never get it off the ground. But if we make some changes to the design and cut back on weight—here, here and here—then it just might work!"

"Uh huh," Ayana replied with a laugh, not really sure what Tyler was talking about.

It was a tough job. Even with everyone pitching in to help, it still took them most of the day to finish cutting, gluing, weaving, tying and even sewing the clumsy-looking contraption together.

"Voila!" Tyler announced proudly as he and Qiaohui fitted the last pieces into place and took a step back to view their handiwork.

The giant sky lantern looked terrible. It was nothing like the elegant and beautiful small lanterns that they'd seen rising toward the heavens the night before. This one was clunky and ugly, patched together with three dozen different colours of rice paper in who knew how many different types of sizes. Imagine the crappiest, most ragtag, tattered sweater or quilt that you've ever found in a second-hand shop and you *still* won't even be close to how horrible this looked.

It was going to work. Tyler was sure of it. And like Qiaohui, he had never been afraid of detailed work. They were both smiling ear-to-ear at the thought of accomplishing such a masterpiece.

"It might look awful," he said, turning his head skyward to gaze up the face of the towering cliffs. "But it will get us where we need to go."

"So that's it?" Ayana asked. "Now we just hop in and float up to the top of the cliffs?"

Tyler nodded.

"Exactly," he said. "We'll leave first thing tomorrow morning. We'll take it out to the meadow outside the garden walls to fill it with hot air, and then...."

Ayana gulped.

"...and then we're up and away!" Tyler continued excitedly.

It's not the UP that I'm afraid of, Ayana thought. *It's the down.*

With night time quickly approaching, the group carefully put their tools and building materials away and headed for the dining room for something to eat before bedtime. Ayana was amazed to see the table set with some simple bowls of rice and vegetables already waiting for them. Along with all of her hard work on their makeshift flying machine, Qiaohui had also managed to cook a meal. And not only that, Qiaohui had also found time to do their laundry. Much to Ayana's surprise, her clothes were neatly stacked at the foot of her bed when she returned to her bedroom to turn in for the night.

It's so unbelievably peaceful here, she thought after she'd slipped into some silk pajamas and was safe and warm under the covers. *I wish we could stay forever.*

Outside her window, Ayana could see the face of the moon clock shining its pale silver light onto her bed. The minute hand had moved ever so slightly since the last time she'd seen it. The time was now eight and a half minutes past two—a definite reminder that time was passing slowly in the real world, and that she and Tyler had to find a way home again.

With *Mongo* curled up outside her door and *Kami* neatly folded up for the night on her pillow, Ayana slowly drifted off to sleep with the sound of the crickets chirping outside in the garden. She dreamt a strange dream of an enormous sky lantern in the shape of a dragon flying Tyler and her to the top of the cliffs.

That has to be a good omen, Ayana thought as she rubbed her eyes and sat up in bed the next morning. Outside in the courtyard she could hear Tyler and the others already hard at work preparing things for their first test flight.

"Why are you guys awake so early?!?" Ayana joked after she changed into her normal clothes and went out to join them.

"It's nearly noon!" Tyler called out, laughing. He and Qiaohui were busy folding the sky lantern into as small a bundle as possible so they could carry it out to the meadow at the foot of the cliffs.

"It will take quite some time for the lantern to fill with hot air, so why don't we have a late lunch out in the meadow?" Mr. Zheng suggested, gesturing to a gigantic picnic basket sitting nearby that Qiaohui had presumably prepared.

Ayana couldn't think of anything more perfect than that and happily carried the incredibly large picnic basket out to the meadow while the others somehow managed to lug the heavy deflated sky lantern between them.

Once out in the meadow, Tyler and Mr. Zheng set up the lower frame of the sky lantern over a large coal stove to catch the rising hot air while Ayana helped Qiaohui unload the picnic basket. They spread a blanket on a patch of grass and set places for everyone with cups of tea and small plates of sweet dim sum pastries.

"It's working!" Tyler said proudly as he and Mr. Zheng came over to join them. Ayana looked past him and saw that he was right. The rising hot air from the stove was very slowly but surely filling the patchwork sky lantern like a balloon. It was a slow process, and it soon became obvious that it was going to take most of the day, but Ayana could see that it was definitely working.

"Mr. Zheng wasn't kidding," Ayana said. "That's really gonna take a long time."

"All the more time for us to enjoy this lovely day," Mr. Zheng replied.

And so they sat together and ate and talked and laughed while the sky lantern gradually grew larger and larger, its colourful patchwork sides billowing in the afternoon breeze as it rose slowly in the air. After lunch, Ayana played with the dragons while Tyler tended to the sky lantern.

"This is really going to work," Tyler called out excitedly.

Mr. Zheng smiled.

"I never had any doubt," he replied.

"I did," Ayana muttered under her breath with a chuckle.

She and Mr. Zheng laughed as they watched Tyler's extensive launch preparations.

Qiaohui rose to her feet and bowed apologetically to Ayana.

"Qiaohui wants me to tell you that she will now go to prepare a gift and some dinner to take with you," Mr. Zheng explained as Qiaohui smiled and fawned over Ayana.

"Oh, she doesn't have to do that!" Ayana cried.

"She insists," Mr. Zheng said, smiling as well. "We are very grateful to have the two of you here. We so rarely have visitors."

Ayana could feel tears creeping into her eyes. It hadn't occurred to her that when she and Tyler got into the basket of the sky lantern, they would actually have to say goodbye to their two extremely gracious hosts.

"We are so grateful for you and for everything you've done for us," Ayana replied. "The food and clothes and just... everything! She doesn't need to do anything else for us!"

"It is her pleasure," Mr. Zheng replied as Qiaohui bowed again and headed back down the meadow in the direction of the house.

"She really doesn't have to," Ayana said again.

Mr. Zheng leaned in close to Ayana and whispered a secret to her.

"Qiaohui very much insists on showing her gratitude." He chuckled. "And believe me when I say that there is no use trying to resist her."

For some reason this made Ayana laugh as she watched Qiaohui disappear through the gates of the garden wall.

"I think we'll be ready to go in another hour or so," Tyler said, walking back toward them with the enormous sky lantern filling the sky behind him.

"Will it still be daylight?" Ayana asked. She wasn't sure she wanted to go on a balloon ride in the darkness.

"It should be fine," Tyler replied. "There's plenty of time left before darkness falls."

"Okay," Ayana replied, feeling better.

"The *real* question is how we will ever be able to thank Mr. Zheng and Qiaohui for everything they've done for us," Tyler said.

"We were just discussing the very same thing...." Ayana said when suddenly they heard a loud commotion from the trees at the far end of the meadow.

"What on earth is that?" Mr. Zheng asked, all of them rising to their feet in time to see a large powerful animal burst out of the trees and scamper across the meadow toward them.

"What is it?!" Ayana asked as she gathered the dragons together protectively.

"It's a wolf," Tyler replied, staying close to Mr. Zheng and Ayana.

"Stay close, all of you, please," Mr. Zheng said, frowning as they watched the huge animal scurrying toward them.

Ayana didn't need to be told twice; she moved closer to Mr. Zheng. The wolf was big and frightening, with long gangly legs and powerful jaws lined with sharp white teeth. Against her better judgement, Ayana suddenly wished that Chara was there with them. Chara wasn't afraid of anything.

"*Help me! Help me! Please help me!*" the wolf cried as it loped toward them.

"Is the wolf *talking* to us?!?" Ayana asked in disbelief. She wasn't sure because she hadn't actually heard any sound. It was as though the wolf was speaking to them directly in their thoughts.

"He is," Mr. Zheng replied simply, still frowning.

"*Please! I am hurt and I need help!*" the wolf said again as it scuffled to a stop in front of them. "*There are hunters chasing me! Please!*"

Despite its formidable size the wolf looked very frightened and kept glancing over its shoulder nervously. Ayana looked at the wolf's haunches and saw the broken tip of an arrow protruding from a dark wound.

"He's hurt!" she cried, and moved to rush forward to help. Mr. Zheng pulled her back.

"It's a wolf," he cautioned. "Whether it's wounded or not, it is still a wolf and always will be. That is simply its nature."

"But we have to help!" Ayana cried. "We can't just leave him for the hunters!"

Mr. Zheng's frown faded ever so slightly. The seconds passed, and it soon became a smile.

"You have a good heart," he said, placing his hand on Ayana's forehead. "That is your nature."

Ayana looked up and smiled.

"*Please, I beg you!*" the wolf cried, his desperate eyes darting toward the trees. "*The hunters are almost upon us! You must help me!*"

"In here," Mr. Zheng replied as he flipped open the lid of the picnic basket. "Jump in here and we will hide you."

"*Oh, thank you, thank you!*" The wolf eagerly limped to the basket and leapt inside it. Mr. Zheng closed the lid and gestured to Ayana and Tyler to sit on the picnic blanket while he poured them each a cup of tea.

chapter twenty-one
the nature of things

"Be still, now," Mr. Zheng said, nodding almost imperceptibly toward the opposite end of the meadow where a group of five or six men emerged from the trees wearing dark green tunics and strange round hats, each adorned with a single swept-back peacock plume. In their strong hands, they each gripped a long bow with one brightly fletched arrow at the ready and a quiver of replacements at their side.

"You there!" the lead hunter called out to them as they approached cautiously. The men stared in wonder at the enormous sky lantern hovering over the meadow, casting a shadow upon them in the late afternoon sun.

"Hello!" Mr. Zheng called back to the hunters, raising his hand cheerfully in greeting.

"What is this here?" the lead hunter asked as he and his group approached the picnic blanket. He laughed and did a double take when he saw the strange assortment of dragons reclining on the grass.

"It is a picnic," Mr. Zheng replied with a friendly smile. "A perfect amusement for such a lovely day as this, don't you think?"

The hunter scoffed.

"A perfect day for hunting, if you ask me," he said. "Not for picnics with children and...."

He stopped in mid-sentence, staring at the dragons.

"... and whatever these strange creatures might be," he continued, laughing warmly.

"To each his own," Mr. Zheng replied with a gracious nod and smile.

"We are hunting a wolf that has been harassing our hen houses of late," the hunter continued. "One of our arrows struck true and wounded him, but he somehow managed to escape, and we've tracked him here. Have you seen any sign of him?"

Ayana resisted the urge to glance at the nearby picnic basket.

154

Tyler took a sip of his tea and tried to stay cool.

"A wolf? Goodness, no," Mr. Zheng replied with a singsong chuckle. "Naturally we would have run for home and abandoned our little outing at the first sign of any such thing."

The hunter smirked.

"Naturally," he said, chortling with laughter. "I apologise for disturbing your afternoon tea."

"Think nothing of it," Mr. Zheng replied.

"The wolf is still out there," the hunter warned. "Make certain to stay on the alert for the remainder of the day and move indoors before darkness falls."

"We most assuredly will," Mr. Zheng replied. "Thank you."

The hunter took another look at them and the dragons then gave them all a polite bow and raised his arm as a signal for his men to follow him. Everyone stayed silent as the hunters moved off and disappeared into the trees.

For the longest time no one moved or made a sound, then suddenly the lid of the picnic basket burst open and the nose of the great wolf emerged.

"*Is it safe?*" the wolf asked. "*Have the hunters left?*"

Mr. Zheng scanned the tree line and, seeing no sign of movement there, he nodded.

"It is safe," he said. "You may come out again."

"*Thank goodness,*" the wolf cried as he leapt out of the basket and stretched his legs. He bit at the broken tip of the arrow that was still lodged in his right haunch in an effort to pull it out.

"Let me help you with that," Mr. Zheng said, reaching over and deftly pulling the arrow free with one quick motion of his hand.

"*Oh, thank you, thank you,*" the wolf said as he licked the wound. "*That is the second time that you have helped me. Perhaps you can help me for a third time as well.*"

"We can certainly try," Mr. Zheng replied amicably. "But I don't know what else we could possibly do for you."

The wolf looked at Mr. Zheng and Ayana and Tyler with a strange expression on his face. Something about it made Ayana's blood run cold.

"*All of this running from those hunters has made me very hungry,*" the wolf said, springing back to its feet again and taking a few threatening steps closer. "*And with this wound of mine, I shall never be able to catch myself some dinner.*"

"We are happy to share whatever food we have with you," Mr. Zheng said, gesturing to the leftover pastries on the picnic blanket.

"*But you must know that I am a carnivore,*" the wolf

continued, taking another step forward. *"All of these vegetarian foods are of no interest to me."*

Ayana and Tyler closed ranks with Mr. Zheng, gripping the seams of his cloak fearfully.

"What do you propose, then?" Mr. Zheng asked calmly.

The wolf stopped and stretched his mouth in a wide grin—a terrible and awful grin that made Ayana and Tyler's knees weak.

"I think I'll make dinner out of the three of you," the wolf replied, stepping menacingly toward them again. *"And still have enough left over for lunch and dinner tomorrow."*

"You ungrateful beast!" Ayana cried indignantly, her fear momentarily overwhelmed by a flash of sudden burning anger at the wolf's lack of gratitude. "How dare you?!? We just saved you from those hunters!"

The wolf turned to Ayana and seemed to smirk.

"And for that I am eternally grateful," the wolf replied. *"But you should have listened to the old man when he said that it was simply my nature to be a wolf."*

The wolf was close now, almost on top of them, growling with his lips pulled back hungrily and his sharp teeth dripping with saliva. Ayana thought of running, but she knew that even in its wounded condition, the wolf would easily run her down.

"Wait!!!" they suddenly heard a voice shouting from behind them.

Please be the hunters come back to save us! Ayana thought desperately and spun her head around. But it wasn't the hunters.

"What is going on here?" the voice bellowed.

It was Qiaohui returning from the house with a small basket of food and a flat, delicate package wrapped with string. Ayana's jaw dropped open in utter astonishment at hearing Qiaohui speak for the first time, not to mention from the sheer raw power of her voice.

"What's going on here is none of your concern!" the wolf replied, growling. *"These three are about to be my dinner, and unless you want to become my dinner too, I suggest that you mind your own business!"*

Qiaohui continued walking briskly and fearlessly toward them.

"What right do you have to eat these three helpless humans?" Qiaohui asked, sticking her face directly into the wolf's.

"I am a wolf!" the wolf replied furiously. *"It is in my nature to eat whatever it is that I want to eat!"*

Qiaohui took one step back and thought this over. She was smiling strangely and nodding her head.

"It is true," she agreed. "You are a wolf, and it is your nature to eat these three humans. You are right. This is none of my concern, and I will be on my way and leave you to it. Who am I to interfere with the natural order of things, after all?"

Ayana couldn't believe her ears.

"*Very good,*" the wolf replied, nodding as they watched Qiaohui walk off again.

"Wait a minute!" Ayana cried. "He didn't tell you the whole story!"

Qiaohui stopped dead in her tracks.

"What's this?" she asked, turning toward the wolf again. "Is there more to this situation than you've already explained to me?"

"*Perhaps a few details here and there,*" the wolf replied sheepishly. "*But it doesn't matter. It doesn't change a thing.*"

Qiaohui put her hands on her hips and waited.

"Please, do tell," she said.

"*I have been on the run all day from hunters who seek to kill me,*" the wolf explained in detail. "*They succeeded in wounding me and although I ran and ran and ran, I simply couldn't escape them and was convinced that all was lost and they would surely catch me.*"

The wolf paused for a moment to lick his lips hungrily.

"*But then I happened across these three out here in the meadow having a picnic,*" the wolf continued. "*I begged them to help me. The old man here didn't want to, of course, for he is wise, and he knew that a wolf is a wolf, and I could not do anything other than act according to my wolf-like nature. But the young girl here convinced him that they had to help, and so they hid me in that picnic basket over there until the hunters passed by in the course of tracking me, none the wiser of my hiding place, and I was saved.*"

"And then?" Qiaohui asked.

The wolf bared his teeth and growled.

"*And then you came along,*" the wolf replied. "*Just as I was about to eat these three.*"

Qiaohui rubbed her chin and pondered the wolf's story. She turned to Ayana and the others with a dismayed frown on her wizened face.

"I am afraid that the wolf is right," she said. "None of what he's told me changes anything. You may have saved this wolf's life by hiding him from the hunters, but the old man here was most certainly right in saying that a wolf has no choice other than to be a wolf. It is simply his nature."

Ayana wanted to punch someone. She'd had enough of this it's-his-nature-to-be-a-wolf crap.

"But it's not fair!" she cried.

Qiaohui shrugged her shoulders helplessly.

"No, it's not fair," she admitted. "But unless there is something else to the story that you're not telling me, I am afraid that I have to agree with the wolf and let him eat you."

Qiaohui looked at them and waited.

"Is there something more to the story?" she finally asked. "Something the wolf hasn't told me?"

Ayana and Tyler stared at their shoes and shook their heads.

"No, ma'am," Ayana said. "What he said was absolutely true."

"Strange. I would have thought otherwise," Qiaohui said with a surprised look on her face. "I mean, I can hardly believe that this big powerful wolf actually fit into that tiny little picnic basket. I was sure that he must be lying."

"*Lying?!?*" the wolf cried resentfully. "*I may be many things, but I am most certainly not a liar!*"

Qiaohui shrugged her shoulders again.

"What does it matter if you are lying or not," she said, walking off again. "Unless someone here is willing to tell me the truth, then there's nothing I can do but agree with you."

"But we *are* telling the truth!" Tyler cried. "He *did* fit in that basket!"

Qiaohui huffed.

"I am sorry," she said. "I just don't believe it. Look at how big he is and how small that basket is!"

The wolf growled viciously.

"*Old woman!*" he snarled. "*You would be wise not to anger me! Look here! See how I fit perfectly into this picnic basket!*"

The wolf dashed over to the picnic basket and leapt inside, the same as he had done fifteen minutes earlier. The lid clapped shut and hid him perfectly out of sight

"*Do you see now?*" the wolf snapped from inside the basket. "*Now do you believe it?*"

"Yes, you're right. I can see it now," Qiaohui replied as she raced across the picnic blanket in a completely unexpected burst of movement and fastened the lid tightly shut. She then pulled a length of rope out from somewhere in her flowing robes and whipped it around the entire basket, knotting it and trapping the enraged wolf inside.

"*Grrrraaaahhhh!*" the wolf snarled furiously. "*Let me out of here!!!*"

Ayana and Tyler were completely stunned. They looked up at Qiaohui to see her grinning at them from ear to ear.

Mr. Zheng put his hand on Ayana's shoulder and smiled warmly.

"For many years I have studied and meditated and contemplated the universe in an attempt to gain wisdom," he said, speaking softly while the infuriated wolf howled and growled horribly from inside the basket, nearly tipping it over in his unrestrained fury. "Some of us require so many decades of dedication to find wisdom, while others are able to gain it naturally."

Ayana began to smile.

"Qiaohui is one of those to whom wisdom comes easily," Mr. Zheng said. "It is simply her nature."

chapter twenty-two
victorian london

Ayana was amazed by Qiaohui's cool, calm handling of the wolf situation but unfortunately, the group didn't have much time to reflect on it because no sooner had the wolf been taken care of than the ropes anchoring the sky lantern to the ground came loose against the force of the powerful lantern trying to pull free.

Tyler ran over and stomped on the bamboo stakes holding the ropes down, securing them in the soft earth. The lantern was completely off the ground now, filling the sky above them.

"You must go," Mr. Zheng said as he watched the enormous contraption yanking and tugging on its harnesses like a thoroughbred racehorse itching to run.

"Now?" Ayana cried. "So soon?"

Both Mr. Zheng and Tyler nodded emphatically.

"You cannot wait any longer," Mr. Zheng said, pointing to the sun riding low in the sky. "Soon the sun will set and the night air will turn colder. That will make it more difficult for the air in the lantern to stay hot."

"Not to mention that we don't want to be navigating around in the dark," Tyler added. "We have to go now, or stay here another day and go through all of this again tomorrow."

Ayana looked around from face to face in desperation. She wasn't ready to go yet.

"But...." Ayana started to say.

"Shhh, my child," soothed Mr. Zheng. "This is how it must be."

Ayana knew he was right. But she still couldn't bear the thought of saying goodbye.

"I will miss you all so much," she said, not caring that they saw the tears welling in her eyes. She threw her arms around Qiaohui first then Mr. Zheng.

"This is for you," Mr. Zheng said, gesturing to Qiaohui who was holding out the flat package that Ayana had seen her carrying earlier.

"What is it?" Ayana asked as she carefully removed the strings and unfolded the wrapping paper.

"A gift," Mr. Zheng said simply.

Ayana peeled back the last of the paper and saw the most amazing thing pressed between two thin sheets of opaque rice paper. It was a replica of Mr. Zheng's garden meticulously cut out from a single sheet of paper and painted by hand. Every detail was there—the pond, the fish, the black bamboo, and of course the red pagoda. The intricacy of the paper cutting was unbelievable. Ayana had seen Qiaohui snipping furiously with a pair of old rusty scissors earlier in the day, but never in a million years would she have guessed that this was what she was working on.

"I... I don't... I don't know what to say...." Ayana was full on crying now, and speechless.

"It's so beautiful," Tyler gasped, looking over Ayana's shoulder with quite a few tears in his eyes as well.

"And here is some dinner to take with you," Mr. Zheng said as Qiaohui handed Tyler a small picnic basket. "But now you really must go. I wish we had more time, but there is a time for everything in life, and the time for you to sail off into the heavens is now."

Ayana sobbed and wrapped her arms around Mr. Zheng and Qiaohui for a second time. She didn't want to let them go, but somehow she was finally able to pull herself away. Tyler hugged them too then hurried off to fix the rope harness to *Mongo* and tie it securely to the basket of the sky lantern.

"What about him?" Ayana asked as *Kami* came fluttering over to land on her shoulder. She pointed toward the picnic basket where the angry wolf was trapped inside. The basket was still shaking and howling.

"Don't worry about him," Mr. Zheng replied. "We'll set him free again when the time is right."

"Only when it's safe—promise?" Ayana said and helped pull Tyler into the sky lantern basket after her.

"Of course," Mr. Zheng replied, smiling with a warmth that made Ayana want to jump out of the basket and stay with them forever in their beautiful little garden oasis.

With the added weight of Ayana and Tyler in the basket, the sky lantern was pulling at the ropes now with much less urgency, but it was clear that it still was straining to fly free.

"Thank you... both of you... for everything!" Ayana cried as Mr. Zheng pulled the bamboo stakes free, and she and Tyler lifted off the ground and rose slowly into the air.

"Yes, thank you!" Tyler shouted as he reached up to open the air vents on the charcoal stove. With the influx of fresh oxygen, the coals flared brightly and the sky lantern rose ever so slightly faster.

Ayana was expecting a more abrupt and dramatic departure, but unlike a normal hot air balloon with its huge flaming burners to heat the trapped air quickly, their sky lantern had a far more modest heat source. The result was a very slow and gradual ascent that left her and Tyler waving almost endlessly to Mr. Zheng and Qiaohui as the lantern lifted above the trees at a snail's pace.

Things began to speed up a little bit once *Mongo* lifted into the air and pulled them up behind him. Flying next to him, *Vapor* and *Dune Buggy* glided in long circles around the sky lantern, keeping an eye on things and looking worried.

"Goodbye!! Thank you!!!" Ayana cried one last time, not even sure if they could hear her any more. By now they had climbed quite high, and with *Mongo*'s help they were ascending the face of the cliffs more quickly now.

Ayana stared down at Mr. Zheng and Qiaohui until they had completely disappeared from sight. She missed them already.

"How long do you think it will take to reach the top of the cliff?" Ayana asked, trying to see past the huge lantern above them. Tyler shrugged.

"I honestly have absolutely no idea," he admitted as they watched the rough grey face of the stone cliff gliding past them. Occasionally, they passed several small ledges with scruffy-looking trees clinging desperately to the rock face, their roots frantically clawing into every nook and cranny and holding on tight.

On and on they went. Down below they could see the jungle world at the foot of the desk stretched out in front of them. In the distance beyond, the pale sands of the desert stretched out toward the enormous waterfall cascading from the edge of Tyler's bed.

"I think I see a sandworm," Tyler laughed, pointing into the distance.

Ayana tried to see what he was talking about but she couldn't be sure. It might have been a sandworm. But it also might have been the shadow of a long dune catching the rays of the setting sun.

"We must be at least halfway there," Ayana said. She was staring off to their right where a large flat plateau of rock had opened in front of them. It looked remarkably like the seat of Tyler's desk chair, at least to Ayana anyway.

"Why?" Tyler asked. "Because we're higher than the bed now?"

Ayana turned and looked where Tyler was looking. He was

right. They were now higher than the surface of his bed. They could see the endless chain of tiny islands dotting the surface of the sapphire blue sea, including the island forest of the pop-up book where they'd first arrived in this strange book world.

"Shouldn't we be almost at the top if we're higher than the bed?" Ayana asked, frowning as she tried to visualise the layout of Tyler's bedroom.

Tyler shook his head.

"My bed is only about half as high as my desk," he said. "So, I guess we're halfway there."

Ayana nodded.

Makes sense, she thought. *I guess.*

By now, the sun was brushing against the horizon at the far end of the wide blue ocean that stretched across Tyler's bed. It looked like it was going to be a breath-taking sunset, but Ayana was worried about how long it was taking them to reach the top. She tried again to see around the big fat lantern above them, but it was no use.

"It's gonna be dark soon," she said.

Tyler nodded.

"Don't worry," he said, trying to reassure her. "Why don't we eat something and watch the sunset?"

Ayana frowned. She would have preferred to just stand there worrying, but she knew that was pointless.

"All right," she replied and helped Tyler unpack the little picnic basket that Qiaohui had prepared. There was a pot of tea, of course, and two beautifully painted teacups, and bamboo baskets filled with dim sum and pastries.

"Why is everything in this world so beautiful?" Ayana asked as they munched on dim sum and sipped their tea. The sun now slipped below the horizon, filling the sky with a blaze of purple and orange that sparkled off the dazzling surface of the distant sea.

Tyler grinned.

"It's a world of books," he said. "How could it be anything different?"

Little by little, the colour began to fade from the distant clouds at the horizon, and the world descended into darkness. Far off to their left the moon clock slowly came into view and the sky filled with a million stars.

Tyler opened the vents on the charcoal stove all the way now. The air had quickly turned cold once the sun went down, and the last thing they wanted was to float all the way back down to Mr. Zheng's house again.

Suddenly, from somewhere up above, they heard *Mongo* bleating excitedly.

"I hope that's the top of your desk," Ayana said as both she and Tyler leaned out over the edge of the sky lantern basket to see what was going on.

"It is!" Tyler cried out.

It was so dark that she and Tyler could barely see their hands in front of their faces, but as the sky lantern crested the clifftop, the never-ending blackness of the cliff walls was immediately replaced with a twinkling ocean of lights spread out in front of them. At first Ayana thought they were stars, but she quickly realised that what she was looking at was a city, and that the ocean of lights was, in fact, the burning lamps of thousands upon thousands of houses and street lights.

As they rose higher, *Mongo* flew to a lower altitude and pulled the sky lantern horizontally across the landscape of chimneys and church spires. Smoke was curling up from every building, filling the air with an acrid odour of burning wood and coal that invaded Ayana's nostrils and made her want to sneeze.

"What is this place?" she wondered.

"It's London, Victorian London, to be exact," Tyler answered, pointing out across a wide river that wound its way across the landscape. "See Big Ben over there?"

"Of course," Ayana replied, staring at the distinctive gothic clock tower. She remembered seeing it days earlier from the top of the trees in the pop-up forest. Back then, it had seemed so far away, but now they were nearly on top of it.

"And St. Paul's cathedral over there?" Tyler said, pointing to an enormous moonlit church dome in the distance to their right.

"But why London?" she asked. "And what does *Victorian* London mean?"

"It means London during the reign of Queen Victoria," Tyler explained as they sailed silently over the dark rooftops. "In the late 1800s."

Ayana nodded and stared out across the surreal scene laid out in front of them.

"But why London in the late 1800s?" she asked again. "I mean, what is a book about Victorian London doing on top of your desk?"

Tyler grinned like someone who was incredibly thrilled to be exactly where they were at that particular moment in time. Back in the desert world, he'd been excited, but now he was nearly ecstatic. Clearly, there was something about being in Victorian London that made him very, very happy.

"Sherlock Holmes," he said simply, waving his hand across the dark and smoky city below them. "This is the London of Sherlock Holmes."

chapter twenty-three
mr. jabez wilson

Ayana and Tyler and the dragons spent the night in one of London's many big parks. When they cruised over the rooftops the night before, Tyler seemed to know exactly which park was the one he wanted and expertly guided *Mongo* to it.

"Why don't we just keep going all the way to Professor Möbius's clockwork tower?" Ayana suggested. "It must be somewhere up ahead, plus isn't it where we need to go anyway?"

Tyler shook his head and pointed to the tired wooden dragon pulling them along and slowly losing the strength he needed to stay aloft.

"*Mongo* is completely exhausted," he said. "Besides, don't you want to have a look around Sherlock's London?!?"

Ayana looked at *Mongo* and immediately saw that Tyler was right. Every swish of his big wooden wings seemed to cause him pain. They needed to get him on the ground for a rest. Tyler turned down the heat on the charcoal stove as they glided past Big Ben and Westminster Abbey, gradually reducing their altitude until he and *Mongo* brought them in for a nice soft landing on a wide-open stretch of grass in a park in the north end of London.

Once they were on the ground, Tyler and Ayana (and the dragons too—except *Mongo*, who was too tired) worked quickly to deflate the enormous sky lantern and get it out of sight before anyone noticed it. Thankfully, it was a quiet night and the park was completely deserted, so they didn't have much trouble flattening the gigantic paper monstrosity before folding it and stashing it in the woods nearby.

After getting everyone and everything safely hidden among the trees, Tyler immediately wanted to set off exploring the city.

"Just imagine it, Ayana!" he cried excitedly. "Somewhere out there right now the game is afoot! Sherlock and Doctor Watson are prowling the foggy streets of the city in pursuit of their latest adventure!"

"I just think we should wait until morning," Ayana argued. "The streets of *modern* London would hardly be appropriate for two kids our age to be roaming in the middle of the night. Just imagine what it must have been like in Sherlock Holmes's London!"

"Oh, come on!" Tyler replied. "It can't be that bad, can it?"

In truth, Tyler knew deep down that Ayana was right. They really had no idea what was out there, and it would be far better for them to just stay put until daylight and then set out to explore the city. So they curled up for the night inside the folds of the sky lantern and snuggled between the various dragons for warmth.

Late the next morning, Tyler was second-guessing their decision to wait for daylight because Ayana seemed to be sleeping forever. He was anxious to get out and see the city.

Okay, enough of this, Tyler finally thought, growing tired of waiting.

"Oops, sorry," Tyler whispered as he 'accidentally' kicked Ayana's foot on purpose.

"Grmmmmmmmmhhh," Ayana groaned and immediately fell back asleep again.

Tyler rolled his eyes and kicked her again.

"Ooops, sorry," Tyler said, a bit more loudly this time.

"Grrrrmmmmh!!!!" Ayana groaned again and subconsciously kicked him back.

The dragons were staring at Tyler in confusion.

"I'm trying to wake her up!" he whispered at them defensively. "It's going to be lunchtime before we get out and start exploring!"

"I can hear you, Tyler," Ayana said, still lying motionless with her eyes shut.

"Then why don't you wake up?" Tyler suggested politely.

"Because I'm having a really great dream where I'm about to kick my friend Tyler's butt for trying to wake me up all morning," she replied and promptly kicked Tyler playfully in the shins.

"Ow! That hurt!" Tyler cried, pulling away from Ayana as she finally sat up, stretching her arms and looking around with sleepy eyes.

"What's the big hurry, anyway?" she asked, reaching for Tyler's backpack and pulling out one of the leftover pastries from their dinner the night before.

"There's somewhere I wanna go," Tyler replied, grabbing a pastry of his own and quickly stuffing his face with it.

"Where?" Ayana asked.

Tyler grinned.

"To see Sherlock Holmes, of course!" he replied.

Ayana just chewed her pastry and stared at him.

"Why on earth would we do that?" she asked.

"Isn't that why we came here?" Tyler replied. "To meet the greatest detective of all time?"

"Okay, okay," Ayana said, dusting her hands off and letting Tyler pull her to her feet. "Let's go see Sherlock Holmes."

They left the dragons in the trees (how could they possibly explain walking around with *them* in central London?) and promised to be back as soon as possible. Then they set off through the park toward the city.

Tyler couldn't have been happier. He was almost skipping along in excitement as they walked past morning strollers in the park, all of them dressed in particularly uncomfortable-looking and overly fancy clothes. A few gentlemen in overcoats and top hats tipped their hats to Ayana as they passed by, but for the most part the two of them were completely ignored.

"They must think we're some kind of homeless street urchins or something," Tyler said.

"They have a point!" Ayana laughed. "Isn't that exactly what we are right now?"

Tyler had to laugh too. Ayana was right.

"Here we are," Tyler cried excitedly as they passed through a final archway of trees. Ahead of them was a long street stretching into the distance with row houses lining each side. The streets were cobblestone, and the hard wheels of horse-drawn carriages clattered and made a terrible racket as they drove back and forth across them. Compared to the tranquillity of the park, the streets were a chaos of frenetic activity and putrid smells.

"Watch out!" Tyler cried as Ayana stepped into the street and was very nearly flattened by an oncoming horse carriage.

"Thanks," Ayana replied breathlessly as they carefully looked both ways and raced across the street when the first opportunity presented itself.

"See there?" Tyler asked; he was pointing to a street sign plaque mounted high on the side of one of the buildings.

"Baker Street," Ayana read. "This is where Sherlock Holmes lives!"

"Yes!" Tyler cried. "Right up there at number 221B!"

Tyler grabbed Ayana's hand and eagerly pulled her through the throngs of people making their way up and down the sidewalk.

"This is it...." Tyler said, and then he froze.

"What is it?" Ayana's body was tense with fear at Tyler's

sudden reaction. She followed his gaze and saw that he was staring at the open door of number 221 Baker Street with eyes as wide as dinner plates.

Walking down the front steps was a very large older man in a shabby brown overcoat. His face was bloated and red with tiny eyes staring out, but by far the most remarkable thing about the man's appearance was his unusually fiery red hair.

"Good day to you, sir," Tyler said as the bulky man passed by. The man nodded curtly in response and planted a faded top hat on his head as he headed down the street in the opposite direction.

"Jabez Wilson!" Tyler whispered excitedly. "Can you believe it?!?"

"Okay," Ayana shrugged. She had no idea who that was.

"That means...." Tyler said, thinking aloud.

Ayana waited patiently.

"That means...?" she asked expectantly.

"That means we somehow have to get to Fleet Street," he replied, grabbing Ayana's hand again and rushing down the street. "And then to Aldersgate."

"Okay," Ayana replied, struggling to keep her feet under her as Tyler dragged her along. "And why do we have to do that?"

"To see if I'm right," Tyler said, moving faster now, ducking left and right through the crowds of pedestrians. "And if I am, then in about an hour Sherlock Holmes and Doctor Watson are going to leave their rooming house and catch an underground train to Aldersgate. I want to get there before they do, but first I have to see if I'm right. And the only way we'll know that is if we go to Fleet Street first."

"Okay," Ayana replied, laughing at how little sense Tyler was making. But he was clearly having the time of his life, so who was she to ruin his fun?

"It would be fastest if we took the Underground," Tyler said, ducking through an iron archway and down some steps into Baker Street Station. "But unfortunately, to do that we need some money to buy a ticket."

Tyler was eyeing the uniformed conductor manning the entrance to the Underground platform.

"Who needs money?" Ayana asked as she casually wandered toward the gates.

"Are you crazy?" Tyler hissed at her. But Ayana wasn't listening. She was waiting for an opportune moment to jump over and sneak inside.

Ayana didn't have to wait long before a perfect opportunity

presented itself. A very tall and elegantly dressed woman approached the conductor and inquired as to the frequency of trains on the upcoming bank holiday. The man graciously obliged her by producing a train schedule from inside his breast pocket, and the two of them immediately began going over it in great detail.

While they were preoccupied with the schedules, Ayana glanced around to make sure the coast was clear and then quickly lifted herself up and over the wrought-iron barrier leading to the platforms. She strolled nonchalantly along the other side, signalling to Tyler to follow her lead.

Tyler gulped and looked around to see if anyone had noticed. No one had. Plenty of people were coming and going, but none of them were particularly interested in what two young street urchins might be doing.

"I'm the one who must be crazy," Tyler muttered, and he slipped over the barrier when he was sure that no one was looking.

"What took you so long?" Ayana joked as she and Tyler headed for the train platforms.

"You're lucky this is 1890," Tyler said as he hurried over to a route map pinned to a board. "When I was in London last year, you would *never* have gotten away with sneaking onto the Underground trains."

Tyler stopped in front of the map and examined it carefully. The routes in 1890 weren't entirely the same as those that he'd seen when his parents had taken him to London the year before. There were far fewer of them, for one thing, and they didn't exactly follow the same routes he was used to, but the important question was whether or not any of them could take them where they needed to go.

"There!" Tyler cried triumphantly. "Blackfriars! That's close to Fleet Street. That's the train we need."

"Platform two, then," Ayana said, suddenly aware of the rattle and thunder of an approaching train somewhere below them.

"That's us," Tyler cried, and the two of them sprinted up the platform and down some stairs to reach the arriving train on the other platform just in time.

"Come on!" Ayana said as she tried to pull Tyler onto the wooden train car. Tyler was watching the train conductor as he impatiently waited for everyone to get on or off the cars.

"What if they check for tickets once we're on the train?" Tyler asked.

Ayana frowned and yanked Tyler on board.

"Then we make a run for it," she said and stepped into the inside of the car and found a pair of seats for them. "Don't be so worried all the time."

As it turned out Tyler worried for nothing. Either the conductor wasn't supposed to check for tickets on the train or he was too lazy to do so. Whatever it was, twenty minutes later the rattling, clanking train car pulled into Blackfriars Station and the two of them stepped off onto another dingy platform just like the one they'd left behind in Baker Street.

A few minutes later, they stepped out again into the fresher outside air of the city, and Tyler struggled to orient himself.

"Everything is so different from when I was here," he said, staring at the confusion and crowds swarming all around the streets. "But if that's the river there, then we want to go the opposite direction—this way."

Ayana followed Tyler as he dashed up the street. Through the low masonry buildings to the right of her, she caught the occasional glimpse of the domed roof of St. Paul's Cathedral. Unlike Tyler, she had never been to London before, and only knew the famous landmarks that she'd seen in television and movies.

"And down here, this is it. This is Fleet Street," Tyler cried as they turned a corner onto a busy thoroughfare jammed with horse carts, pedestrians and beggars.

"Okay, so what now?" Ayana asked.

Tyler frowned and scanned all around them.

"When my parents brought me to London, we went on a walking tour of Sherlock Holmes locations and one for Harry Potter too. But everything just looks so different now. I don't know if I can figure it out."

"We'll have to ask for directions from someone, then," Ayana said. "What are we looking for?"

"Pope's Court," Tyler replied, still looking around for something that looked familiar. "Just off Fleet Street."

Ayana didn't waste any time waiting for Tyler to figure things out. She knew better after spending too many hours driving around aimlessly with her father who also simply refused to just stop and ask directions.

"Excuse me, sir?" Ayana asked the next gentleman she saw passing by. "Can you tell me where Pope's Court is?"

The man completely ignored her, sidestepping around her like she wasn't even there.

"Excuse me...?" Ayana asked someone else, but with the same result.

The people in Sherlock Holmes London sure are rude, she thought as she stepped right in front of the next man and refused to let him pass.

"Can you tell me where Pope's Court is, please?" she asked, darting left and right to keep the man from getting past her.

The man tried to ignore her but quickly grew frustrated and caved in.

"It's just over there—to the right," he said, pointing up the street before pushing Ayana out of his way and moving on.

"Yes! It's right up there!" Tyler cried and hurried up the street in the direction the man had just pointed.

Ayana rolled her eyes.

Just like my dad, she thought, always conveniently figuring it out after she or her mother finally asked someone for directions.

Ayana hurried after Tyler and caught up with him just as he turned the corner off Fleet Street and into the small, enclosed courtyard beyond.

"It's one of the buildings here," Tyler said as he moved from doorway to doorway in search of something.

"What number are we looking for?" Ayana asked.

"I don't remember," Tyler replied, shaking his head. "But we're looking for...."

Tyler stopped short in mid-sentence and stared off into space.

"What is it, Tyler?" Ayana asked, worried.

"I'm so stupid!" he cried. "It's not even here! Jabez took it with him when he visited Sherlock Holmes!"

Ayana was confused. "*What* isn't here?" she asked.

Tyler was about to answer but at that exact moment Mr. Jabez Wilson, the corpulent red-headed man they'd seen half an hour earlier coming out of Sherlock Holme's house on Baker Street rounded the corner behind Tyler and marched right up to the wooden door at number seven, Pope's Court.

They couldn't believe their eyes.

Mr. Wilson didn't notice either of them standing there. He was red-faced and agitated, pounding on the door with his meaty right hand with a frightening amount of force. He waited a minute or two, puffing for breath. After three minutes, there was still no answer, so he pounded again.

Only after thumping on the door a total of three times did Mr. Wilson finally decide to give up and walk off again. But before he did so, he took a square of cardboard out of the pocket of his threadbare overcoat and reached up to pin it to a panel at the centre of the door.

That done, Mr. Jabez Wilson huffed angrily and tramped down the steps and around the corner back toward Fleet Street.

"What was *that* all about?" Ayana asked, amazed at the red-haired man's obviously extreme frustration.

"This," Tyler said, pointing to the little square of cardboard that Mr. Wilson had left tacked to the door. "This is what I came here looking for, and it proves that we are on the right track."

Ayana stepped forward to read the writing on the little card. The message was simple, but it didn't make any sense.

The card read:

THE RED-HEADED LEAGUE IS DISSOLVED. OCTOBER 9, 1890

chapter twenty-four
the great consulting detective

"So what does *that* mean?" Ayana asked as Tyler grabbed her hand again and dragged her toward Fleet Street. "What on earth is the Red-Headed League? And where are we going now?!?"

"Saxe-Coburg Square," Tyler replied. "Near Aldersgate Station. That's where we're going."

"Another Underground train?" Ayana teased.

Tyler shook his head.

"Not this time," he said. "This time we can walk. But we have to hurry if we're gonna beat Sherlock and Watson there."

"Okay," Ayana replied, gradually getting used to feeling a little lost and behind the ball in Sherlockian London. "But what about the Red-Headed League? What is that about?"

"It's a sort of club for red-headed men," Tyler explained as they darted to and fro through pedestrians and horse carts. "It was founded by an American millionaire named Ezekiah Hopkins who had very red hair. When he died he wanted to set up some kind of trust fund to take care of other men with similarly red hair."

"What kind of trust fund?" Ayana asked. "Like free money?"

"Not quite *free* money," Tyler replied, shaking his head. "Anyone who was successfully accepted into the league was expected to perform a certain kind of work for a set number of hours a day."

"What kind of easy work?" Ayana asked.

Tyler dodged the wheels of a horse carriage and yanked Ayana across a busy street before continuing.

"Copying out the contents of the *Encyclopaedia Britannica*," Tyler said. "Starting at A and ending at Z, as much as one could do in four hours each and every day from ten to two then picking up where they left off the very next day."

Ayana stared at the back of Tyler's head in disbelief.

"You're kidding, right?" she asked.

Tyler shook his head.

"Not at all," he called over his shoulder. "Completely serious. And Mr. Jabez Wilson has been doing exactly that for the past two months, although he must be a bit slow because he hasn't even reached the B section in the encyclopaedia yet."

"And now?" Ayana asked. "The Red-Headed League has been dissolved and Mr. Wilson is out of work?"

Tyler nodded in reply.

"Exactly," he said. "Except that the whole thing is just a ruse. There actually is no such thing as the Red-Headed League in the first place."

"What?!?" Ayana cried as Tyler suddenly came to a halt and stopped to check his bearings.

"Here it is!" Tyler cried, off and running, stepping off the busy main road and down an alley to a grubby little square lined on all sides with low grimy brick houses.

Ayana hurried after him and was surprised to see a very familiar-looking pair of men standing in front of a corner house on which a dirty brown board was displayed with the words JABEZ WILSON—PAWNBROKER.

In truth, there was actually no good reason why Ayana would find those two particular men to be so familiar to her. She had never laid eyes on either of them in her entire life. And yet, she knew with absolute certainty from the very first moment she saw them that the tall, lean man with a thin face like a fox was Sherlock Holmes, and the bushy-whiskered sturdy man at his side was Dr. Watson.

Ayana stared in disbelief as the two men walked briskly toward them. Tyler seemed even more stunned and simply stood there absolutely speechless.

"Evidently," Dr. Watson said to his bright-eyed companion as the two men made their way toward Ayana and Tyler, "Mister Wilson's assistant counts for a good deal in this mystery of the Red-headed League. I am sure that you inquired your way merely in order that you might see him."

"Not him," Sherlock replied.

"What then?" Dr Watson inquired.

"The knees of his trousers," Sherlock answered.

"And what did you see?" Watson asked.

"What I expected to see," Sherlock replied cryptically.

"Why did you beat the pavement?" Watson persisted.

"My dear doctor, this is a time for observation, not for talk," Sherlock Holmes snapped impatiently as the two men disappeared around the corner. "We are spies in an enemy's country. We know something of Saxe-Coburg Square. Let us now explore the parts which lie behind it."

Without another word, the two men turned the corner toward the busy street that Ayana and Tyler had just come from.

"Come on!" Tyler cried, and raced after Sherlock and Holmes.

Ayana sprinted after Tyler and soon caught up to him around the next corner where Sherlock was standing and counting down the row of buildings with one long, skeletal finger.

"Let me see," Sherlock was saying as Ayana and Tyler approached him. "I should like just to remember the order of the houses here. It is a hobby of mine to have an exact knowledge of London. There is Mortimer's, the tobacconist, the little newspaper shop...."

"The bank!" Tyler cried out, interrupting Sherlock's train of thought.

"What's that, boy?" the world-famous detective said, eyeing Tyler up and down. "What's that you say?"

"The bank," Tyler repeated, striding up to Mr. Holmes confidently. "It's the bank they're after."

For the briefest of moments, Sherlock Holmes looked completely taken aback, but the expression evaporated so quickly that Ayana couldn't be sure if it had actually been real or if she'd imagined it. Dr. Watson, on the other hand, looked bewildered.

"What's that, boy?" Watson snapped as he raised his cane toward Tyler. "Scurry along, you filthy beggar!"

Sherlock put has hand on Watson's elbow and restrained him.

"What about the bank?" Sherlock asked Tyler, leaning toward him and examining his unusual clothing with great interest.

"The City and Suburban Bank," Tyler explained, pointing to a sign displayed prominently on one of the buildings behind them. "That's what John Clay and his gang are after."

For a fleeting instant that same look of astonishment flashed across Holmes's face again. Ayana could hardly believe her ears. Tyler was like a completely new person in Sherlock Holmes's London—totally in his element and speaking with greater confidence and vocabulary than she had ever heard him use. He sounded like such an adult.

Sherlock's eyes narrowed and turned serious.

"What do you know of Mister John Clay?" Sherlock asked, his voice grave and tense.

"I know that it was his knees that you were interested in seeing just now when you met him at the door of Mr. Wilson's pawn brokerage," Tyler replied. "You wanted to see what condition his trousers were in—whether they were clean and in good condition or worn from hours of kneeling and digging."

"You are quite right," Sherlock remarked with the thinnest of smiles flickering at the edges of his lips.

Tyler stomped the pavement with his foot.

"Nothing hollow down there," Tyler observed. "Therefore, all indicators point to the bank as being the intended target for Mister Clay and his cohorts. That's the reason for the ruse. They want to get the owner, Mister Wilson, out of the way for four hours every day so they can dig a tunnel from the basement of his business on the opposite side of these buildings to the Coburg Square branch of the City and Suburban Bank, where they clearly intend to break through at some point in the very near future and make off with the contents of the bank's basement vaults, perhaps even this evening. After all, why else would they choose today to dissolve the fictitious Red-Headed League?"

No one spoke a word. And Ayana was completely speechless, as was Dr. Watson as well, apparently.

Sherlock Holmes smiled.

"Astonishing," he said after a brief moment's pause. "And pray tell how exactly did you arrive at such startling conclusions as the ones you have just laid out before us?"

Tyler grinned.

"It was elementary, my dear Holmes," he replied with a smirk, and Ayana burst into laughter despite her best efforts to contain it. "Once you eliminate the impossible, whatever remains, however improbable, must be the truth."

This only made Ayana laugh harder.

Sherlock ignored Ayana's outbursts of amusement and leaned in very close to Tyler to look directly in his eyes.

"You seem to be uncommonly clever for someone so young," he said with a warm smile. "I suspect that you and I may have a great deal to discuss; however, at this moment, my companion, the good doctor and I, have an appointment to experience the delicacy and harmony of Sarasate at Saint James's Hall. Perhaps you would be able to spare me some moments tomorrow for a bite of lunch and some friendly conversation."

"Most definitely," Tyler replied with a grin. "It would be my pleasure."

"Very good then," Sherlock said, drawing himself up to his full imposing height. "Shall we say twelve o'clock at my rooms in Baker Street?"

"Agreed," Tyler replied.

"Until tomorrow, then," Sherlock said, turning on his heel.

"But first...." Tyler said, stopping him before he and Watson could stalk off down the street. "My friend and I here are new to the city and are in desperate need of lodgings."

A smirk began to grow on Sherlock's angular face.

"Very well," he said. "I do believe that one of the rooming houses across from mine has some vacant rooms."

Sherlock whistled for a hansom cab, pulling open the side door after the carriage had rolled up next to them at the curb. Ayana and Tyler quickly climbed inside while Holmes instructed the driver on where to take them, giving him some money for his troubles and to pay the landlady of the rooming house on their behalf.

"That takes care of it," Sherlock said, closing the door behind them. "Until tomorrow, then; for now, the good doctor and I are off to violin-land."

"Thank you, Mr. Holmes!" Ayana cried, leaning out of the window as the horse carriage rattled off down the cobbled street, leaving a very perplexed Dr. Watson and his companion standing at the curb.

Ayana collapsed into her seat in a fit of laughter.

"I can't believe you!" she shrieked in amusement.

Tyler just grinned proudly.

"It was nothing, really," he said. "I mean, don't forget that I *have* read all the stories already. It's not like I actually figured out the whole case by myself."

"Still!" Ayana replied. "That was just classic! You were totally messing with his head! Did you see how confused he was?!?"

Tyler shook his head but still couldn't help but grin.

"No one confuses the great Sherlock Holmes for very long," he replied. "All I did was tell him all the things that he already knew."

"And that's what's so funny about it!" Ayana squealed.

"I guess," Tyler replied, still grinning.

Tyler didn't stop smiling the whole way back to Baker Street. Once they arrived, the coachman took them to the door of one of the row houses just up from 221B and explained the situation to the landlady. The woman's name was Mrs. Stuyvesant, and she welcomed Ayana and Tyler into her home with much enthusiasm.

"Any friends of Mr. Holmes are friends of mine!" she cackled ecstatically. "Do you have any bags with you? No? You're dressed quite strangely. Are you sure you have no change of clothes?"

Reassured that neither Ayana nor Tyler had any other clothing, Mrs. Stuyvesant showed them to their rooms.

"Would you like a spot of bread and cheese to tide you over until dinner time?" she asked.

"Oh yes, please," Ayana replied eagerly. Her stomach was growling.

"Me too, please," Tyler said. "Thank you very much."

"It is my pleasure, darlings," Mrs. Stuyvesant replied, and she hurried down the steep staircase.

"Excuse me, Mrs. Stuyvesant," Tyler called after her before she could get too far.

"Yes, child?" she replied.

"Is there any access to the roof from here?" Tyler asked. "I have a fondness for watching the night sky and may wish to spend some time up there stargazing."

Ayana was again impressed at how quickly Tyler had adapted his manner of speaking to better fit into this strange new world they found themselves in.

"Yes, of course," Mrs. Stuyvesant replied, pointing to an opening in the ceiling of the hallway from which a folding stair emerged. "It's right through there. Go on up any time, but be sure to latch the door closed when you return so as to keep out any burglars."

"Of course," Tyler replied graciously. "Thank you again."

"Of course, darlings," Mrs. Stuyvesant called out as she continued down the stairs to her pantry to fetch them some food.

Ayana waited for Mrs. Stuyvesant to reach the bottom of the stairs before she turned to Tyler again.

"What do we need the roof for?" she asked. "Are you seriously going up there to look at the stars?"

Tyler laughed.

"It's for the dragons!" he said. "We'll go back and get them after dark. They can stay up there, and no one will even know they're there."

Ayana smiled and looked across at Tyler for a very long time.

"What?" Tyler asked, blushing at all the attention. "Why are you staring at me?"

"Maybe Sherlock was right after all," Ayana said, looking at Tyler in admiration. "You really *are* uncommonly clever for someone so young."

chapter twenty-five
the fog dragon

After a quick lunch of Mrs. Stuyvesant's excellent cheese, Ayana and Tyler headed back out to the streets of London and into nearby Regent's Park to check on the dragons.

The four of them were still hiding in the woods exactly as they had left them a few hours earlier. Ayana snuggled with each of them as they pranced and pawed about her excitedly.

"We are glad to see you too!" Ayana cried happily as she played with them. "Yes we are!"

The two of them spent the rest of the afternoon with the dragons, waiting for nightfall so they could sneak them back to their rooming house on Baker Street. It was a lovely afternoon for napping and reading, and Tyler had brought with him some books from Mrs. Stuyvesant's personal library.

"You know what? This Mr. Darcy is kind of a jerk," Ayana said as she angrily put *Pride and Prejudice* down, leaning back on the folded sky lantern with her hands behind her head so she could look up at the sky through the trees.

"He's not so bad," Tyler assured her. "He gets better later."

"Pfff. Once a jerk, always a jerk," Ayana scoffed. "What other books do you have?"

"*Wuthering Heights.*"

"Pass."

"*Little Women?*"

"Pass."

"*Huckleberry Finn?*"

Ayana hesitated.

"Pass," she said after a few more seconds. "Don't they have any *good* books in this century?"

"They have lots of good books!" Tyler protested. "We're *IN* one of those good books right at this very moment, in fact!"

"Whatever," Ayana replied stubbornly. "What else do you have?"

"*Frankenstein*?" Tyler asked, picking up the last two possibilities. "*Dr. Jekyll and Mr. Hyde*?"

Ayana thought this over for a moment.

"*Frankenstein*," she said finally. "That's dark. I love dark."

Tyler handed the book over, and the two of them read for a bit longer while the dragons curled up and snoozed all around them. But eventually the sun went down and it became too dark for them to read. It was time for them to sneak back to their rooming house.

Tyler stuck his head out of the bushes to make sure the coast was clear while Ayana lined up all the dragons in a row.

"Okay, here's the plan," Tyler said to the dragons. "All of you fly up into the air and follow me and Ayana back to Baker Street."

The dragons nodded in unison.

"Once we're inside, we'll head up to the roof and signal you from there. When we do that, you guys just fly down and join us, okay?"

The dragons nodded again.

"Okay, let's go," Tyler said, and all of them crawled out through the bushes onto the open grass. One by one, the dragons spread their wings and flew into the night sky, disappearing almost immediately against the background of stars.

Ayana and Taylor hurried through the park, nervously looking over their shoulders as they did so. Somehow, the park seemed a lot less friendly in the darkness than it did in broad daylight.

Soon they were under the light of the gas lamps on Baker Street and galloping up the stairs of Mrs. Stuyvesant's boarding house.

"Give me a boost," Ayana said when they reached the door leading to the roof.

Tyler threaded his fingers together and lifted Ayana by one leg so she could grab the rope that unfolded the ladder stairs.

"Come on," she cried as she pulled herself up the steps and unlatched the door.

The two of them stepped out onto the roof and immediately began scanning the sky for any sign of the dragons. It didn't take long before they spotted *Mongo* gliding toward them with the others not far behind.

Mongo wheeled his body around to hover for a moment before gently lowering himself to the rooftop. His wings were flapping furiously, and Ayana and Tyler had to shield their eyes from the dirt and soot flying everywhere. Fortunately, the other three dragons kicked up a lot less dust when they settled in for a landing.

"There's plenty of room up here for them," Tyler commented as the dragons got busy sniffing around and exploring the top of the roof. "And that low wall around the outside of the roof will keep them out of sight during the daytime."

"It's perfect," Ayana agreed.

Just then, they heard the sound of Mrs. Stuyvesant's voice floating up to them from the stairwell. She was calling them for dinner.

"We'll be right back," Ayana assured the dragons as she and Tyler climbed down the stairs and found Mrs. Stuyvesant in their room serving a light dinner of cold pheasant sandwiches and tea.

"Here you are, loves," Mrs. Stuyvesant twittered pleasantly as she set out the sandwiches and teacups. "And will you be needing anything else this evening?"

Tyler's mouth was already full of a huge bite of sandwich.

"Ow!" he cried as he bit down on something hard. Fishing it out of his mouth, he examined it then tossed it onto the plate where it landed with a tinny metallic clank.

"Watch out for the buckshot, dear," Mrs. Stuyvesant chuckled as she closed the door behind her. "I tried to pluck all of it out, but I might have missed some here and there."

"Why don't we take all this up and eat it on the roof," Ayana suggested once Mrs. Stuyvesant's footsteps had faded away.

"Okay!" Tyler grabbed the plate of sandwiches while Ayana grabbed the tea. Getting all of it up the shaky fold-down stairs was a bit of a challenge, but somehow they managed and were soon overlooking the rooftops of the city, their backs leaning against *Mongo* and their dragon friends surrounding them as they wolfed down their sandwiches and tea.

"It's kinda nice up here, actually," Ayana said as she lifted *Kami* onto her shoulder so she could see the view.

Tyler nodded in agreement.

"Maybe we should sleep up here so the dragons don't get lonely," Ayana mused. "I mean, we did leave them all alone in the park for half the day. It's the least we can do."

The dragons seemed happy with that idea.

"We can grab some blankets and have a kind of mini campout," Tyler suggested. "Although it might be kind of cold tonight. There's a fog coming in."

Tyler nodded in the direction of the river where a dense wall of fog was slowly enveloping the city, creeping between the buildings until only little islands of chimneys were visible across a vast billowing ocean of moonlit white.

"Now *that's* the London I imagine when I think of Sherlock Holmes," Ayana said. "Foggy dark cobblestone streets at night."

"Well you won't have to wait long to see it," Tyler said with a laugh. "In a half hour or so that fog is gonna be all the way up here to Baker Street."

Ayana smiled and leaned against *Mongo*, closing her eyes and resting for a moment.

"Wasn't there a fog dragon?" she asked dreamily.

"A fog dragon?" Tyler asked, not sure what she was talking about.

"In *THE BOOK*. Wasn't one of the dragons of the month a fog dragon?"

Tyler sat up straight, his mouth frozen in mid chew.

"I think so," Tyler replied, thinking. "In fact, definitely yes. I think it was the second or third spell we saw when we first looked through the book, and we couldn't conjure it because we didn't have any fog."

The two of them stared out toward the silently advancing sea of fog.

"I'll get *THE BOOK*," Tyler said with a grin and disappeared down the ladder. He reappeared thirty seconds later with *THE BOOK* and a small oil lamp in his hands and sat down next to Ayana so they could read it together.

the fog dragon

category: ethereal dragon
difficulty: easy
classification: epic

the fog dragon is one of a most unusual category of dragon known as the 'ethereal dragons' who have no fixed size or form thanks to the extreme range of their compressibility. while they generally prefer to remain fairly small in size, their potential for stretching themselves out over very large spaces is nearly limitless. in fact, perhaps the next fog bank you see is actually a fog dragon in disguise.

required material(s): fog (the natural kind)

Once they'd finished reading, Ayana and Tyler gazed out at the oncoming fog and wondered. The cloud of misty white was creeping up Baker Street directly toward them, heralding its arrival by sending a cold chill through the warm night air.

"Is that a fog dragon or just normal fog?!?" Ayana asked.

Tyler wasn't sure.

"I guess there's only one way to find out," he said. "We try the spell. If it works, it's fog."

"And if not?" Ayana asked.

Tyler shrugged.

"When have dragons ever done anything to hurt us?" he said.

Good point, Ayana thought as she dusted herself off and skipped over to join Tyler at the edge of the roof overlooking the foggy streets.

"The spell is actually pretty simple," he said, spreading *THE BOOK* out in front of them on the parapet so they could go over the steps. "If we'd had some fog, we totally could have done this when we first got *THE BOOK.*"

Ayana leaned on her elbows and checked the spell as well. Tyler was right—the spell was dead simple and consisted only of standard figures and motions that the two of them probably could have done in their sleep at that point.

"Let's do it!" Ayana said, excited at the prospect of acquiring another dragon for their collection.

"Okay. What do we wanna call it?" Tyler asked. He picked up a loose brick to weigh *THE BOOK* down and turned to face Ayana with his hands at the ready.

Ayana closed her eyes and thought this over very carefully.

"*Peaball,*" she finally answered.

"*Peaball*?!??" Tyler replied, totally confused. "Where does that come from?!??"

"It's fog, right?" Ayana explained with a smirk.

"Yeah...." Tyler said.

"A fog so thick it's like pea soup...." Ayana continued, waiting for Tyler to follow her train of thought. "And I bet he'll be a goofy dragon, like a goofball. Pea soup? Goofball? Get it?"

Tyler grinned. "I like it," he said. "Let's do it."

Ayana raised her hands and they started the spell together. That was probably the most interesting thing about the steps of that particular spell—the fact that each motion was carried out simultaneously instead of sequentially, which was the case with most other conjurings.

The whole thing took no more than thirty seconds, but as they finished the final sweeping motion, Ayana and Tyler stood there staring at each other blankly.

Nothing had happened.

"Did it work?" Ayana whispered. She couldn't believe that they'd actually screwed up such a simple spell.

"We must have messed something up somewhere," Tyler said with a frown as he bent over *THE BOOK* to double check.

"Tyler! Look!" Ayana cried as she pointed out across the buildings and rooftops of the city.

Tyler lifted his head and saw the most amazing thing. The fog seemed to be swirling and spinning toward them, filling every available space for hundreds of feet in every direction. It looked just like water flowing down the drain, and the epicentre of the giant spiralling cloud was the space right between them where their hands had just been.

Little by little, the fog was sucked toward them like some giant nebula falling slowly through a black hole. The longer it continued, the faster it got until the air around Ayana and Tyler was spinning like a maniacal whirling dervish, finally collapsing in on itself in a bright flash of moonlight that very nearly knocked the two of them over.

"What happened?!?" Ayana cried, shielding her eyes. They were both momentarily blinded. It took a second or two for her eyes to recover, and then she saw a small misty white dragon perched on the low wall next to them. At first Ayana thought it was a cat, but a second later it spread its wings and she knew that it was most definitely a dragon—a celestially beautiful dragon with twinkles of starlight glittering off its misty gossamer wings.

"It's unbelievable," Tyler whispered as he and Ayana moved closer.

Ayana put out her hand and *Peaball* leaned his snout down to lick it. His tiny tongue was cold and tickly on her palm.

"He's perfect," Ayana replied as she glanced at the rest of their beautiful and perfect dragons who were watching curiously from the other side of the roof. "Just like all of our dragons are."

Ayana smiled and let *Peaball* climb onto her hand so that she could carry him back to meet his new friends.

chapter twenty-six
a very queer mongrel

"Please come in, both of you," the great consulting detective, Sherlock Holmes, welcomed Ayana and Tyler into his sitting room and waved them over toward a pair of comfortable-looking armchairs arranged near the fireplace. Dr. Watson was there too, enthusiastically welcoming both of them with a warm and robust shake of each of their hands as formal introductions were made all around.

"Please do sit down," Dr. Watson invited them, smiling broadly. "As you can see, Mrs. Hudson, the landlady, has prepared some delicious chilled quail and morsels of cheese for us while we carry out our discussion this afternoon."

"Quail is like pheasant, right?" Ayana asked with a grin as she took her seat across from Tyler.

"Quite right," Watson replied. "Both are game birds, although in truth I much prefer the texture of quail."

"Watch out for the buckshot," Ayana joked as she glanced over at Tyler.

"Yes, quite right," Watson said with a hearty laugh.

Ayana and Tyler settled into their chairs while Dr. Watson took a seat not far away and Sherlock took his place just across from them in another of the armchairs.

"As my faithful companion, Doctor Watson, could tell you," Sherlock said, "it is my habit, upon meeting a person, to make certain deductions as to their background and character based on my observations of their mannerisms and dress."

"Quite so," Dr Watson agreed gruffly. "In fact, I have often remarked that Holmes himself likely would have been burned at the stake had he been born two centuries earlier."

Sherlock scoffed at the notion.

"My friend's fondness for embellishment aside," he said, "it is rightly true that as a rule, my deductions, arrived at in this manner, almost always prove to be unvaryingly accurate."

Sherlock leaned forward in his chair and looked Ayana and Tyler up and down, assessing them.

"But I must admit," the great detective continued, "that aside from the obvious fact that the two of you come from well-to-do but by no means wealthy families of Eastern European heritage, but who now live—and you were born in—one of the former British colonies in North America, or perhaps Canada or California, and that you have recently returned from China, I am afraid I am at a loss to make any further deductions about you."

Ayana glanced at Tyler.

What is he talking about?!? her expression said.

Tyler smiled.

"Our recent haircuts and general appearance of cleanliness," Tyler explained. "Reveal to Mr. Holmes that despite our current homeless condition, we must come from families that are of at least the upper middle class, although not well-off enough that we have adopted the pretensions and mannerisms of the wealthy."

Sherlock nodded his head in assent.

"Our accents and manner of speaking, as well as our command of the English language," Tyler continued, "identify us as being from, and born in, the former British colonies in North America, or in our particular case, from Canada."

"Quite so," Sherlock interjected with another approving nod.

"The ink stains on my fingertips and palms," Tyler continued again, lifting his hands up for all to see, "are most certainly from some rather specific variety of ink used only in Chinese calligraphy, thus revealing that of the two of us, at least I have recently been in China."

Tyler smiled proudly and looked to Sherlock for confirmation, but the great detective simply pursed his lips and shook his head.

"You are on the right track, my boy," Sherlock said. "But not quite on the mark. It was the ink stains from your recent dabblings in calligraphy that gave a hint, particularly the very specific shade of deep black that you have apparently used. I have at one time made a study of the various inks of the world and have even written a monograph on the subject, and as such, I can tell you that this particular ink you have used is of a variety that is peculiar only to certain parts of China. However, the fact that you have used an ink originating in China is by no means a reliable indicator that you have recently travelled there."

Tyler was stumped.

"How, then?" he asked. "What gave it away?"

Sherlock grabbed a poker from the cold fireplace and used it to tap Ayana on her left shoe.

"*Phyllostachys Nigra*," he announced. "Otherwise known as black bamboo."

Ayana and Tyler leaned forward and stared at her shoe. Sherlock was right. There were tiny bits of bamboo shavings embedded in the laces of Ayana's shoes. Two days earlier, she and Tyler had sat in the courtyard of Mr. Zheng's house and used his pocketknife to shave off bits of the bamboo's outer black shell to use in making the ink for the paper dragon.

Sherlock leaned back in his chair again and replaced the poker to its stand next to the fireplace.

"Those bamboo cuttings are fairly recent, I observe," Sherlock explained. "Within the past two months at least, and as far as I know, live specimens of that particular species of bamboo can only be found in certain parts of China."

"Remarkable," Dr. Watson cried exuberantly between sips of tea.

"There is only one of your deductions that I don't understand," Tyler said, frowning as he turned to face Holmes once again. "It's why you'd think we were of Eastern European heritage."

"Why, your clothes, of course!" Sherlock replied. "I must admit that the manner of your dress is what vexes me the most, for it is unusual in the extreme. I have never seen such unusual fashions as this, but judging from their cut and general appearance, I would only venture to say that they must originate from somewhere on the continent, some obscure city far off in the east—Zagreb perhaps, or Ljubljana, or Belgrade."

Tyler and Ayana looked at each other and laughed.

"Something like that," Tyler replied, unable to think of a suitable or convincing explanation for their twenty-first century clothing.

"But what I find most remarkable," Sherlock said, leaning further forward in his chair with the hint of a gleam in his eyes, "is your singularly impressive grasp of the fundamentals of what I once referred to as the Science of Deduction and Analysis. Never before have I met anyone with such clarity of observational focus so very much like my own. Why, I'd be willing to wager a sovereign that you can tell us how many steps there are leading up to this room from the hall below."

Tyler grinned like someone who'd just been asked the winning question on a game show and he already knew the answer.

"Seventeen, of course,"

"Remarkable," Sherlock Holmes replied, digging into the

pockets of his smoking jacket to extract a shiny coin and flipping it over to Tyler. "And from someone of such tender years, no less."

"If I did not already know of your methods, Holmes, I would swear this was witchcraft!" Dr. Watson exclaimed heartily.

Ayana leaned close to Tyler so they could both admire the gleaming gold coin that Tyler had just been given.

"I'd wager a sovereign to know how you knew the answer to that," Ayana muttered to Tyler under her breath.

"He knew the answer simply because he is a keen observer," Sherlock interjected, his hearing clearly as sharp as his intellect. "Most people could walk up and down those stairs a hundred times, seeing them clearly each time yet failing to observe precisely how many steps there are. But your friend here is different. There is a very clear distinction between seeing and observing, and your friend obviously not only sees but also observes the world that surrounds him."

Tyler's face was flushed and glowing with pride.

"I must admit that I would be most interested in observing your methods and process at work," Sherlock continued, leaning even further toward Tyler. "My practise has been somewhat busy as of late, so perhaps some time within the next fortnight or two, I could interest you in taking a look at some suitably trivial case with me. The full fee would be paid directly to you, of course."

Tyler's face now flushed for a different reason. *"Never believe your own press,"* he'd often heard his father say. He was now quickly starting to understand the full meaning of that particular phrase.

What if the case turns out to be one that Dr. Watson never wrote about? Tyler thought in a panic. *I won't know any of the answers!*

"You are very kind, Mister Holmes, but I couldn't possibly interfere with your practise...." Tyler stammered in response.

"Nonsense, my boy," Sherlock replied with a dismissive wave of his hand. "My only regret is that we must wait some time before we can bear witness to the employment of your impressive powers of deduction. You see, for the next several weeks my mind will be occupied with more pressing matters involving a true Napoleon of crime at the pinnacle of half that is evil and nearly all that is undetected in this great city. This man is a genius, a philosopher and an abstract thinker who sits at the centre of his great foul web of a thousand nefarious radiations, and he knows well every quiver of each of them."

"Professor Moriarty," Tyler whispered reverentially.

The great consulting detective sat bolt upright in his armchair, startled.

"You know of Professor Moriarty?" Sherlock replied, his surprised reaction uncharacteristically vigorous.

"Of course!" Tyler replied. "He is the most dangerous man in all of London! In fact, he'd be fully notorious if only any of the poor souls of this city had ever heard of him."

"My boy, this is astounding!" Sherlock replied. "For therein lies the man's true genius. He and his nefarious enterprises pervade London, and yet no one has ever heard of him. Please do tell what you may know of him and his illegal undertakings. Any detail you might add to my imperfect understanding of his great criminal organisation would be most welcome and appreciated."

Tyler tried to think of something useful. The problem was that, despite the fact that Professor Moriarty was undoubtedly Sherlock Holmes's archenemy and true nemesis in every sense of the word, in all of the original Sherlock Holmes stories there was hardly any mention of him at all, much less any helpful details that Tyler could provide that Sherlock himself wouldn't already know.

"Anything, my boy.... anything at all," Sherlock prompted Tyler encouragingly.

Tyler suddenly remembered something that Sherlock Holmes himself had once said—or, more accurately, would one day say in the near future, under their present circumstances—and that gave him a clever idea of how to get out of having to provide Sherlock with any further information.

Tyler shook his head slowly.

"Unfortunately, I am afraid there is very little to tell," he responded cheerlessly. "The professor surrounds himself with a fence of safeguards so cunningly devised that it would be impossible to get evidence to convict him in a court of law. He is one of the greatest schemers of all time, and yet he is so aloof from general suspicion that to call him a criminal would be uttering libel in the eyes of the law."

Sherlock fell back into his chair, nodding his head slowly and with wholehearted agreement.

"You are more right than you know, my boy," he said despondently. "In fact, just this past week I have made considerable efforts to penetrate the veil of protection and secrecy surrounding the wicked professor but to no avail."

Tyler's ears perked up.

"Exactly what efforts were these, if I may ask?" he said, hoping for some detail from one of the stories that might prompt his memory so that he could be of some help.

Sherlock settled deeper into his armchair and waved a single bony hand dejectedly.

"Oh, there is no point in telling," he replied with a miserable groan. "All of my efforts proved to be completely fruitless in the end."

"You must forgive my friend," Dr. Watson interrupted. "Although his intellect has virtually no equal, he is himself quite prone to mood swings."

"Still," Tyler replied, sitting forward in his chair eagerly. "I would be very interested to know what efforts he made this past week."

"Me too," Ayana chimed in. She was loving every second of this.

"Very well, then, if you must know," Sherlock replied, sitting up straight and instantly regaining his former vigour. "As Doctor Watson knows well, I have cast my own sort of web across the city of London—an informal intelligence network of informants who provide me with information when and if it comes into their possession. And it was from this network that not one week ago I came into the knowledge that each day at four o'clock a certain heavily curtained horse carriage draws up in front of the Union Club on Trafalgar Square. The cab waits there for a man to emerge from the building and jump inside. This mysterious man is a very highly placed envoy of none other than Professor Moriarty himself, and he carries with him the information and proceeds garnered in the course of the previous day's criminal activities."

Sherlock Holmes took a moment to pause and lean forward in his chair to speak his next lines in a low, conspiratorial tone.

"That man and that horse carriage could lead us straight to the headquarters of Professor Moriarty's vast network of criminal enterprises."

Sherlock leaned back again and stared out at the others from the shadow of one of the chair's protruding wingtips.

"I don't understand," Tyler replied after thinking this through for a moment. "Is Professor Moriarty not a seemingly respected citizen? Is the location of his home not something easily knowable?"

"Of course, my boy!" Sherlock replied, springing to life once again. "His home I know well and have visited in disguise several times. But it is not his home that I seek, but rather the epicentre of all his extensive criminal ventures. It is that which lies hidden from all the world."

Tyler nodded in understanding.

"Can you not just follow the carriage and see where it leads?" Ayana asked.

"Why, yes, of course, my dear lady," Sherlock came alive once again. "I have tried, oh have I tried. But the precautions taken by the driver and occupant of that particular horse cart are considerable. Endless random turns are made throughout the lanes and avenues to confuse anyone who might attempt to follow them. They ride along the busiest thoroughfares and confuse the eye of any prospective trackers by losing themselves among the dozens of other identical horse carriages that ply the city streets. I have tried every means at my disposal to overcome their tricks, but thus far I've turned up short."

Sherlock slumped back in his chair again, depressed.

"There must be something," Ayana said, glancing at Tyler hopefully, but he just shrugged and looked rather helpless.

"What's wrong?" she whispered directly into Tyler's ear so Sherlock couldn't hear. "Why don't you tell them the answer?"

Tyler cupped his hand over Ayana's ear and whispered, "I have no idea what the answer is. This doesn't sound like any of the Sherlock Holmes stories I've ever read."

Ayana thought about this for a second then whispered a reply.

"That doesn't mean that the answer isn't in one of those stories." She gave him a knowing look and leaned back in her chair.

Tyler stared off through the windows of 221B Baker Street. His mind was deep in thought as he watched the clouds sailing across the distant sky.

Is there something out there? he thought. *Something in one of the other stories that would help in this situation?*

And then, quite suddenly, he had it.

"What if you were somehow able to coat the wheels of the carriage with something that has a very distinctive smell?" Tyler said, thinking of just such a future occasion in one of the stories where the great detective would do this very same thing for a completely different reason.

Sherlock leaned forward attentively.

"Why, yes! An odoriferous agent of some kind!" he exclaimed. "Some essential oil of aniseed, perhaps."

That's just what I was thinking, Tyler thought with a smile. Aniseed was precisely what Sherlock had used in the other story that he'd just been thinking of.

"The carriage would then go on its way," Tyler continued, "twisting and turning to throw off anyone following it, but of course this time you wouldn't have to follow it at all. All you would have to do is wait an hour or two then use a bloodhound to track the scent."

Just as Tyler had known that Sherlock would use aniseed oil for one of his cases some years in the future, he also knew that Sherlock had previously employed the talents of a special bloodhound to trace the scent of a murderer.

"Quite right, my boy!" Sherlock replied, his eyes bright with anticipation. "And, in fact, I know of such a bloodhound already, a very queer mongrel with the most amazing power of scent. I would rather have his help than that of the whole detective force of London, but unfortunately he is currently out of the city with his owner on holiday in Cornwall and will not return until three days hence. By then Moriarty may have changed his *modus operandi*, and there may not be a carriage to follow, if that hasn't happened already."

"Don't you know of any other bloodhounds that are capable of tracking a scent?" Ayana asked.

Sherlock Holmes shook his head sullenly.

"I am afraid that I do not," he said, "nor any other animals capable of such tracking prowess."

Ayana and Tyler glanced knowingly at each other.

"Well, today may be your lucky day, then, sir," Tyler replied with a grin, "because my friend and I *DO* happen to know of just such an animal."

chapter twenty-seven
something like that

"Are you sure this is such a good idea?" Ayana asked as she and Tyler and Dr. Watson watched the streets of London racing past them from the inside of a horse-drawn hansom cab. It was a quarter to four, and with any luck they would arrive at Trafalgar Square in plenty of time to observe Professor Moriarty's carriage pulling up in front of the Union Club.

Tyler shrugged and smiled. He wasn't sure whether it was a good idea or not, to be honest, but he was having too much fun to care.

Sherlock was travelling separately from the rest of them. After a brief discussion in his sitting room, the plans had been firmly laid and he had shooed them out of the house into a waiting cab before they could protest. The carriage clattered and bumped through the streets of London, jarring Ayana and Tyler's teeth as they swept past street signs with names so familiar that Ayana knew them well, despite the fact that she had never been to London. First they cruised down Oxford Street and past Piccadilly Circus, then finally out into the open air plaza of Trafalgar Square where they rattled to a halt right at the base of the Nelson Column.

"Here we are, then!" Dr. Watson announced cheerily as they piled out of the carriage and stood near the base of one of the column's great bronze lion statues.

"Which one's the Union Club?" Ayana asked, scanning the frenetic traffic and crowds all around.

Dr. Watson pointed to an imposing masonry building occupying the entire western end of the square.

"It's that building right there," he said. "Now mind yourselves to act as naturally as possible. We don't want anyone getting their nerves up thinking we're spying on them."

The three of them tried to mill about the plaza as casually as possible, stealing glances toward the Union Club. Ayana and Tyler slouched with their hands stuffed into their pockets while Dr.

194

Watson puffed his chest out proudly and slipped his fingers elegantly into the pockets of his waistcoat.

"Spare a penny for an old cripple?" Ayana heard a terrible grating voice squawking from behind her. She spun around to find a horribly deformed woman in colourful gypsy clothing standing next to her with one scarred and dirty palm extended.

Ayana squealed in surprise and disgust and pulled away.

"Off with you, vile woman!" Dr. Watson cried, banging his walking stick on the pavement to send the frightful visitor off.

"Hello, Mr. Holmes," Tyler said with a grin. "May I be the first to compliment you on your most excellent disguise."

The old woman shuffled off, and Ayana turned to Tyler.

"Tyler, that's not...." she began to say.

Just then, the old woman turned around so that no one could see her face but the three of them, and she began to transform, her wrinkles filling out and the malformations of her face straightening. Dr. Watson and Ayana could barely contain their astonishment. Standing before them was none other than Sherlock Holmes himself.

"You never fail to surprise me, my boy," Sherlock said to Tyler with a grin. "You have an impeccably keen eye, and you never trust yourself to general impressions. You instead rightly concentrate on the details."

Tyler nodded graciously, blushing.

"Be watchful, now," Sherlock cried, his face instantly morphing back into that of the disfigured and unfortunate soul he'd been when he first approached them. "The game is afoot! Four o'clock is nearly upon us. Meet me in my sitting room once this is all over."

With that, the old woman shuffled off, mumbling incoherently to herself as she stumbled toward the western end of the square.

Ayana turned to Tyler, her eyes wide with surprise and admiration. "Tyler! How did you know that was Sherlock Holmes?!? It didn't look anything like him!"

Tyler laughed under his breath.

"I actually *didn't* know," he replied with a shrug. "It was a lucky guess. But knowing of Sherlock's love for disguises, I thought it was a pretty good assumption."

Ayana shook her head in wonder as she stared at her friend.

"Look here," they heard Dr. Watson say just as the bells of a nearby clock tower began to chime. "Be careful not to arouse suspicion, but see that carriage just entering the square? The one with the heavy curtains drawn at every window?"

Ayana and Tyler glanced at the carriage without turning their heads. Dr. Watson was indeed right. A large black carriage with dark curtains pulled across the windows was rounding the corner just across from them. The driver quickly slipped to the curb directly in front of the Union Club and pulled the horses to a sudden halt.

"Keep a careful eye on Sherlock," Tyler whispered. "Let's see what he does."

The three of them watched as Sherlock Holmes hobbled gracelessly across the street in his old woman disguise, lurching between the oncoming traffic until "she" reached the opposite side at the precise moment that the black carriage came to a halt at the curb.

"There! Did you see it?!??" Tyler whispered as Sherlock suddenly stumbled, grabbing on to the rear wheel of the carriage for support before quickly righting himself and staggering down the street, muttering nonsense as he went.

"What??!? What happened?!??" Ayana cried. "I didn't see it!"

Just then, a respectable-looking man in a dark suit and top hat emerged from the main doors of the Union Club and hurried down the steps toward the waiting carriage. Tucked under his arm was a heavy-looking black metal box with a large lock fixed to the front of it, holding it securely closed. The man ducked and disappeared into the back of the waiting carriage. The instant the door was closed the driver immediately flicked his whip and the horses sprang forward, pulling the carriage quickly out into the traffic then speeding off around the next corner and disappearing from view.

"Are you sure Sherlock actually did something?!?" Ayana asked, turning to Tyler as soon as the carriage was out of sight. "I didn't see a thing."

"Nor did I!!" Dr. Watson exclaimed. "It all happened so quickly." He pointed toward a small white church at the northwest corner of the square. "Listen now, the clock chimes of Saint Martin-in-the-Fields have only just this moment finished ringing the hour. The whole affair was done in mere seconds!"

Tyler was grinning from ear to ear and nodding eagerly.

"I am sure he did something," he said. "It was fast, but I saw it. Just as the carriage pulled up, he took a small glass bottle from underneath the shawl he was wearing. He then pretended to trip and reached for the wheel to keep from falling down, pouring some liquid from the bottle along the front half of the wheel. And then he poured the rest of it over the back half as he walked away before he stuffed the bottle back under his shawl again."

"My boy, that's remarkable," Dr. Watson exclaimed. "You truly do have a keen eye for observation."

"Not at all," Tyler replied, remembering his father's advice not to believe one's own press. "I merely saw what all of us already expected to see."

"Well, whatever explanation you put on it, it's most certainly astounding to me," Dr. Watson replied with a chuckle.

"Me too," Ayana agreed.

"Right then, you two," Dr. Watson said as he whistled for a cab. "You heard what Holmes said. It's back to Baker Street for us."

Another hansom cab identical to the first one pulled to a stop in front of them and they quickly piled inside.

"Can we take a different route this time?" Ayana asked, pointing toward the distinctive clock tower in the distance at the end of the street. "Can we go past Big Ben?"

"Of course, my dear," Dr. Watson replied with a smile, and he shouted instructions to the driver. "My good man, it's Baker Street for us, but take the scenic route by way of the parks and Constitution Hill."

"Very good, sir!" the driver called out, and cracked his whip across the backs of the horses to set off.

Ayana stuck her head out of the open window and watched in awe as they approached the Houses of Parliament, rolled past Buckingham Palace and Hyde Park, then finally headed down Oxford Street before turning left onto Baker Street, pulling up in front of 221B just a few minutes later.

Ayana and Tyler jumped out of the cab and waited while Dr. Watson paid the driver then rang the house bell. Mrs. Hudson the landlady answered the door and directed them up the stairs to where Sherlock Holmes was already waiting for them, tweed-suited and respectable as always, his clever old-woman disguise already a distant memory. Laughing heartily, he beckoned them to come in and have a seat.

"Well, all of you are looking at a right fool, I must say," Sherlock laughed.

"What is it, Holmes?" Dr. Watson asked as he hung his bowler hat and overcoat on the coat stand. "Has something happened?"

"Goodness yes, you could say that," Sherlock replied, still chuckling to himself. "I spilled half the bottle of aniseed oil on my hand when I nearly fell to the cobblestones not half an hour ago in Trafalgar Square."

"You tripped?!?" Tyler asked, surprised. "I thought you did

that on purpose to disguise what you were actually doing."

"That was my intention, my boy!" Sherlock laughed in reply. "To feign a slip on the paving stones to conceal my true actions, but then in my efforts to maintain the wobbly and lurching gait that was appropriate to my disguise, I tripped on the uneven pavement and nearly plummeted to disaster. Thank goodness that carriage wheel was there or I'd have broken a leg for certain."

Ayana burst into laughter. For some reason she found this incredibly funny. So did the others as well and for a moment they all laughed at Holmes's unfortunate accident.

"The short of it is that I now have a fine *cologne du aniseed* all over my left hand that will linger with me for a week or more," Sherlock added, extending his long fingers. "But so be it. Such are the hazards of the occupation."

Sherlock turned in his chair to face Tyler directly.

"So tell me, my boy, where can we find this bloodhound of yours to track the scent of the professor's mysterious carriage?"

"We'll have to wait until after dark...." Tyler started to say as he looked over at the windows where bright daylight was still streaming in.

"Agreed," Sherlock replied. "So much the better to mask our approach to Professor Moriarty's headquarters."

"Right, yes," Tyler said, although that hadn't been the reason he had been thinking of. Thus far, only Ayana and Tyler were aware that the animal they were planning on using was their sand dragon, *Dune Buggy*. The enthusiastic little dragon had already proven himself to be an excellent tracker with a superb sense of smell, and should easily be able to track the scent of the aniseed on the wheels of Moriarty's horse carriage. The only problem was that they obviously couldn't take him out in the daylight.

"And I should also mention that the animal in question is not exactly a bloodhound," Tyler added.

"A Basset Hound, perhaps?" Sherlock asked.

"Not quite," Tyler replied, glancing at Ayana nervously.

"A beagle?" Sherlock suggested eagerly. "A fox terrier?"

"Not a dog at all, actually," Ayana interjected, trying to bail Tyler out. "This is more of a flying animal than one that runs around on the ground."

"A bird! Splendid!" Sherlock cried in obvious delight. "I always suspected that the avian sense of smell was quite refined."

Ayana looked at Tyler with an uncomfortable wry smile.

"It is a bird then, isn't it?" Sherlock asked.

"Something like that," Tyler replied.

chapter twenty-eight
something worth seeing

Dune Buggy was perched on Ayana's lap completely covered with a small tablecloth as she, Tyler, Dr. Watson and Sherlock Holmes clattered down Oxford Street in a hansom cab for the third time that day. Dr. Watson was eyeing the hooded animal with nervous suspicion.

"This is a bird of some fair size, I must say," Dr. Watson said, clearing his throat apprehensively. "Is it a golden eagle, perhaps?"

"I would venture that it must be a vulture of some kind," Sherlock observed. "A California condor, perhaps, based not only on its size and the fact that our two young friends originate from the North American continent, but also on the fact that it apparently possesses a keen sense of smell. I have taken the liberty since our last meeting to educate myself regarding the olfactory senses of the condor and can report that they are apparently capable of smelling fresh carrion at a distance of many miles."

"Half a sovereign to the victor, then," Dr. Watson proposed.

"Very well," Sherlock replied agreeably.

"Well, which is it, then?" Dr. Watson demanded of Ayana with a grin, anxious to settle the wager. "An eagle or a condor?"

Ayana and Tyler looked at each other and laughed.

"I'm afraid you're both mistaken," Tyler replied. "This is more of a desert animal."

"An Egyptian vulture, then?" Dr. Watson suggested hopefully. "I could tell you tales of those terrible harbingers of death from my time in Afghanistan that would make your hair turn white."

Tyler shook his head. "I'm afraid that's still not it," he said.

Dr. Watson harrumphed and sat back in his chair with his arms folded across his chest to silently brood as he contemplated the identity of the strange bird. Sherlock Holmes, on the other hand, was content to leave the identity of the mysterious animal a secret for the time being and simply leaned forward in his chair to ask a more practical question.

"Exactly how is it that you plan to track this bird from the ground once we arrive in Trafalgar Square?" Sherlock asked, pointing out of the cab's windows at the pitch black sky. "Or will the creature have to stay close to the ground so that we can follow it easily?"

Ayana panicked for a moment. She hadn't thought of that. Once *Dune Buggy* was up in the air flying after the scent, they'd never be able to see him in the dark. She looked at Tyler with questioning eyes.

"I have a small red light that we will attach to his leg," Tyler answered on Ayana's behalf. "We'll be able to see that from quite a distance."

Thus assured, Sherlock sat back and gazed out to where the Nelson Column was now gliding into view.

"We're there," Sherlock announced undramatically. "Trafalgar Square."

With a clattering racket, the hansom cab pulled up to the curb just across from the Union Club.

"Okay," Tyler said as he stared across the street to where Moriarty's black-curtained carriage had briefly stood earlier in the day. "Our animal is very shy and easily spooked by strangers, so it's best if you and Doctor Watson stay here while we take him across the street to set him free."

Sherlock nodded in understanding.

"Come on," Tyler said to Ayana as he pushed the door open and stepped out onto the street. Ayana held out her arm to give *Dune Buggy* a solid roost as she carefully climbed down from the cab with Tyler's help.

"Let's go," Ayana said as they quickly glanced both ways for traffic then dashed across the street to the opposite side.

Kneeling on the sidewalk together, they arranged themselves as best as they could to block the view of Sherlock and Dr. Watson, who were watching with interest from the open window of the horse carriage.

Ayana uncovered *Dune Buggy*'s head. He looked up at them with typical dragon hyperactive happiness.

"Okay, boy," Ayana said, and she held the empty bottle of aniseed oil to his nose so he could sniff it. "Can you smell that?"

The dragon nodded excitedly.

Ayana shifted *Dune Buggy* a little closer to the street to where Moriarty's carriage had been standing a few hours earlier.

"Can you smell the same smell there on the street?" Ayana asked.

The dragon nodded again, even more excitedly this time.

"Can you track it for us, *Dune Buggy*?" Tyler asked.

The dragon nodded emphatically, twisting and itching to be set free.

"Okay, good boy." Tyler smiled and reached into his backpack to take out one of his small battery-operated bike lights. He fixed the light onto *Dune Buggy*'s leg and secured the Velcro closures.

"Is that okay, boy?" Ayana asked. "Does it hurt?"

Dune Buggy shook his head and seemed to smile as he squirmed around excitedly, flapping his wings and trying to get free.

"Okay, boy!" Tyler cried as he pulled the tablecloth off the eager dragon. "Follow the scent!"

Dune Buggy flapped his wings again, more forcefully this time, and in seconds he was airborne, sailing through the air majestically and making straight for the hansom cab on the opposite side of the street.

"What's he doing?!??" Ayana gasped as they watched *Dune Buggy* sail straight in through the open window of the cab where Sherlock and Dr. Watson were waiting.

"I don't know!" Tyler replied as they raced across the street, narrowly avoiding being hit by another passing horse carriage. "We can't let them see him!"

"It's a bit too late for that," Ayana commented cynically as they dashed to the side of the carriage and stood on tiptoe to peer inside.

Dr. Watson and Sherlock Holmes were sitting in the back of the carriage on opposite sides facing each other. Dr. Watson was recoiling from the sight of the dragon with a look of absolute astonishment and confusion on his mutton-chop-whiskered face as he stared across at the small sand coloured dragon balanced on Sherlock Holmes's right knee. Sherlock Holmes simply sat stoically and with a slightly bemused look on his face as the dragon nudged his aniseed-scented left hand with his little nose.

Dune Buggy looked proudly at Ayana and Tyler, and Ayana understood immediately.

"The aniseed oil on Sherlock's hand!" she cried with a wide grin. "He smelled it! Good boy! You led us right to it!"

Tyler smiled wryly and looked at Dr. Watson and Sherlock in embarrassment.

"I am so sorry, Mr. Holmes," Tyler stammered. "I should have anticipated this."

"Think nothing of it, my boy," Sherlock replied, a smile

quivering at the edges of his lips. "I should very much have done the same."

Sherlock Holmes lifted his arm out for *Dune Buggy* to climb onto it, and he carefully handed the dragon back to Ayana.

"This magnificent animal is yours, I believe," the great detective said.

"Thank you," Ayana replied as *Dune Buggy* climbed off Sherlock's arm and onto hers.

"We'll try this again, of course," Tyler stuttered, still blushing bright red in humiliation. "And set him on the right track this time."

Sherlock Holmes nodded graciously.

"Holmes, this is outrageous!" Dr. Watson exclaimed as he gaped at *Dune Buggy* with a bewildered and slightly horrified expression on his face. "This creature is completely unnatural!"

"In my experience, Watson," Sherlock said, as the amusement on his face grew more robust, "there is nothing so unnatural as the commonplace. We have clearly underestimated the extent of experience that our young friends here possess. This exquisite specimen is clearly some exotic flying lizard from the Dutch island archipelagos of the Far East; Sumatra, perhaps, or Java."

Sherlock gave Tyler a wink.

"Something like that," Tyler replied in obvious relief.

"Quite so, Holmes," Dr. Watson sputtered apologetically as he shifted his weight in his seat to regain his composure. "I am sorry to have lost my head there for a moment."

"Please carry on," Sherlock said to Ayana and Tyler with a wave of his left hand. "Can your wonderful flying friend track the *other* trail of this scent—the one that will lead us to Professor Moriarty?"

Tyler was about to answer but *Dune Buggy* beat him to it, nodding his little head enthusiastically.

"Right, then," Sherlock replied. "Shall we proceed?"

The little dragon nodded again and pushed off Ayana's arm. He soared into the air and circled over Trafalgar Square a few times before spiralling farther upward until only the red light on his leg was visible. As the others watched from the ground, the red light circled a few more times before heading west.

"Driver, follow that light, if you will!" Sherlock cried as he pulled Ayana and Tyler into the carriage and closed the door.

"Will do, Mr. Holmes, sir!" the driver called back as he snapped his whip, and the carriage sped off under an archway and down the Mall in the direction of Buckingham Palace.

As they raced along through the streets of London, all eyes were on the sky above, their heads poked out through the open windows and the wind flying in their hair. The hour was late and the streets of the city were mostly deserted as they flew past Hyde Park and the Royal Albert Hall then west toward Windsor. As they travelled farther to the west, the lights of the city thinned out, and they found themselves racing across the darkened English countryside instead.

On and on *Dune Buggy* flew until finally the red light in the sky began to spiral slowly down toward the ground again. They were nearing the end of the trail.

"My good man!" Sherlock called out to the driver of the carriage. "Extinguish those head-lamps, will you? We don't want to risk being spotted."

The driver quickly did as he was ordered, and the carriage continued at a much reduced speed, carefully navigating the dark back roads by the light of the moon and stars. It was slow going, but soon they passed over the top of a small hill and caught sight of *Dune Buggy*'s red light fluttering down into a patch of trees and bushes at the edge of a well-lit country estate nestled in a picturesque valley.

"This must be it!" Sherlock cried. "Moriarty's headquarters! From here we'll continue on foot."

The others nodded and quietly lowered themselves out of the carriage while Sherlock helped the driver turn the horses around in the darkness and sent them back down the hill a short distance until them were out of sight.

"Come on, then," Sherlock whispered as they set off toward the lights of the estate, taking care to remain in the shadows lining the darkened road. They walked single file with Sherlock taking the lead, moving as graceful and quiet as a cat. Ayana and Tyler were next, moving with the lithe silence of the very young. Dr. Watson brought up the rear, moving with the measured and methodical care of a military man.

Not a word was spoken as they continued down into the valley. Ayana was careful to keep an eye on where she was stepping but couldn't help but be transfixed by the amazing view spread out before them. High above them was the usual breath-taking array of stars that she could never possibly grow bored of seeing. Somewhere behind them, the silvery light of the moon clock shone down upon them, the hands on its face now showing the time as ten minutes past two. But the most remarkable thing about the view from the crest of that hill, as they gazed out across the dark and lonely English countryside, was the rocky crag looming high above the landscape and the enormous metal-domed clockwork towering at the summit of it.

It was Professor Möbius's laboratory, and they were now so close that they could almost touch it.

Tyler tapped Ayana on the shoulder and pointed toward it, his eyes gleaming with excitement. Ayana nodded in reply with a wide smile. They were almost there.

"Careful now, everyone," Sherlock whispered in an almost inaudible voice as they crossed a bridge over a small stream and reached the perimeter of the country estate. "Look sharp. We cannot afford to expose ourselves now."

Holmes led the way along a row of trees and a fence that lined the road at the edge of the estate. Beyond the trees, stretching all the way toward the very large multi-winged house, was a wide-open lawn, completely devoid of any vegetation and bathed in light from several gas lamps. The reason for the open lawn and lights was clear—any approaching intruders or trespassers would be spotted immediately and dealt with accordingly.

A few minutes later the little group reached the spot where they'd seen *Dune Buggy* come in for a landing. He was sitting proudly next to the side gate where Moriarty's carriage had driven in earlier that day.

Good boy! You did it! Ayana said wordlessly as Tyler stepped forward to remove the bike light from *Dune Buggy's* leg.

Sherlock waved at them to follow him a bit farther up the side of the road until he stopped behind a thick patch of shrubbery growing next to the fence.

"We'll have better cover here," he whispered as everyone silently knelt behind the bushes. "What do you make of it, Watson? How many guards do you see?"

Guards?!? Tyler thought. He hadn't seen a thing.

Dr. Watson squinted into the darkness.

"Four, Holmes," he finally replied. "Two standing on opposite sides of the main doors, one by the carriage house, and a fourth off to the left near the southern wing."

"Six," Sherlock replied. "One more at the foot of the trees along the stream and another on the roof, plus, who knows how many more around the back of the buildings."

"Quite right," Watson said with a quiet sigh. "Your theory appears to be correct. It is quite possible that this is Moriarty's headquarters."

"It is more than possible," Sherlock observed. "It is highly probable. However, as of yet we have no reliable data, and it is a capital mistake to theorise before one has reliable data. In such cases one insensibly twists facts to suit theories instead of building theories to suit facts."

"But pray tell, precisely how do you propose to obtain reliable data?" Watson asked.

"Such a daunting assortment of sentinels," Sherlock said with a dismayed shake of his head as he scanned the perimeter of the house and lawn. "I have to admit that I cannot see how we can possibly make any approach to the house without giving the whole game away. And this is with the cover of darkness to assist us. In daylight such an attempt would be unthinkable."

Sherlock settled onto the grass, deep in thought.

The minutes passed, one by one, until finally Holmes spoke.

"It cannot be done," he reported forlornly. "I have considered every possible scenario and means available for making an approach to the house, and not a one of them exists that doesn't end with me in shackles before the local constabulary for trespassing, or worse."

"There must be something!" Tyler whispered.

Sherlock gloomily shook his head.

"I'm afraid not, my boy," he said. "I'll have to retire from the field of battle for the moment and formulate a workable plan that will allow me to return another time in victory. In the meantime, I can only hope that Moriarty will not catch the slightest hint of our sniffing around his lair or else he will pick up the whole operation and move it elsewhere, and all of this will have been in vain."

"We must act tonight, then," Tyler said. "You and I both know what a cunning and formidable adversary Moriarty is."

"You are quite right, my boy," Sherlock replied despondently. "But try as I might I can see no possibility available to us. Perhaps if *Aeolus* himself were to blow a thick London fog our way to camouflage my approach then we could be successful, but I'm afraid that barring divine intervention, I can see no solution to this particular quandary."

"Wait a minute," Tyler said, his eyes flashing brightly. "What did you say?"

"I said, I can see no solution...." Sherlock began to say.

"No, I mean about the fog," Tyler clarified.

Sherlock frowned, puzzled.

"I said that if *Aeolus* himself were to blow a thick London fog our way to camouflage my approach, then perhaps we could be successful," Sherlock repeated. "A blanket of thick fog across the house and lawns would most certainly render the visibility of the various guards and lookouts virtually useless. But unfortunately, one cannot simply summon a fog at will, unless one is a deity of ancient Greek mythology."

Tyler glanced at Ayana. They were both grinning.

"What if I told you that my friend and I can do exactly that?" Tyler asked.

Sherlock leaned forward and raised his eyebrows incredulously.

"Quite right," he said simply. "Well *that* would be something worth seeing, then, wouldn't it?"

chapter twenty-nine
pure witchcraft

After everyone had snuck back over the crest of the hill to the carriage, Ayana sat with *Dune Buggy* to have a serious heart-to-heart conversation.

"I need to ask you something really important," Ayana said.

Dune Buggy sat in front of her and listened intently.

"Can you find your way back to London and back to our rooming house on Baker Street?"

Dune Buggy nodded yes.

"And can you find your way back here again and bring the other dragons with you?" Ayana continued.

Dune Buggy nodded again.

So it was decided. Off *Dune Buggy* went, leaving Ayana and Tyler sitting with Dr. Watson and Holmes in the back of the horse-drawn carriage waiting for him to return with all the other dragons. *Vapor*, *Mongo*, *Dune Buggy*, *Kami* and *Peaball* were all on their way, but it was really *Peaball* that Ayana and Tyler needed the most. He was going to help Sherlock Holmes sneak up close to Moriarty's headquarters.

"Here they come," Ayana said a little more than an hour later. She had been watching intently out of the windows of the carriage for any sign of the dragons returning.

There was a commotion and fluttering of wings outside as the five dragons of various sizes settled down on the grass next to the road.

Ayana leapt from her seat and pushed open the door of the carriage. She jumped down to the ground and hurried over to greet the dragons with hugs all around. Tyler was right behind her, but Dr. Watson and Sherlock Holmes maintained a cautious distance.

"Come on, *Peaball*," Ayana said, holding out her hand so the little dragon could climb onto it. "There's some people I want you to meet."

Ayana walked toward the carriage.

"*Peaball*, this is Mister Holmes and Doctor Watson." Ayana held up the dragon for them to see.

Dr. Watson couldn't believe his eyes.

"Holmes!" he cried. "I'm sure you'll insist that there is some logical reason for all things, but surely this is proof of something that must defy all possible efforts at explanation!"

Holmes remained stoic.

"Sometimes," Sherlock observed as he leaned in to examine the tiny fog dragon, "an explanation turns out to be quite simple, despite the fact that at first sight it seems almost inexplicable."

Sherlock leaned in closer, turning his head left then right to view *Peaball* from all possible angles.

"That said, however," Sherlock added as he stood up straight again, "I will admit that at the present moment I am at a loss to find any rational explanation for this."

"Quite so!" Dr. Watson replied, sounding vindicated.

Holmes held up his hand to stop the doctor before he could comment further.

"However, that does not mean that such an explanation does not exist," he cautioned. "Our present desire for understanding aside, we are still faced with the more immediate situation of what to do about confirming that the house in the valley over the next hill is, in fact, the lair and criminal headquarters of the nefarious Professor Moriarty. And in this regard, this young man and young lady have assured us that they have an appropriate solution that they've now brought readily to hand."

Ayana was having a hard time following what Sherlock was saying. Beneath his calm exterior, she sensed an ever so slight ruffling of his nerves, and his unnecessarily wordy reply to Dr. Watson seemed to be evidence of that.

"We do have a solution," Ayana assured them. "And a good one; isn't that right, *Peaball*?"

The little dragon nodded his head and seemed to smile.

"Well, then," Sherlock said. "Who are we to doubt that when the evidence of such fantastical things as this have been laid before us? Will you ask your small... *dragon*... friend whether he is willing to help us?"

Holmes's voice faltered slightly when he said the word dragon aloud.

Peaball nodded enthusiastically.

"Well, that settles it then," Sherlock said with a gleam in his eye. "We must carefully make our way back down into the valley—

myself, Doctor Watson, Ayana, Tyler... and *Peaball*."

Sherlock's obvious discomfort made Ayana want to giggle.

"Wait!" Tyler cried and hurried over to clarify a few final details with Holmes. "And we have a deal, right? Once you've confirmed that this house is indeed Moriarty's, then you and your horse carriage will take us—all of us—as far as you can in the direction we need to go?"

Sherlock nodded affirmatively.

"As far as we are able to," he agreed wholeheartedly as he looked over his shoulder toward Professor Möbius's monstrous clockwork tower in the distance.

"Okay, then!" Tyler said with eagerness. "Then let's get to it, shall we?"

"Our time is limited," Sherlock agreed. "It will not be many hours until daybreak."

Ayana cradled *Peaball* in the curve of her elbow and gave the other dragons a hand signal to stay behind and wait for them.

"We'll be back, I promise," she told them, and off the little group of humans went again, back over the hill and down along the road.

This time, when they reached the bridge and crossed over the stream to the edge of Moriarty's estate, Ayana was able to spot the various guards that Dr. Watson and Holmes had referred to earlier. She could see one man, nothing more than just a black outline, standing near the trees upstream from them. Another man stood at the corner of the house, ready and alert. Then they saw another one.... and another. The dark silhouettes of the guards seemed to be everywhere she looked as her imagination ran wild with speculation.

Just breathe, Ayana told herself, and she closed her eyes and cleared her head of the phantom men in the shadows.

"Stop here," Sherlock whispered as he stopped behind a low thicket of bushes just outside the fence around Moriarty's compound. "Based on the lay of the land and the respective locations of the sentinels, it's best if I make my approach to the house from here."

Ayana and Tyler knelt in the grass, safely out of sight behind the bushes. Dr. Watson and Holmes crouched on either side of them.

All eyes turned to Ayana and *Peaball*.

"Very well, my lady," Sherlock said with a hint of a smile. "Your dragon friend here promised to summon a thick London fog for us. I am quite ready whenever you are."

Ayana nodded and lifted *Peaball* to her face to whisper directly to him.

"Are you ready, little guy?" she asked.

Peaball nodded.

"Okay, go," Ayana said, and she extended her arm so that *Peaball* had room to flap his wings and lift himself into the air.

Once he was airborne, *Peaball* hovered in place for a few seconds then slowly dissolved right in front of their eyes. It was a bit like watching a drop of food colouring dissolve in water, spreading out at first with dark wisps and tentacles curling here and there, until slowly *Peaball* disappeared completely from view and a thick blanket of fog filled the air around them.

"Good heavens, Holmes!" Dr. Watson cried, barely able to keep his voice low in his horror and surprise. "This is pure witchcraft!"

Sherlock merely observed and said nothing.

"Perhaps you are right and the creature we followed out here earlier tonight was some strange flying lizard from the Far East," Dr. Watson continued. "And perhaps there is also some reasonable explanation for the odd assortment of strange creatures waiting for us back at the carriage, but this, Holmes! There is no possible explanation for this except pure sorcery."

Sherlock still said nothing as the fog thickened and spread across the landscape.

"Holmes! Have you nothing to say to all of this?!?" Dr. Watson exclaimed. "These are dragons, Holmes! This is pure magic!"

A flicker of a smile played at the edges of Sherlock Holmes's thin lips.

"England is a land of dragons, is it not?" he said simply.

The four of them watched as the fog grew massive in size, filling the ditch where they were sitting then coursing toward the small stream where it snaked across the surface of the water and filled the entire lawn surrounding the country estate. In a matter of minutes, the fog had completely filled the entire valley, and Ayana and Tyler could barely see their hands in front of their faces, much less anything else.

Coming from the direction of the country estate they could hear low voices speaking to each other. The fog had apparently created some confusion amongst the sentinels.

"I'm off," they heard Sherlock whisper from somewhere nearby in the fog. "The commotion at the house will work to my advantage. I will return as quickly as I am able, but if I am not back before the first glimmers of sunrise, take the carriage back to the city and contact Scotland Yard."

"Very well," they heard Dr. Watson reply.

And with that, Sherlock Holmes disappeared silently into the night.

It was eerie sitting there in the darkness and fog. Dr. Watson was still there, Ayana knew, because she could hear him breathing. But Tyler was completely silent.

Ayana reached out her hand and slipped it into Tyler's. He smiled at this even though he knew she was only doing it for reassurance.

The minutes passed by slowly, and Ayana started to daydream about what she would do once they got back to the real world. In a way, it would be sad to leave this magical book world behind, but she had to admit that she was missing fast food and sleeping in her own bed. She was even missing school, which is something that she never thought would be possible.

"It's done," a voice suddenly whispered from somewhere in the thick fog nearby, making Ayana and Tyler (and Watson too) nearly jump out of their skins.

It was Sherlock. He was back.

"Okay," Ayana whispered, letting go of Tyler's hand and holding out her palm. "We're done, *Peaball*. You can come back now."

Slowly the all-encompassing fog dissipated, snaking down the open lawn toward the stream and inching toward the road as *Peaball* returned to his dragon form. Within a few minutes, the air had cleared completely, and the little misty moonlit dragon was sitting on Ayana's palm right where he started.

It was a relief to be able to see the others again. Dr. Watson was there, as sturdy as ever, and Sherlock too, looking none the worse for wear following his excursion to the house.

"It's best if we wait a few minutes here," Sherlock said. "I overheard quite some puzzlement at the house as to the provenance of the strange fog that had descended upon the land. They fear it was a kind of apocalyptical sign or some other nonsense. I believe it would be prudent to wait for things to settle down again and return to normal."

"Quite right, Holmes," Dr. Watson agreed. "But you have said nothing as to the results of your investigation of the house itself. Don't leave us all in suspense. Is it Moriarty's lair or not?"

Sherlock Holmes merely smiled and slowly rubbed his long, nervous fingers together.

"Let us just say, my dear Watson," he finally replied, "that once we deliver these two young friends of ours and their remarkable companions to their destination, we shall be making a very early morning call on Mr. Lestrade of Scotland Yard."

Sherlock lingered on this thought for a moment to consider it further.

"We should perhaps stop by a baker on the way," he said after a pause. "I hear the pastries in this particular county are most excellent."

chapter thirty
the entire story

"I'm afraid that this is where we must leave you," Sherlock Holmes announced as he helped Ayana and Tyler down from the back of the horse carriage.

Several hours had passed since their exploits at Professor Moriarty's country estate, during which time they had clacked and rattled to the west, making only one small detour along the way to stop into a small village where Sherlock had spotted the lights of a bakery shop with people inside working in the wee morning hours. After scaring the baker and his assistant half out of their wits by appearing suddenly out of the shadows, he had somehow convinced them to sell some of their scones and Banbury cakes for an early morning breakfast.

Ayana and Tyler jumped to the ground and stared up at the looming spire of Professor Möbius's clockwork tower standing atop the rocky crags above them. It was still quite a way off, but certainly within walking distance over rough ground. Not that there was much choice but to walk anyway—there was simply no more road anymore. The landscape ahead was too uneven, pitted and cratered like the surface of the moon.

"Thank you very much, Mr. Holmes," Ayana said, fighting the urge to burst into tears. These adventures seemed to be full of many painful goodbyes.

"Yes, thank you so very much, Mr. Holmes," Tyler chimed in. "And to you as well, Dr. Watson. I don't know how we can ever repay you."

"It's been a true pleasure, I assure you," Dr. Watson said, handing a pair of paper-wrapped parcels to Tyler. "Take these breads and pastries with you. You appear to have a long climb ahead, and you'll need your strength."

"Thank you, Doctor," Tyler replied.

"And please drop in if you should pass through London again," Sherlock Holmes said, stepping forward to shake Tyler's hand. "I regret that you and I were unable to work on a case together. Perhaps next time?"

"Perhaps," Tyler smiled and shook Holmes's hand firmly.

"And to you, my lady," Sherlock said, turning to shake Ayana's hand as well. But much to Sherlock's surprise and mild discomfort, Ayana simply threw her arms around him in a big friendly hug.

"Oh, well, there you go," Dr. Watson mumbled in surprise as Ayana threw her arms around him next. "Thank you very much, my dear."

"We will miss you," Ayana said, wiping a tear from the corner of her eye. "Both of you."

"We'll see each other again," Dr. Watson assured Ayana with a whiskery smile as he looked from her to Tyler to the collection of dragons who were sitting patiently nearby. "All of you."

"Right, then," Sherlock said, pulling open the door of the carriage for Dr. Watson. "I'm afraid that Watson and I have an urgent appointment with Inspector Lestrade back in London. With any luck we'll have the despicable Professor Moriarty and his gang locked up in the clink before the week is out, and the world will be a better place, not to mention my own personal satisfaction for having subdued such a treacherous villain."

"Thank you again!" Ayana cried as Sherlock and Dr. Watson climbed into the back of the carriage. The driver snapped his whip one last time, and they set off back in the direction of the city.

Ayana and Tyler watched the carriage until it was nearly out of sight, waiting until they saw Sherlock's leather gloved hand appear one final time out of the open window in a farewell wave.

"Well, that's it," Tyler said as the carriage disappeared over a hill, and everything was quiet once again. "We should get going."

Off toward the east the sun was almost set to rise, giving them plenty of light for the climb up the ragged, uneven stones that lay between them and Professor Möbius's tower.

Tyler stuffed the pastries into his backpack and hefted it onto his shoulders as he started to climb. Ayana took one last look back and then followed along behind him.

It was a tough climb—at least for Ayana and Tyler it was. The dragons had it much easier. *Kami* was riding on Ayana's left shoulder and *Peaball* on her right, balancing themselves like surfers as she clambered from one rock to the next. *Vapor*, *Mongo* and *Dune Buggy* had it easy as well, simply flying a short distance ahead of the rest of the group then watching and waiting for them to catch up before flying on again.

They climbed for a while then stopped to rest. They then climbed a bit more and stopped to rest again. On the third rest stop, they ate some of the scones that Dr. Watson had given them. They were making good progress.

"You know, I was wrong," Tyler said as they took their sixth rest stop of the day and were now munching on the delicious currant-filled Banbury cakes. "Not all books have villains."

"What?" Ayana asked, brushing some crumbs from her sleeve.

"Remember what I said about all books having a villain?" Tyler asked.

Ayana nodded.

"Even Sherlock Holmes," she said.

"*Especially* Sherlock Holmes," Tyler agreed. "But I just realised that I was wrong. Not all books have a villain."

"What books don't?" Ayana asked.

Tyler pointed up the steep incline of rocks ahead of them.

"Professor Möbius's books," he said. "They're science books, not made-up stories. There's no villains in any of them."

Ayana chuckled and nodded.

"Okay," she said. "Then all made-up stories have villains, I guess."

"I guess," Tyler agreed as he finished eating and pulled his backpack on again. "Shall we?"

Ayana nodded, and the two of them continued their climb up the rock face.

Three rest stops later they ate the last of the pastries then set off again with *Mongo* and the other dragons flying ahead as usual and stopping at the next convenient resting place. But this time something was different. *Mongo* was bleating and looking down on them from above, wagging his head excitedly from side to side.

"I think they've reached the top!" Ayana said. "Look at *Mongo*."

Tyler glanced up and saw *Mongo* and the other dragons peering down at them with happy and excited expressions on their faces.

"That's a relief," Tyler said, smiling broadly as they scrambled the rest of the way up to where the dragons were waiting.

Ayana had been right. They *were* at the top—finally.

Stretched out in front of them was the sprawling complex of industrial-looking buildings and gadgets and machines that made up Professor Möbius's laboratories and living quarters. Now that they were closer, they could see that the whole thing looked surprisingly like some kind of clockwork castle with spires and battlements and turrets arranged seemingly at random all around the perimeter. Looking down on all of this was the enormous domed tower they'd seen days before from the pop-up forest.

"It's incredible," Ayana whispered as Tyler helped her up the last few feet to the summit. "Is all of this for one man?"

Tyler shrugged his shoulders.

"I guess there's only one way to find out," he said, pointing to an inconspicuous little door in the wall of the huge mechanical fortress. Hanging next to the door was a bell with a pull-rope and a plaque that read:

Professor Doctor Linus Aloysius von Möbius PhD, ME, MD, MS, BE, BLA

"What do all those letters mean?" Ayana asked as they approached the door cautiously.

"I'm not sure," Tyler replied. "But I think it means he went to school for a long time."

"And why is his name so long?" Ayana asked.

Tyler shrugged.

"In his books he's always just Professor Möbius," he replied.

"So what do we do now?" Ayana asked as they reached the innocuous little doorway. From behind it, they could hear the muffled hum of machinery.

"We ring the bell, I guess," Tyler replied, reaching up to pull the cord.

Tyler clanged the bell three times then let go of the rope and stepped back to wait.

"Is anything happening?" Ayana whispered. All she could hear was the hum of machines.

"Listen!" Tyler replied. Fading in slowly they could both hear the sound of approaching footsteps.

The footsteps stopped, and from the opposite side of the door they could hear a series of locks being sprung. One after the other the locks were disengaged until suddenly the door swung open to reveal a tall thin man with dark, silver-grey hair. He was wearing a long white lab coat that tapered at the sides and flared out at the bottom. On his forehead was a pair of round goggles that were pushed up to reveal a pair of piercing pale blue eyes.

"Yes?" the man asked cordially, his eyes darting from Ayana to Tyler, then opening wide as he saw the collection of dragons standing behind them. "How may I help you?"

"Professor Möbius?" Tyler asked.

"Yes, yes, my apologies." Professor Möbius smiled. "I am he."

Tyler grinned.

"My name is Tyler Travers," he said, speaking fast and excitedly as he introduced everyone. "And this is my friend Ayana Fall. And these are our dragons—*Vapor*, *Mongo*, *Dune Buggy*, *Kami* and *Peaball*. We've come a very long way to meet you, sir. We're hoping that you can help us."

Professor Möbius smiled warmly and opened the door a bit wider so he could welcome everyone inside.

"It is a pleasure to meet all of you," he said as Ayana and the dragons shuffled past him and into a large domed room filled with every imaginable assortment of computers, monitors, blinking lights, spinning gadgets and clockwork gears. "Please come in, all of you. I was just making some tea. Perhaps we can discuss things over a cup of Earl Grey?"

"Of course!" Tyler replied, following the others into the room. Professor Möbius closed the door and directed them to a series of chairs gathered around a large table scattered with blueprints and sketches. The dragons spread themselves out next to *Mongo* who lay down on the floor just behind Ayana.

"Your friend said your name was Ayana?" Professor Möbius asked as he poured cups of tea and brought them over on an elaborate bronze tray.

"Yes, that's right," Ayana replied.

"Interesting," Professor Möbius said. "Until just the other day I had never heard of this name before. But then during the course of one of my latest projects I happened across it."

Ayana and Tyler were listening intently.

"Can I ask where?" Tyler said curiously. "I mean where you came across the name Ayana?"

Professor Möbius smiled.

"It's better if I show you," he said. He strode over to a panel of controls hanging from a complicated mechanical arm and motioned Tyler and Ayana to remain standing near the table at the centre of the room. "I can only assume you've seen my very tall observatory tower outside. You can hardly miss it."

"Yes," Tyler replied. "You can see it from miles away."

"Well, normally I use the tower strictly for astronomical observations and experiments," Professor Möbius continued. "But just the other day I got it into my head that I should aim the various telescopes toward the ground instead of at the skies. I wanted to use them to draft a map of the world. That would be a pretty handy thing to have, I figured."

"Definitely handy," Tyler agreed.

"I have only just begun," Professor Möbius said. "You can see a quick sketch I made—it's lying right there on the table—of the places I've examined so far."

Tyler grabbed the sketch, and Ayana slid next to him to peer over his shoulder.

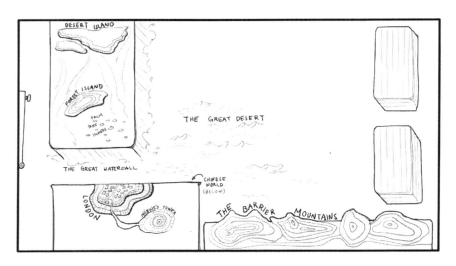

"Look!" cried Ayana. "The pop-up forest! The sea of islands! The waterfall, the desert, the jungle, the city of London...."

"We've just come from these places, Professor," Tyler said.

Professor Möbius smiled as he adjusted the buttons and levers and computer screens on his control panel.

"I'm not at all surprised," he replied. "Because *this* is where I saw the name Ayana just three days ago."

The professor spun his floating control panel around on its arm mounts so that Ayana and Tyler could see the large monitor display. In the middle of the display was an image of a heavily forested island in the middle of a beautiful blue sea.

"This is the large island I marked in my sketch as *Forest Island*," Professor Möbius explained. I believe Ayana just referred to it as the pop-up forest."

Ayana nodded.

"Because the trees there look like trees from a pop-up book," she said.

Professor Möbius nodded.

"That makes sense," he said. "But look at this."

Professor Möbius spun a knob and the image zoomed in toward the island, closer and closer until they could see only the trees. Then he zoomed the image until they could see the branches and leaves. Finally he zoomed in on a small clearing in the forest where a very familiar tree was located—a tree with small white cards dangling from every branch.

The Wishing Tree.

"A very unusual tree, don't you think?" Professor Möbius asked.

"It's the Wishing Tree!" Tyler cried. "We were just there!"

"As I thought." Professor Möbius smiled as he zoomed in further. They could see the leaves of the tree now and the individual cards close up. So close, in fact, that they could even read them.

The professor moved the image around until he found what he was looking for.

I wish that Ayana could be whole again.

It was Tyler's wish card—the one he had written almost a week earlier and hung from the tree with his own two hands.

"And that," Professor Möbius said, "is where I first encountered the name Ayana."

Ayana stared at Tyler who was now blushing bright red.

"I can only assume that you are this same Ayana," the professor said.

Ayana nodded her head slowly.

"I'm pretty sure that refers to me, yes," she said. "Right, Tyler?"

Tyler lowered his head in embarrassment.

"Yes," he said quietly, wishing that a hole could open up in the floor and suck him into it.

"I thought as much," Professor Möbius said, pushing the control panel away again and taking a seat across the table from Ayana and Tyler. "Which means that the two of you have really come a long way to see me."

"You have no idea!" Ayana laughed.

"Which leads me to my next question," Professor Möbius said. "You said that you need my help, but I cannot imagine what it is that I could possibly help you with."

"To get home," Tyler said, still blushing bright red and staring at the floor. "We need your help to get us home again."

"I see," the professor replied as he took a sip of his tea. "And where exactly *is* home?"

Tyler lifted his head and looked at Ayana. He tried to see in her face any sign of what she might be thinking, but she was harder to read than a closed book.

"I'd better start from the beginning, I guess," Tyler said.

"Sensible," Professor Möbius agreed.

And so Tyler began to tell him the story, the *entire* story starting from the very, very beginning in the maze of bookshelves at the back of the old library where the very unlikely friendship between he and Ayana had first begun and where the *THE BOOK* had serendipitously fallen into their hands.

Epilogue
welcome to the real world

Ayana handed *THE BOOK* to Professor Möbius just as Tyler was nearing the end of his long retelling of the entire course of their adventures.

"And then I pulled the bell cord next to that door over there," Tyler said. "A few seconds later you answered, and here we are."

Professor Möbius smiled as he listened to the end of Tyler and Ayana's story. As he listened, he silently leafed through *THE BOOK* then set it down on the table in front of him, leaning back in his chair with his fingers tented in front of his face as he struggled to absorb everything he'd just been told.

For a long moment, no one said anything. Ayana stifled a yawn. Neither she nor Tyler had slept in almost twenty-four hours.

"What a remarkable story," Professor Möbius finally said, shaking his head in disbelief. "It is really, truly remarkable."

"So, do you think you can help us?" Tyler asked as he put his hand over his mouth. Ayana's yawn was contagious.

Professor Möbius leaned forward on his elbows and looked Ayana and Tyler solemnly in the eyes.

"To be honest with you, I cannot imagine what I can possibly do to help you get home again."

Ayana's heart sank.

"But," the professor continued, "I promise that the three of us will put our heads together and do our best to figure it out. I'm sure we'll be able to think of something."

Ayana felt a bit better hearing that. So did Tyler.

"Thank you, Professor," Ayana said, yawning again.

"Perhaps what I need is just a few hours on my own to peruse this extraordinary book of yours and see what I can think of," Professor Möbius said. "In the meantime, perhaps the best thing for the two of you is to get some sleep. You're both yawning like the dickens!"

Ayana wasn't sure exactly what that meant, but she was too

exhausted and tired to figure it out.

"It probably won't surprise you," Professor Möbius continued, "that in a building as big as this one there are a few spare guest bedrooms. Why don't I show all of you up to some of those and you can get a few hours of sleep before we come up with a plan of attack for this problem."

"That would be awesome," Ayana heard herself saying drowsily. Right at that moment, she could think of no place she'd rather be than curled up in a nice warm bed.

"Good idea," Tyler said, suppressing another yawn.

"Follow me, then!" the professor called out as he jumped up from his chair. "All of you! Even you dragons!"

Ayana somehow dragged herself out of her chair and fell in with the others as they walked over to a large elevator on the far side of the room. Professor Möbius pushed a button and the doors opened shortly afterward. They all squeezed inside somehow, and the doors closed behind them.

"Thirty-second floor please," the professor said aloud.

"Thirty-second floor," a tinny woman's voice responded, and the elevator began to move.

Ayana's ears popped slightly as the air pressure changed with the altitude. Seconds later the doors opened, and the professor stepped out into a long curving hallway.

"Right through here," the professor said cheerfully and showed them into a small sitting room with doors on either end leading to private bedrooms. "I hope this will be comfortable enough."

"It's perfect," Ayana said with a weary smile as she eyed the bed in the room off the right-hand side. *Mongo* and the other dragons were already making themselves comfortable on the various chairs and sofas.

"Yes, it's definitely perfect," Tyler agreed. "It certainly beats sleeping out in the woods."

Professor Möbius laughed.

"That it does," he said. "Good night, then. Sleep well. I'll be back for you in a few hours."

"Okay," Tyler replied. "Thank you again, Professor Möbius. I don't know how we can repay you for your kindness."

The professor scoffed.

"You've repaid me plenty enough already," he said. "But there's just one last thing before I leave you up here all alone."

Ayana and Tyler turned toward the professor, listening.

"*Ropav*," the professor said.

"Pardon me?" Tyler asked.

"*Ognom,*" the professor continued.

"What are you saying?" Ayana asked, frowning.

"*Yggubenud. Imak. Llabaep.*" The professor rattled off the remaining names in one go.

As Professor Möbius spoke each dragon's name backward, the dragon instantly winked out of existence, *Peaball* last of all, disappearing into thin air leaving only Ayana and Tyler and the professor standing in the room.

"What are you doing?!??" Ayana shrieked as she looked desperately around for the vanished dragons. "*Peaball*?!?? *Vapor*?!??"

"What are you doing Professor?!?" Tyler cried. "What's going on?!??"

The professor just smiled and took a step backward and out into the hall, pushing a button on the outside as he did so. In a sudden violent hiss of steam, a set of bars slammed heavily shut over the doorframe, trapping Ayana and Tyler inside.

"What are you doing?!??" Ayana screamed, tears flowing down her face as she threw herself against the bars. "Why are you doing this?!?"

"You know why," the professor said as he took another step backward to put some space between himself and Ayana's clawing fingers. "A few days ago when I hit upon the idea of turning my telescopes downward, I was amazed at this vast and beautiful world that I found stretched out in front of me. There was so much promise in it; so much potential. It seemed almost endless."

Ayana was gripping the bars in a furious panic now, her fingers slowly turning white. Tyler was standing right next to her trying to remain calm, frowning in concern.

"I asked myself questions like what lies beyond that great ridge of mountains to the west of here? What are those islands that I can see in the distance? Does anyone live there? Are there caves beyond the walls of water created by the cascading sea waterfalls? I had barely begun to grapple with questions like these when the two of you showed up on my doorstep with your amazing little dragon zoo and told me that everything I can see out there is nothing more than a small bedroom in a much larger universe that you refer to as the *Real World.*"

Tyler listened, growing angrier by the second. Ayana was almost apoplectic with rage.

"And as I listened to your remarkable story, I asked myself another very important set of questions," the professor said. "Such as: What would it be like if I could find my way into this *Real*

World? Imagine what a man with my immense intellect and an army of powerful dragons could accomplish there! I would be virtually unstoppable."

"You can't do that!" Ayana cried, wiping the tears from her face with a quick swipe of her hand.

"Oh, my dear, but I can," Professor Möbius replied with an evil laugh. "And that is precisely what I intend to do."

Fun Facts From The Author For Those Who've Already Read The Book
(aka beware of spoilers)
(aka how to read a message from the author in just six fun facts)

Fun Fact #1: You might have already guessed that there will be more books in this series. I am not sure how many yet, but I can definitely tell you that I am extremely excited about this particular idea. (Just ask my friends — I've been driving them crazy with my enthusiasm for months.) How many do YOU think there should be? Five? Seven? Let me know what you think.

Fun Fact #2: Obviously a number of the scenes in this story take place in magical little book worlds that are based on some famous and classic works of literature. *Struwwelpeter*, for example, is a real book written by the German author Heinrich Hoffman in the 19th century. The story of the girl who played with matches and the roving tailor with the giant scissors are just two of the somewhat horrible stories contained in this collection. The point of the stories was to teach a lesson about the dangers and consequences of misbehaving. Another favourite of mine is called "*Die Geschichte von Hans Guck-in-die-Luft*" about a boy who always has his head in a book and never looks where he's going. Eventually he falls in a river and learns an important lesson. What's the lesson? Don't read books? No, just kidding. The lesson is to watch where you're going. This is also a good one for all of us who walk around in life with our eyes glued to our smartphones.

Fun Fact #2a: Some of the other classic works of literature that are included in this book include: the Dune series by Frank Herbert, The Wolf of Zhongshan (an ancient Chinese folk tale), and of course (obviously) Sherlock Holmes by Sir Arthur Conan Doyle.

Fun Fact #2b: Some of the language and dialogue in the Sherlock Holmes section of this book is taken straight from the original stories — an homage to the great consulting detective. If you've never read any Sherlock Holmes stories before then put this book down right now and go do so because Sherlock is totally awesome.

Fun Fact #2c: Professor Möbius and the series of science books that are mentioned in this book are not real.

Fun Fact #3: Sometimes when I am writing a book I listen to a particular song over and over and over again. The song doesn't really have anything to do with the book itself, but I use it more like a mantra to block out the outside world and help me concentrate.

Fun Fact #3a: The song that I listened to over and over and over again while writing this book was Coldplay's Sky Full Of Stars. (In fact, I am listening to it right at this very second as I write these final words.)

Fun Fact #4: I have a favourite line in this book. It is this one:

"*Perhaps,*" the wolf replied sheepishly.

Fun Fact #5: The Wishing Tree is real. It is in Port Costa, California, just up the street from a haunted hotel. (38°02'45.9"N 122°11'02.8"W)

Fun Fact #6: If you don't already know it, make sure and check out the official website for this book:

www.dragonofthemonthclub.com

Featured on this website every month (on the 13th, of course) will be a new Dragon Of The Month, chosen from entries submitted by fans. Draw a picture! Write a story! Take a photograph! Bake some cookies! Mold a dragon out of clay! Knit one out of yarn! Make one out of LEGO! Whatever you want! Just let your imagination run wild because anything goes - the more creative the better! Check out the website to see how you can enter.

dragon of the month club registration form

name:
favourite colour:
favourite food:
favourite animal:
favourite jelly bean:
favourite flavour of ice cream:
favourite school subject:
swim or fly:
cake or pie:

signed: _____

dragon of the month club registration form

name:
favourite colour:
favourite food:
favourite animal:
favourite jelly bean:
favourite flavour of ice cream:
favourite school subject:
swim or fly:
cake or pie:

signed: _____

Made in the USA
Lexington, KY
08 August 2015